What Readers Are Saying!

"Speedsuit Powers is therapeutic and a breath of fresh air. I didn't want to put it down! The story ties together different issues that youth and adults face in a way that is believable, moving and motivating. I know students will read this book and be transformed! I give it two thumbs up!" **– Dr. Sharnnia Artis, Author of Moving from Ordinary to Extraordinary, Ohio**

"Speedsuit Powers is amazing. My son read the book and was unable to put the book down. His teacher wants to read the book after hearing my son's enthusiasm about the book during his classroom presentation!!!"
– Sandra Blockman, NY

"Just letting you know how much my 14 year old son enjoyed your book and can't wait for your next book. Congratulations to you Allen!!!"
– Dionne Samuels-Reid, NY

"Allen Paul Weaver III has so cleverly addressed the issue of bullying in his novel, Speedsuit Powers. He's done this by allowing his main character, Curtis, to use his intelligence to outwit and befriend his nemesis, Treyshawn, with the support of his school, friends and family."
– J. Helen Perkins, ED.D., Associate Professor of Reading & Urban Literacy, TN

"Speedsuit Powers is an inspiring read! It captures and brings to light a hidden obstacle facing many of today's youth. This book sends a message of hope that in spite of circumstances, youth can achieve and succeed."
– Daren Jaime, Anchor and Host of Perspectives, Bronxnet Television, NY

"Allen created a fun character for young people to read and enjoy. The novel gives young people that spark to have a dream. The character goes through his trials and tribulations, but it shows the heart of a winner. I will be waiting for Book 2."
– Eric Cooper, Knight Seeker novel series, NJ

"Speedsuit Powers Book 1 is amazing!! After 5 hours, I have been inspired beyond reason. Even as a college student, I can relate to his story of seeking understanding about who I am and what I want to do. I have always known that I wanted to be great, and Curtis inspires me to become my very best."
– Lexi Sampson, College Student, Kansas

"This book is a must read!!!! It is inspiring and action packed from the first page until the ending. This book is amazing and teaches something new on every page. I truly recommend this novel to anyone!"
– Sadasia M., College Student, NY

"This is a "must read" book for all persons on all levels especially our youth who experience being bullied daily. This book will keep you wide-awake at night wondering what's next! I have truly never read such an inspirational, motivating novel before such as this. The humor contained within also had my children looking at me "suspiciously" wondering what was so interesting and emotional. My daughter who prefers movies over reading books has decided to read this novel. Needless to say, we are eagerly looking for a Part 2 to Speedsuit Powers or at least a movie! Thank you Allen!"

– Zelda Revell, NY

"Speedsuit Powers is an engaging, well written story about a group of young people who use teamwork and inner strength to overcome obstacles and grow together. While the story itself and the characters grab your interest, the underlying message of the book will stay with you. It's a great read, and will be a wonderful choice for young people."

– Jillian Bryson, VA

"What an incredible story. Not only of invention, excitement and drama, but one that gets at some of the real issues that affect teenagers now like bullying, loss and a sense of their place in this world. Our hero Curtis is a fine example of being the best of what we can be and striving for what is important. You can become great by keeping people down (e.g. Bullying, criticism) or by raising up people around you (e.g. Encouragement, understanding and concern). Our hero Curtis opts for the latter, sharing many of the traits of the author." **– Paul Hartley, NY**

Speedsuit Powers is an amazing story that is not only a must read for today's youth, but offers a great opportunity for adults to come along for the ride." **– Nicole Colon, NY**

"Speedsuit Powers is an epic urban adventure story. I highly recommend it!" **– Dorette Saunders, NY**

"I read Speedsuit Powers in 4 hours! This book is amazing! It will encourage and inspire you as I was. I highly recommend this book!"

– Jae Robinson, NY

"Everyone that has a child in their household needs to order this book! It is a great book on teaching children how to deal with bullies. I cannot put this book down!" **– Helena Woods, NY**

"Speedsuit Powers is a great book that I could not put down! I found a lot of myself in Curtis. I definitely feel this book is something that both adults and teenagers can relate to. I am definitely looking forward to the next two installments" **– Jen K., NY**

"What a great story! Curtis, Kelly and the other characters will inspire kids to dream big and stand firm during tough times. Speedsuit Powers will make a great gift for any kid who is about to start high school – it's not too late to put it on their summer reading list! It makes me wish that I had paid more attention in my physics class. I hope to see Speedsuit Powers on the big screen!" **– Frank Gomez, NY**

"Speedsuit Powers shows that anyone, including those that have physical difficulties, can overcome the obstacles they face and create a better future for themselves and for everyone around them. It's an incredible story of

triumph, family and courage. People need to read it!"
– Christopher Graham, College Student, Bronx, NY

"WOW! I really don't know where to start, other than to say that
Speedsuit Powers changed my entire direction. I serve on the prior
Memphis City School Board, now the Unified Shelby County School Board.
I have taken on Bullying as my personal campaign. While Bullying has been
around forever, we must do everything in our power to stop it!
We can no longer just talk about it, read about it, and/or watch it… we
must take action! Great job on the Book, and the Movie!"
– Stephanie Gatewood, Memphis, TN

"It's not very often that a book grabs you, takes you for a really intense
ride, and leaves you breathless and waiting for the movie and sequel book.
But that is the strength of Speedsuit Powers! I read it in less than 5 hours
because I could not put the book down. I had to see how the characters
ultimately developed. I was not disappointed.

Mr. Weaver is to be commended for creating a realistic fiction work that
tackles serious issues with integrity: Bullying, the education system, family
dynamics, violence, mentoring, nurturing and ultimately, and supporting the
creativity that lives in each child.

Speedsuit Powers made me reflect fondly on the people who influenced
me during my formative years and in present day. Mr. Weaver respectfully
presents counselors who truly counsel, teachers who challenge their
students, students who bring out the best and worst in us, and mothers/
fathers who struggle, hope and work towards something better for
themselves.

The protagonist is real and believable. Supporting characters are well
developed and even the antagonist is a fully developed and recognizable
character, who draws you into his dark reality.

I've said enough…Go buy two books - one for yourself, and one to
influence a youth within your reach." **– Donna Jackson, Parent &
Community Organizer, NY**

SPEEDSUIT POWERS

Special Illustrated Edition

Speedsuit Powers
Powersuit Series: Book One

By: Allen Paul Weaver III

This book is a work of fiction. Any references to historical events, real people, or real locales are used fictitiously. Other names, characters, places, and incidents are the product of the author's imagination, and any resemblance to actual events or locales or persons, living or dead, is entirely coincidental.

The poem, "What About Your Dreams" was written by Allen Paul Weaver III and is from the book, Transition: Breaking Through the Barriers.

Conceptual designs for cover art and backmatter illustrations created by:
Allen Paul Weaver III / Radiant City Studios, LLC

Chapter Illustrations drawn by:
Shawn Alleyne

Cover art designed by:
Shawn Alleyne, Blair Smith & Jeff Tyler

Interior design:
Robert Giorgio

Speedsuit Powers
Powersuit Series: Book One
Copyright © 2009 by Allen Paul Weaver III

Speedsuit Powers
Special Illustrated Edition
Copyright © 2014 by Allen Paul Weaver III

Published by: Radiant City Studios, LLC

Books may be ordered by contacting:
Allen Paul Weaver III at **www.allenpaulweaveriii.com**

ISBN: 978-0-9961045-0-0 (pbk)

Printed in the United States of America

To our youth who are struggling to survive
while trying to hold on to their dreams…

"Who are you running from?"
"Where are you running to?"

To Candace,
Do your best so the
miracles can happen!
Allen Paul Weaver MD
3/19/17

Contents:

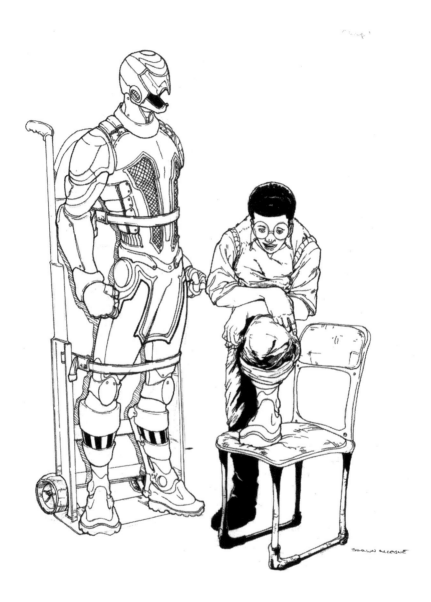

Prologue

Sports Magazine. May 2011.

FINALLY! THE STORY YOU'VE BEEN WAITING for is here. Sports Magazine brings you the exclusive interview with the one and only, Curtis 'Speedsuit' Powers. Strap on your seatbelt because things are about to move fast!

Curtis is the fastest man alive—not quite faster than a speeding bullet—yet he can outrun you, your dog, your bicycle, and even keep up with your car on the thruway. But how does he do it? This young man, who's barely old enough to drive, has used his keen intellect to create a high-tech outfit: the Mach-1 Speedsuit.

Sports Magazine caught up with Curtis and got him to slow down long enough to talk. Here's what he had to say:

SM: So, Curtis, how does it feel to be named the fastest man alive?

CP: It feels great; especially since I battle with asthma. Besides, technically I'm only the fastest man alive when I'm wearing the Speedsuit.

SM: Was your intent, at the beginning of your invention, to become the fastest man alive?

CP: (Laughing). Not really. I mean, I've always *wanted* to be fast and thought about some ways to do it; but the idea for the Speedsuit hit me after I built a pair of running boots in the 9th grade to outrun a bully.

SM: A bully? Sounds like some serious motivation.

CP: (Laughing). It wasn't funny then, but looking back—you can do a lot with the right motivation.

SM: Speaking about that—setting the land speed record has brought you a lot of attention.

CP: Yes, it has.

SM: How does it feel to be a household name?

CP: Still getting used to it. Before the world record, nobody knew who I was; now a lot of people recognize me. I've always liked my privacy. I've had to adjust.

SM: We heard that you'll be doing an exhibition run and carrying the torch at the 2012 Olympics next year in London.

CP: I'm excited about that!

SM: What about the television or movie deal?

CP: There's talk of it...

SM: And a book?

CP: You never know.

SM: You're only 17 and yet your story is resonating with so many people.

CP: Yeah, that's the amazing part!

SM: Students from across the country have said that you inspire them. Who inspires you?

CP: Wow... I can think of a few people—my father, for one. He spent a lot of time with my brother and me before he died. My mother inspires me because every day she holds our family together while working and going to school.

My brother, Omar, inspires me, too. We both took it hard when our dad died, but he went off the deep end and almost didn't make it back.

SM: Why does he inspire you?

CP: Dad drilled into our heads that we should take responsibility for our actions. He did that.

SM: Anyone else?

CP: My friend Kelly and my physics teacher, Mr. Grabowski.

SM: Why them?

CP: I was a new kid at school and Kelly was the first person to be my friend and show me the ropes. Mr. G made learning more interesting and helped me create my boot and suit designs. And when other students made fun of me because I liked learning, he would encourage me to see my future and seek out practical, real-world applications for my ideas.

SM: So you were considered a geek in high school?

CP: Oh, yeah! (Laughing). For 9th and part of 10th grade, definitely! But as other students learned about my inventions through my exhibition runs at track meets, they began to think I was cool.

SM: Speaking of cool, what would you say to other students reading this article?

CP: It's not fun when people make fun of you, but don't let that be an excuse for not doing your best. Try to surround yourself with people who support you, not people who only want to use you. I wouldn't be where I am today if people didn't help me.

SM: That's excellent advice for students everywhere. Now for the question that is on everyone's mind... How does the Speedsuit work?

CP: The million-dollar question. Well... I can't tell you specifics, because of patents that are pending, but I can share the concept: the suit uses the energy that's shed when a person runs—and adds to it with some serious kick! From the bottom up, the entire suit is built for speed.

SM: It's amazing that technology exists which makes this possible. How do you stop? That seems a bit dangerous.

CP: (Laughing). I've had several accidents while testing things out. One sent me to the emergency room.

SM: That sounds serious! What kind of injuries did you sustain?

CP: I fractured both my legs and an arm.

SM: It sounds like running fast can be real dangerous.

CP: There's definitely a learning curve. You really have to move a different way when you're in the suit.

SM: Well Curtis, we are out of time. Thanks for slowing down enough to talk with us mere mortals. We look forward to seeing what your future holds.

CP: Me too, thanks for having me.

SM: We'll see you at the 2012 Olympics!

Chapter One
The New Kid

THE ALARM CLOCK GOES OFF JUST before dawn… It sits on a makeshift stand next to the bed—blaring its squawking drone—which is ignored for several minutes before a massive array of covers, comics, magazines, and textbooks begin moving. An arm lurches out from beneath the fabric mass and slams hard on the snooze button. Next to the clock, a calendar sits— the date circled with orange ink: Tuesday, September 9, 2008—the first day of school.

"Curtis! Wake up!" a woman's voice yells from down the short hallway. The form beneath the covers moves just enough to get his mouth out into the open.

"Five more minutes, Mom…!" He pulls his face back underneath the covers as he hears the click-clack of his mother's shoes approaching. A moment later she forcefully uses the door like a shovel to push aside a large clump of clothes on the floor.

"Curtis, your room is a mess! When you come home today, I want it cleaned. Do you hear me?"

"Yes, Mom…" he moans from beneath the sheets.

"And you don't have five minutes. You need to get up right now! I don't want you to be late on your first day."

"Ok. Two minutes… please!"

"I made your favorite breakfast…" she says cheerily, "but if you're not in the kitchen in two minutes, I'll find something else to do with it."

"All right, I'm up!" He throws back the covers with a grunt, and sits up, causing some of his books to slide off the bed—hitting the floor with a thud. His mom can't help but smile as she sees his hair—matted and disheveled.

"Two minutes or your food is gone," she says. "I'm serious! I've got to finish getting ready for work; and don't forget I've got class tonight—so I'll be home late."

He turns and looks at his mother. "I can't wait till you finish your degree,

Mom."

"Me too," she says while turning to walk out of his room and back down the hall. "Me too."

Curtis' stomach growls as he thinks about breakfast. He may be sleepy, but that doesn't matter when his favorite meal is waiting for him. He inhales deeply, as the slight aroma whiffs past his nose, and says with a smile, "Yep! I can smell it from here!"

The phone rings.

"That could be your brother," mom yells from down the hall, "he said he'd try to call this morning!"

Curtis jumps up and runs down the hall, barely missing a collision with his mother. "Try not to kill yourself!"

He gets to the kitchen, checks the caller ID and quickly picks up the phone.

"Omar!" Curtis smiles from ear to ear.

"Hey, little brother! How are things going?"

"Good! Mom's being pushy though," he says sarcastically.

"Nothing new there," Omar laughs, "you know she's just anxious about your first day."

"Yeah, I know." Curtis moves his mother's textbook to the table and settles into the chair next to the phone.

"You ready?" his older brother probes.

"I guess so. I wish Dad was here."

"Yeah... me too. Things would be a lot easier if he was. But listen, you're the man of the house while I'm away. Don't worry about the new school. You got this."

"I hope so."

"Trust me, little bro. Would I lead you wrong?"

Curtis laughs. "Well..."

Omar laughs as well. "Let me rephrase that. Would I intentionally lead you wrong?"

"That's a better way of saying it. No. You wouldn't."

"All right, then."

"So how's the navy today?" he asks excitedly, "are you doing anything new?"

2

"Now you know I'm always doing something exciting. I just finished working on a Harrier's jet engine yesterday."

"A Harrier jet! You got to email me a picture!"

"I'll see what I can do."

"You ever see one take off?"

"A bunch of times; take off and landing."

"Wow… I've only seen one on TV."

"Yeah, it's pretty amazing to see it up close. The thrust from the engine is crazy! If you stand too close it'll knock you on your backside."

They both laugh before Omar continues.

"But listen, you gotta get going. I don't want you to be late for school. My ship is pulling out of port later today, so I'll call you in a few days."

"Hey."

"Yeah?"

Curtis' eyes tear up. "I… miss you."

"I miss you too, bro. Can you put Mom on the phone?"

"You got it." Curtis cranes his head out into the hallway. "Ma! Omar's on the phone for you!"

"I got it," she calls from her bedroom. "And don't forget to eat your food! It's in the oven!"

Curtis listens as his mother starts talking; then hangs up the phone and quickly makes his way to the oven. As he opens the door, the warm aroma intensifies around his nose.

"Mmm… I love mom's pancakes." He puts on a protective glove, pulls the warm plate out of the oven and sits it on the table. The butter has already melted as he pours a hefty serving of maple syrup. In his hurry, he forgot his journal and runs back to his room to get it. Once back at the table, he says a quick prayer and downs a fork-full of pancakes as he opens up the book to the last entry. As he swallows, he wastes no time taking a few gulps from the large glass of milk.

He pauses as he looks down at the page and recalls his first time writing in a journal. It was three years earlier.

"Curtis, you've always loved to write. I think you should start keeping a journal about your thoughts and feelings. It will help you handle your father's death better," said the psychologist.

He reached into his desk drawer, pulled out a notebook and pen and gave them to Curtis. Days passed as the book and pen laid unused on his messy desk. Eventually, Curtis made his way over and stared at them for a long moment before opening the notebook to the first page. He slowly reached for the pen, clicked the tip, and began to write as a tear dropped from his cheek to the page...

June 25, 2005. Entry number one.
    "My dad is dead... and I don't know what to do."

A ray of sunlight pierces the kitchen window, momentarily blinding Curtis—snapping him back to the present. He thinks about the dusty cardboard box sitting underneath his desk. Inside are seven worn notebooks, each with a year on the cover.

"Wow..." Curtis says to himself as he thinks back over the past three years. "Writing has helped keep me from going crazy." He smiles to himself as he begins to write a new entry:

Entry number 1,102. Tuesday September 9, 2008.
    "Maybe today won't be a bad day after all. But I won't know if I don't hurry up and get out of here." He closes the journal, quickly eats the rest of his food, and gets ready for the new day.

As Curtis headed for the train, he thought back to when he, his brother, and his mother first moved into the neighborhood. It was a far cry from their dream home in the suburbs of Teaneck, New Jersey: a five bedroom, three-story house—four if you counted the basement—with a large front yard and an above-ground pool and trampoline in the backyard. Dad had designed it with rooms for everyone and even had his own study.

But that changed after he died. The money bled away—like blood hemorrhaging from a deep wound that wouldn't heal. Mom couldn't keep up with the mortgage payments and there was a problem with dad's life insurance policy. One by one the cable, phone and electricity were cut off, until the house was lost and they had to move out.

They had nowhere to go. Mom was an only child and her parents lived in the mid-west. She couldn't see moving Curtis and Omar out there. They just needed someplace to stay temporarily until the family could get back on their feet.

Help came from Aunt Ophelia, one of dad's sisters. She wanted to move back down South; and would be willing to sub-lease her apartment. It was a small two-bedroom place, but it was better than nothing. There was only one catch… it was in one of the worst areas in the South Bronx.

Loud music played at all times of the day. The sidewalks were overrun with trash and the playgrounds were covered with graffiti. Drug dealers stood on corners and gang members walked boldly on the blocks. Building stairwells and elevators smelled like urine most of the time, and people argued in nearby apartments. And when the police showed up, they arrived in force, not knowing what to expect.

Talk about culture shock! But, it was all the three of them had. Aunt Ophelia made things better by introducing them to other families who lived in the same building and nearby—people who chose to make the most out of their situation. They watched out for the Powers family and over time became close friends.

There was a lot to learn and get used to when the family moved into the neighborhood. Mom took many precautions to ensure her boys' safety. Curtis couldn't go outside by himself; Omar would always have to accompany him and even then they couldn't be out once it got dark. But, that was almost two years ago. Now the family was more at ease—not laid back—just more at ease.

A passing train, in the distance, catches his attention as he walks faster. He often 'lived in his head', but the sounds of the city have a way of snapping his thoughts back to the present. He passes a nearby corner, where two guys stand, wearing the usual urban gear: baggy jeans, fitted hats, name-brand shirts, thick watches and rugged-style boots. He notices them looking at his corduroy pants, faded shirt, jacket and no-name-brand sneakers. They nod in his direction as he approaches.

"What up, Curtis?" one guy says.

He stops for a moment, "How's it going guys?"

They exchange handshakes.

"How's your brother doin'?" the first guy asks.

"Good. I just spoke to him this morning."

"You tell him we said, what's up. Aiight?"

"I will." Curtis looks towards the train station.

"You goin' to school?" the other guy asks.

"First day," Curtis says, while pushing his slightly oversized glasses up on the bridge of his nose. He wished they didn't keep sliding down his face, but money's too tight to get a new pair.

"You're a smart kid. Keep your head in them books and do somethin' with your life. If you got any problems, you let us know."

"Thanks," Curtis says. "Be safe out here."

"Keep your head up, lil' Curt," the first guy says.

Curtis remembers when his brother hung out with those guys; but his thoughts don't stay long as he starts running towards the station. The train is coming in the distance and he hopes he's fast enough.

"Please stand clear of the closing doors!" blares through the muffled speakers as Curtis narrowly clears the doors, presses through the crowd and finds a lone, empty seat between two large women. He'd rather stand, than sit between them, but his heaving chest dictates otherwise.

A full speed run, for a block and a half felt good, but now he's paying the price. He awkwardly forces his way between them and closes his eyes while trying to breathe deeply. The woman to his left is reading a book, while the other talks on her cell phone. *Spanish class sure comes in handy,* he thinks to himself, as he listens to her loud conversation.

The train's brakes release, with a burst of compressed air, and starts pulling out of the station. Curtis winces in pain as he pulls a folded piece of paper from his back pocket, while trying not to disturb the two women. He reads the directions again and scans the station map on the wall. It was just a few days ago when he and his mother took this route, but he still felt nervous—and this nervousness made it difficult to calm his breathing on his own. He needed his inhaler.

"Phssshh..." He breathes in deeply as he brings the pump cylinder from his mouth, replaces the cap and puts it back into his jacket pocket.

"Are you alright?" asks the woman who's reading the book. Curtis notices the textured leather cover and thin, gold lined pages of her book. He nods his head with a slight smile and pushes the rims of his glasses back up on his nose.

"It's just asthma."

"As long as you're alright. I'll be sure to say a prayer for you," she says with a warm smile.

"Thank you, ma'am."

She raises her eyebrows in surprise—it seems to be a lost art among many youth these days... to show basic respect to their elders.

The train goes through the tunnel and rides on the elevated tracks. Buildings blur as Curtis turns and looks out the window. The two women change their positions slightly, to accommodate him.

"Sorry..." he says.

Now on his knees, staring down at the track, Curtis whispers familiar thoughts to himself—like a self-defeating mantra:

All I've ever wanted to do in life was run. Even in my dreams, I hear the sound of sneakers hitting pavement—rhythmic steps like mini explosions propelling me forward—but asthma won't release its grip! Maybe some dreams aren't meant to come true.

The train screeches to a halt, jarring Curtis' thoughts back to the present. He rises from his seat and exits with the crowd of people, walking down a few flights of stairs and passes through the revolving gates. Once on the street, he heads down the block towards the school. He can't help but notice the other students; many wearing the latest styles of clothing, while he looks ordinary. Some look at him and laugh at the way he's dressed.

Curtis tries not to think about them as he focuses his thoughts on his second love: science.

"I wish dad were here," he says to himself. Just as the words leave his mouth, he finds himself suddenly standing in his father's study, back in their New Jersey home. The smell of old and new books fill the air as bookshelves line the wall of the octagonal-shaped room; illuminated by the natural light from four massive skylights in the ceiling.

Curtis scans numerous shelves, which hold several thousand books, magazines and journals on a variety of topics: string theory; particle physics; philosophy; the law of aerodynamics; architecture of ancient civilizations; and so much more... One column of custom shelves, with glass partitions, house detailed replicas of actual buildings designed by his dad. Next to these shelves sits a well-used drafting table, chair and lamp.

Curtis can see everything in his mind, as if he was actually there. In a flash, he and Omar are sitting with their father in front of his drafting table at work.

"Dad!" he exclaims, but no one hears him. He just stands nearby and watches them, looking at schematic drawings of 3D model buildings. He can smell the large format blueprint paper, the ink toner and even the pencil lead. As he draws closer to his father, he smiles when his father begins to speak.

"Boys, don't let anyone steal your dreams from you. If you can dream it, then you can build it. You just have to use your imagination to see all the parts and how they relate to each other."

In another flash, Curtis finds himself standing in his parents' bedroom—in a suit and tie. The only thing he didn't like about going to work with dad was that he and Omar had to wear suits—like he did. It's amazing how clear these memories were and how Curtis could remember the conversation, word for word:

"Dad, why do we have to wear suits?"

"People take you seriously when you are well dressed. They respect you more."

"I don't care what other people think."

"You don't care about what your mother thinks?"

"Dad, you *know* what I mean!"

"Really? *Tell* me what you mean. Don't just assume someone knows what you're talking about. Now, do you care about what your mother thinks?"

"Yeah!"

"What about your brother? I know you care about what he thinks. You always want to do what he's doing."

"Yeah," Curtis says in a softer tone.

"What about me? Do you care about what I think?"

"Yes."

"Well, there you go. What about your friends at school? You care about what they think?"

"Dad, I get the point."

"You do? What is my point, Son?"

"I care about what people think."

"To varying degrees, we all do. But here's the question we need to ask ourselves: 'Is this person whose opinion I value, worthy of me listening to him in the first place?'"

"What do you mean?"

"Basically, does the person have your best interest at heart or are they trying to use you?"

Curtis' eyebrows wrinkle. "How do I know the difference?"

"Now *that* is an even better question! Most people don't care about knowing the difference. If they did, it would help keep them out of a lot of trouble. You think about that for a while. In the meantime, tuck your shirt in and fix your tie; then tell your brother we're leaving in five minutes."

Curtis finds himself standing in front of the school building; a growing line of students wait to pass through the security checkpoint.

"It's early and there's already a line?" He joins the others and grows increasingly uneasy. Being new at a new school isn't fun and making friends is hard. *I need a new project,* he thinks—as a way to divert his attention. But as he looks around, he admits that he does care what others think about him. But how does he tell the difference between those who are for him and those who are against him? Soon, after being scanned, Curtis enters the halls of Rheuman High School for the first time.

"Thank you for coming in early to meet with me, Mr. Powers. I've been looking through your transcripts and I must admit that I'm impressed. I rarely see grades like these. This is simply tremendous! I know your parents must be very proud of you."

"...Yes."

Curtis finds himself seated in front of his guidance counselor, Mrs. Fuller: a very stately looking woman—perhaps in her fifties—regal in her attire, wearing an impeccably starched and creased gray tweed business suit. Her reading glasses sit on the tip of her nose as she leafs through Curtis' transcript folder.

"You are one very smart young man, Curtis. I see you took both biology and chemistry while still in middle school in New Jersey."

"I really like science."

"I can see that. Tell me, how did you cope with being in a class with older students?"

"I mostly kept to myself. The teachers made sure the older students didn't bother me."

"So do you think you're ready for physics?" She takes off her glasses and looks directly at Curtis. "I want to warn you, Mr. Grabowski takes his class very seriously. Most students try to avoid his class and prefer Mr. Peeker because they say he's more personable. Unfortunately for you—or maybe not—Mr. Peeker's class is already full, so you'll *have* to take Mr. Grabowski's class. He will push you, but I think you might be up for the challenge. Am I right, Curtis, do you think you're up for the challenge?"

"I sure hope so."

"Well, the arrangements have been made. I just wanted to make sure. You have several advanced classes, including pre-calculus. That's a formidable workload for a freshman student."

"I can do it," Curtis says assuredly.

Mrs. Fuller smiles. "I like the 'can-do' attitude. I'm pretty sure you can. Just know I'm here if you have any issues—any issues at all. Don't forget to take advantage of extra help if you need it."

"I won't."

She closes his folder and looks at the young boy before her. For all of his apparent confidence, she can see something in his eyes—a bit of uneasiness. She isn't quite sure *why* it's there. Maybe it's the new school or perhaps it's something deeper.

"So, tell me Curtis, what do you want to be when you grow up?"

His face grimaces ever so slightly; but she picks up on the expression immediately.

"I… want to be either an engineer or an architect like my father."

"Those are two excellent choices she says cautiously. Against her better judgment, she asks the next question. "Where does your father work?"

"He used to work for an architectural firm in Manhattan…" his voice trails off.

Is he unemployed? She thinks to herself. *That information isn't in his files. Is he incarcerated? Lord, I hope he's not…*

Curtis can see her eyes—her mind working, trying to put the pieces of the puzzle together. He takes a deep breath as she slowly leans forward in her chair, trying to decide how to phrase her next question.

Curtis cuts to the chase, "My dad died a few years back… when I was in 6th grade."

"I'm so sorry to hear that, Curtis." Images of a horrific car crash assault her mind. "That piece of important information wasn't in your file. It sounds like you and he had a special relationship."

"We did."

She hesitates for a moment as she asks her next question. "Do you... have any siblings?"

"My older brother, Omar; he's in the military."

"Really?" she says relieved, "Which branch?"

"The navy."

"That's wonderful! Are you two close?"

"Very. We like pretty much the same things."

"So he's good in science and math as well?"

"He's studying to be a mechanical engineer."

"Do you get to see him often?"

"Not really, but he tries to call every week. I spoke to him this morning."

"I'm glad you are surrounded by people who are supportive. And your mother? Is she... alive?"

"Yes." Curtis smiles.

"Good," Mrs. Fuller says with a large grin. "What does she do?"

"She works and goes to school for her masters."

"She sounds very ambitious: working full time, going to school and raising two sons on her own after losing your father."

"She's the strongest person I know."

"It's inspiring to hear stories about people who overcome incredible odds, especially women. I'd love to meet your mother some day."

"I'm sure she'd like to meet you too. She knew all my teachers back at my old school."

"It sounds like she's very involved in your education."

"She is."

"If I may ask, how did your father die?"

Instantly, his mind goes back to that day when they first found out.

"Malcolm, I'm afraid I have some bad news," the doctor said as he entered the room. "Are you sure you want your sons in here with you?"

Mr. Powers took his sons' hands in his own—Omar in his right and

Curtis in his left. "They're going to find out anyway. It might as well be now."

"I'm afraid your condition is worse than we thought." the doctor said as he looked up from the paperwork pensively.

Malcolm tried to force a smile for his boys. "How much worse?"

"It's inoperable. Perhaps if we'd caught it sooner…"

Curtis hesitates. "I don't want to talk about my father's death right now."

"I respect your wishes. Losing a parent is never easy. My father died in a car crash a few years after I graduated from college. That was a long time ago, but sometimes it's still difficult to talk about—even now." She struggles to fight back her own tears.

Curtis looks down at his lap. "I'm sorry… I didn't know."

"How could you have known? Our experience may not be exactly the same, but we can relate."

"I keep myself focused on school. It's one of the only things that keep me from going crazy. Besides, doing my best would make my dad happy."

"Your choice to honor your father's memory is admirable," Mrs. Fuller says with a smile. "Thank you for your openness. If you ever need to talk, come and see me."

Curtis nods as his guidance counselor stands up, while grabbing a slip of paper. "Here's your class schedule. Make sure you have a great day, alright?"

"You, too." Curtis stands, takes his schedule, and walks to the office door. He stops and turns back toward her.

"Sometimes I cry and write in my journal." He opens the door and leaves.

Mrs. Fuller watches him walk down the hall as she says to herself, "Me too, Curtis. Me too…" She turns and looks at her overflowing student filing cabinet. *Now that was a breath of fresh air*, she thinks to herself. "So many students; so many problems; so many distractions; so little time. I wish more had motivation like him."

Chapter Two

Enter the Bully

AS THE FIRST BELL OF THE morning rings, the halls of the school are filled with students, teachers, and security personnel.

"Alright, let's keep it moving people! It's the first day of a brand new school year. Let's start it off right! Keep it moving!"

Several hall monitors are inundated with questions from freshmen who have no idea where they should be headed. Over the roar of hundreds of jabbering students, locker doors can be heard slamming as most students make last minute preparations for their first class. As usual, an extra five to ten minutes has been allotted for freshmen that get lost trying to find their way. However, there are those who choose to take this time to goof off.

Treyshawn, a young man who could care less about school, comes around the corner. As he walks with his friends, he readily shoves other students out of his way.

"Watch out, fool! You see me walkin' here?"

A massive hall monitor sees him. "Mr. Jinkins. I'm sure you had an eventful summer, but summer's over. You know the rules, lose the do-rag."

Treyshawn reluctantly pulls it off his head. "I told you about sayin' my last name, Mr. Andre."

"I know you don't like it. And maybe I don't like how you act in my hallway."

"Since when is it your hallway?"

"You see this shirt? What does it say? *Hall Monitor*. That means these are my halls, TJ."

"Don't call me TJ either. You know my name is *Lil' Treacherous*."

Mr. Andre laughs. "That was a good one—*Lil' Treacherous*.... Please. That may be your name in the streets, but this ain't the streets. In here, you're Treyshawn Jinkins, otherwise known as TJ! Now where are your books?"

He smiles slyly and taps on the side of his head. "No need to worry about books; I gots everything I need right here."

"Uh, huh. You must not have much up there because you're on a two-year plan for grade nine."

"Why you disrespectin' me?" Treyshawn cuts back.

"I'm *not* disrespecting you; and you better watch that bass in your voice! You need to focus boy, and leave the other students alone."

"Who you callin' *boy*? I'mma man!"

"Yeah? Well start acting like one. Now get to class before I give you detention."

Treyshawn smiles and nods while turning the corner with his friends. "Man, I can't stand him. Just because he's bigger than everybody don't mean he can push me around. He ain't my father."

It's then that he sees Curtis leaving his locker.

"You gotta be kiddin' me. Check out that kid. See how he dressed?" They approach him. "Hey, you with the glasses and messed up clothes!"

Curtis keeps walking.

"Hey, I'm talkin' to you. I know you hear me!"

Curtis turns and looks at Treyshawn while still moving. "I'm late for class."

"You gon be late, alright; real late if you don't stop walkin' away."

He takes a deep breath, stops and turns around. "Hi, I'm Curtis. What's your name?"

The boys start laughing. "What's my name? Are you serious? You don't need to know my name, Smurtis."

"No. It's Curtis."

"I heard you, but Smurtis sounds better to me."

"Look, I don't want any trouble…"

"Well you got trouble. Now what?"

"I've gotta go." Curtis turns to walk away, but Treyshawn blocks his path.

"You go when I say you go."

"What do you want?" Curtis says defiantly.

"You're pretty bold for a skinny kid. You think you smarter than me? I see all them books you got in your red bag. Looks real heavy!" Treyshawn grabs the bag and throws it to the floor.

"Hey!"

"What? What you gonna do, Smurtis?"

Curtis begins to rub his chest. He tries to take deep breaths. His hands start to sweat as he fights to remain calm and pretend he's not afraid. He sizes up Treyshawn—he's taller and stronger than him.

I can't let him know I have asthma; but his breathing becomes more labored by the second. The next bell rings; classes have started.

"Please... I just... want to go to... class."

"You'll go when I say so." Treyshawn's voice suddenly slows. In reality, it's Curtis' perception that changes as he looks for a hall monitor.

"Just... let... me... go..."

"Why you talking slow? Are you dumb?"

Curtis can't wait any longer as he quickly reaches into his pocket. The other boys jump back, unsure of what he's about to do. Treyshawn grabs his arm as he brings his hand out of his pocket.

"I need... my inhaler..." Curtis says—barely.

Treyshawn lets his arm go as he takes a deep breath and squeezes the pump. "Phssssh..." Just then, Mr. Andre comes around the corner towards them.

"Now how did I know that I'd find you over here Treyshawn?"

"I told you 'bout sayin' my name!"

"And I told you to stop bothering people."

"I'm not, Mr. Andre. I was just talking to my friend here, Smurtis."

The hall monitor looks at the group incredulously and then at Curtis. "Are you alright, Smurtis?"

Curtis takes a deep breath and forces a smile. "Yes sir... I just want to go to class."

"Well you'd better hurry up. The second bell has already rung."

"Thank you... and it's Curtis, not Smurtis."

"Got it. Sorry about that. Have a good day."

Curtis walks away in peace, under the protection of Mr. Andre.

"See you later, Smurtis." Treyshawn says.

"Whew..." Curtis says under his breath. "That was close. I sure hope he's not going to be a problem." He quickly finds his homeroom class and gets situated in the loud room of over forty students.

"Everybody have a seat and be quiet. We have some important information to go over before you all head to your next class," the teacher says.

The room quiets down, except for a few rebellious talkers.

"Young gentlemen in the back of the room. I would hate for you to get detention on your first day of school."

The boys reluctantly quiet down as the teacher starts going over the information. "Take one and pass it back," he says while handing out sheets at the beginning of each row. Just then another student enters the class. Curtis can't help but moan as he sees the student's face. It's Treyshawn.

Several hours later, students rush into a classroom as the second bell rings. The teacher walks over to the door and closes it—as the talking students quiet down and settle into their chairs. They watch the teacher walk back to the front of the classroom. The tension in the room is evident.

"Good morning class," he strikes the black board with his long pointer for emphasis. "My name is Mr. Grabowski, but you can call me *Mr. G.* You are now in my world, *An Introduction to Physics.*

"I'm going to skip past the pleasantries, for the moment, to get to the ground rules. I'm sure most, if not all of you do not want to be here. However, you are here because Mr. Peeker's class was already full. I'm also sure that some of you will drop out... and some will even fail this class. Don't worry," he says sarcastically. "It happens every year.

"Those of you who stick it out, will make it through this class by the skin of your teeth, but you will be better for it. Please understand me, I have no time for jokes and playing around when it is time to be serious and focus on the task at hand. Do not confuse the two. In physics, the time to be serious is most of the time because many of the experiments we will do could be potentially dangerous for a person who doesn't pay attention."

The students sit uncomfortably in their chairs as Mr. G looks around the room. "Having said all of this, let me also state that Physics is *cool.*"

A slight laugh spreads through the class as some of the tension breaks. Mr. Grabowski cuts a quick smile and lightens up a bit.

"Physics doesn't have to be boring. In reality, it can be very exciting.

A hint to you all: the real reason why many students don't like physics is because they don't embrace the beauty of the mathematics and logic that go along with the experiments." A quiet passion exudes from his body language; one he doesn't want to waste.

"Learn to work *with* the equations and understand the logic and you will find that physics is not only fun, it is also a practical tool you can use every day. Now you are probably asking, *why would I want to know about physics?* I'm glad you asked." The class laughs once again.

"Let me tell you why you want to know about physics." He leans in and holds the moment in silence. Several students, including Curtis, lean in waiting for the answer…

"Because everything is physics: when you walk; when you pick something up; when you play a sport or throw a ball!" He pulls a tennis ball from his sweater pocket and tosses it to a student, who clumsily catches it. The class laughs again.

"It's all physics! Nice catch by the way. Now, before I go any further, let me take attendance."

Mr. Grabowski sits at his desk, opens the attendance folder and puts on the glasses that hang around his neck. He starts reading down the list of names and as he speaks, each student answers back. All of the students are in the eleventh or twelfth grade, all except one. When the teacher gets to *that* name, he pauses.

"Ah, yes, how could I forget? Mr. Curtis Powers."

"Here," Curtis responds.

Mr. G raises his head and looks over the rim of his glasses. "Where are you, Curtis?"

Curtis slowly raises his hand.

"It's a pleasure to meet you, Mr. Powers. I've been awaiting your arrival."

He gestures for Curtis to stand as he address the rest of the class. "Please don't say it, please don't say it," Curtis whispers under his breath.

"Class, I want you to meet Mr. Curtis Powers, the only ninth grader in the school who is taking physics."

Suddenly, Curtis feels very nervous as the students look at him intently; some with interest and curiosity and others with disinterest and jealousy.

"You may take your seat, Mr. Powers."

Curtis quickly sits down.

"I've been told that you're a wonder kid when it comes to science and math... Don't worry, we'll have plenty of opportunities to see just how smart you *think* you are."

The class responds with a collective, "Oooooh." Mr. Grabowski sits and moves on with the list. Once done, he stands back up. "Now, who can tell me what physics is?"

The class sits quietly.

"Anyone?"

A girl raises her hand.

"Yes. Oh, for the next few classes, until I get all of your names down, when you answer a question, please state your first and last name before answering the question. Ok, go ahead."

"Joanne Rodriguez. The study of motion?"

"What is the study of motion, Ms. Rodriguez?"

"Physics is the study of motion?"

"Are you asking or are you telling me?"

"Asking...?"

The class laughs again.

"All right, Ms. Rodriguez. You are partly right. Studying motion is a part of physics. Thank you. What about you, Mr. Powers? What is physics?"

"Curtis Powers."

"Yes, Curtis. I just said your name. We all know who you are."

"But you said..."

"Yes, I know what I said," Mr. Grabowski chuckles and takes a deep breath. "Let me qualify my statement. If I do not call out your name, then you can say your name for the class. However, if I call out your name, then there is no need for you to say your name again. Do you see the logic in what I have just said, Curtis?"

"Yes, Mr. G."

"Good. Does everyone else understand?"

The class collectively responds in the affirmative.

"Good. So Mr. Powers, what is physics?"

"Physics is the science that deals with matter, energy, motion, and force."

"Excellent! You're off to a good start, Mr. Powers, but don't get cocky."

A few moments pass before the bell rings and class is dismissed. Mr. Grabowski pulls up a white screen that covers part of the blackboard and points to what's beneath it.

"This is your homework for tomorrow. Make sure it's done."

Most of the students scramble to write down the assignment, while others don't bother. As they exit the classroom, Mr. Grabowski calls Curtis over to his desk. Once the room is clear, he begins to speak.

"Mr. Powers, I want you to know that I am being hard on you for a reason. Many students don't get excited about science anymore. So to see a young man as talented as yourself... it's refreshing." He takes off his glasses and leans back in his chair. "I had a very long talk with Mrs. Fuller about you being in my class. Honestly, I was against it."

Curtis' jaw drops. He almost doesn't know what to say. "Why... didn't you want me in your class?"

"I not sure if you're ready for that answer just yet."

"But I took biology and chemistry already."

"True."

"Now I'm taking pre-calculus!"

"Yes, but as I stated at the beginning of class, most students will either drop out or fail. I have no time for games unless they serve to advance the lesson... Can I trust you, Mr. Powers?"

"With all due respect, can I trust you, Mr. G?"

He smiles slightly and leans back in his chair—pursing his lips. "I'm going to take a risk." Mr. Grabowski breathes deeply and exhales slowly. "Honestly, Curtis, I'm not sure if I'm ready for you."

"Mr. G, none of this makes any sense."

"What I mean to say is that having a young man in my class who loves science is exciting for me. I deal with so many students who only care about their favorite movies, music, or videogames. I don't want to get my hopes up and have them broken if you fail or drop out because you can't keep up with the workload. I don't baby my students. You're smart, but you are also very young."

"I know I'm younger than everyone else, Mr. G, but I can do this. I accept the challenge." Curtis extends his hand. Mr. G looks at it and smiles as he extends his own hand.

"All right," he says as they both shake. "The challenge has been extended and accepted. Welcome to the class, Mr. Powers. I hope this is a race you plan on winning."

"I do, sir."

Mr. Grabowski smiles in delight. "Listen Curtis, if you'd like, you can come here during your lunch period—fourth period right?"

"Yeah."

"Good. I can always use the help of an intelligent student. Are you interested?"

For me, running is both freedom and also a harsh reminder that I am not free. Curtis moves his legs with every ounce of available strength, trying to outrun a young man determined to make his life miserable. Treyshawn's speed is unmatched as he easily grabs Curtis by his shirt collar and book bag.

"Who you runnin' from? Man, you run slower than my grandmother! And just in case you're wondering, I'm one of the fastest cats in this school. So you ain't outrunnin' me! You got that?"

Curtis struggles unsuccessfully to break free from Treyshawn's grip as others walk past and do nothing.

"Where you think you going?"

"I just want to go home! Leave me alone, Treyshawn!"

"Don't you ever say my name! You don't get to say my name ever!" He throws Curtis to the ground. "And I'll never leave you alone!"

"But I didn't do anything to you!" he shouts up from the pavement.

"You didn't do nothin' to me? The moment I saw you in the hall you did somethin' to me! You hurt my eyes wit your sorry clothes and thick glasses! And you walk around wit your books as if you betta than me! But you ain't betta than me!"

Curtis gets back to his feet. "I never said I was better than you!"

"*And...* you just transferred into *my* school."

"How is it your school? We're both in the ninth grade. Did you get left back?"

In a burst of anger, Treyshawn's fist connects squarely with Curtis' jaw, knocking the glasses off his face and sending him back to the concrete.

"Smart talk like that will get you a beat down every time! Get up so I can put my fist to your jaw again!"

"Treyshawn! Leave him alone!"

Both boys turn and see a girl standing nearby, with her arms folded.

"Hey, Kelly." He turns back towards Curtis and points at her. "You're lucky she's here. She's the only reason I don't kick your butt right now. And don't think because you moved here from the 'burbs that you better than me. Every day I see you in my school you pay me ten dollars."

"Ten dollars! I don't have ten dollars!"

"And if you don't pay," he yells louder, "every day you get knocked to the ground!" Treyshawn walks off.

Kelly walks over, picks up Curtis' glasses and extends her hand. Even through his aching jaw and near-sighted vision, he can't help but notice how attractive she is. When he takes her hand, he also notices her strong grip.

"You know he *did* get left back," she says. "This is his second time in the ninth grade."

"I didn't know. I was just talking."

"I'm impressed. People don't usually stand up to him like that."

"Look where it got me. I should have just kept my mouth shut. How am I going to come up with ten dollars every day?"

"Don't worry about that right now. Treyshawn talks a good game, but we'll figure something out. Besides, he did say every day he sees you. The school's a big place," she says with a smile.

Curtis takes out his inhaler. "Phssshh."

"Asthma?"

Curtis nods his head. "Yeah."

"I'm Kelly, by the way."

"…I'm Curtis… You're in ninth grade too?"

"Yep."

"Well, thanks for helping me out."

"No problem. You seem like a nice guy." She hands him his glasses. "Besides, I don't like it when he does that to people."

"How do you know him anyway?"

"Treyshawn and I live on the same block. We've known each other since we were kids; and he still gets on my nerves."

"He's really fast."

"One of the fastest at the school—even made the varsity track team last year."

"As a freshman? Wow, that's fast! So he runs track?"

"Not anymore. He didn't make it two months before he was kicked out because of his attitude."

"Great. It's the first day of school and I've already got a psychopathic maniac, who's faster than everybody, chasing after me! He's like my nemesis!"

"Wow. That's a big word you don't hear much."

"Nemesis? It means someone who-"

"I *know* what it means. I'm just saying I've never heard anyone other than a teacher say it before."

"Sometimes they use the word in comics or science fiction."

"So, you like comics?"

"Yeah... but back to Treyshawn. Has he always been like this?"

"Pretty much. He's got a rough life at home—way too much drama. So I understand *why* he acts the way he does, although I don't agree with it."

"Well, I know a little bit about family drama, so I'll keep that in mind. I may need a bodyguard," Curtis says laughing. "You wouldn't happen to have a big brother who's a *whole lot* stronger than Treyshawn, would you?"

"As a matter of fact," she grins, "I've got two big brothers. And either one of them can handle Treyshawn in their sleep."

As they walk away from the school, Kelly stares shyly at Curtis, "You ever thought about wearing contacts? You have nice eyes."

"I don't know. Maybe I'll try them some day," he sputters, while thinking, *Wow! I definitely care about this girl's opinion!*

Chapter Three
Double Trouble

AFTER DAYS OF STUDYING AND TRYING to keep from getting beat up, Curtis is glad that the first week of school is over. As he walks into the apartment and closes the door, he stands motionless with his eyes closed. He can hear the hum of the refrigerator, the splatter of water droplets in the kitchen sink, and the sound of the wind gently blowing through the curtains in the living room.

"I think mom has class tonight," his voice echoes to no one in particular. As he removes his left sneaker, the duct tape dangles, and the sole flaps open like the mouth of a dead fish. He shakes his head and remembers when buying new sneakers weren't a big deal—but that was a long time ago. Things can change so quickly sometimes, but you learn to make due with what you have until you can get what you want.

He finds a copy of mom's schedule in the kitchen. "Yep. She won't be home until eleven."

Curtis slowly strolls into the living room, plops down on the couch, pulls out his journal and writes:

Entry number 1,120. Friday September 12, 2008.
"I made it through my first week at Rheuman. People are so different than at Colon Prep in New Jersey. It's hard enough trying to make friends, but it wouldn't be so bad if it weren't for Treyshawn! I can't stand him! I've already paid him ten dollars for one day and Kelly helped me avoid him for the rest of the week—thank God for Kelly—but I can't keep this up forever! I wish he'd go jump off a bridge or stand in front of a train somewhere! I know that's not a good thing to wish for, but I still wish it would happen."

The phone rings. Curtis closes his journal and glances at the clock as he darts out of the room to the kitchen. It's almost always the same time every week. He's barely able to keep his enthusiasm as he nearly trips over the chair to get to the receiver.

"Hey, Omar!" he yells into the phone.

Omar pulls his ear away for a second while laughing. "Whoa! That was loud."

"Sorry. Just happy to talk to you."

"That's cool. How was your first week?"

Curtis hesitates. "It was... ok... How are things with you?"

"Not so fast."

"What?" Curtis sits down in the chair.

"You paused."

"No reason."

"A second ago you were yelling in my ear and then you hesitate. What's going on?"

After an awkward moment of silence, Curtis erupts like a busted steam valve!

"There's this guy at school—Treyshawn—he's bothering me! He beat me up once already and said he'll beat me up each day he sees me if I don't pay him ten dollars!"

"Whoa! Some punk's beating up on you? Did you tell Mom about this?"

"What?" Curtis jumps up from his chair. "No! Are you crazy? What can she do? She already has enough to deal with. If I tell her she'll get worried—or worse—she'll go down to the school, get Treyshawn in trouble, and make my life even worse!"

"You got a point, but you can't let him beat you or take your money."

"A girl I met—Kelly—she's been helping me avoid him. But, Omar, he's bigger and stronger than me. I wish dad were here. He'd know what to do."

"Yeah. I wish dad were here, too; but... he's not, so we have to make things work without him."

Curtis winces at his brother's words as he slowly sits down. Omar can sense his brother's hurt.

"Hey, little bro. Are you still there?"

Curtis removes his glasses to rub away his tears.

"Listen," Omar continues, "even though we have to do this without him, that doesn't mean we forget all the lessons he taught us. You get me?"

"Yeah," Curtis says with a deep breath, "I get you."

"Good. Now if this kid is bigger and stronger than you, then you have to use your mind. Try reasoning with him and if that doesn't work, then you'll have to outsmart him. Bullies love to intimidate others to cover up their own weaknesses. Don't be afraid to stand up for yourself, but don't be stupid."

"The last time I stood up to him, he knocked me to the ground."

"All the more reason for you to get up and stand again. Listen, brains over brawn wins out more than the other way around. Don't worry. If you can't reason with this kid or outsmart him, then I'll have to deal with him when I get home."

"You're coming home?" Curtis jumps to his feet. "When?"

"In time for Thanksgiving. It was supposed to be a surprise. That's what I was talking to mom about last week after I spoke to you."

"I can't wait to see you! Two months is such a long time, though."

"Don't worry, it'll fly by faster than you realize. Just focus on your books and don't be afraid to stand up for yourself."

"Right! Stand up for myself, but don't be stupid. Thanks, Omar."

"No problem. That's what big brothers are for."

"Big brothers…"

"You ok?"

"Yeah. You just reminded me of something."

"Something useful, I hope."

"Kelly's got two big brothers. She said Treyshawn is afraid of them. Maybe they'll help me out."

"Good. Check into that. Listen, I have to go. But I'll talk with you next week. If you have an emergency, shoot me an email."

"Thanks, Omar."

"Alright, bro. I'll talk with you soon."

"Bye."

Journal number 1,128. Friday September 26, 2008.
English is just about over. Then it's on to lunch. I sure hope I don't run into

Treyshawn in the hallway or cafeteria.

The students in the hallway move like a colony of ants. On the surface—chaos—but there's a method and a pattern to their movements. Some rush to class while others ease their way to the cafeteria. Curtis rushes to the cafeteria because he didn't have time for breakfast.

"I'm starving!" he says under his breath while trying to run without drawing attention from the hall monitors. "I wonder what's for lunch?" He slows down to double check that he has enough for the meal. "Seven dollars should be enough."

Just then a hand snatches the money!

"Hey!"

He turns around to find Treyshawn standing there with a smirk on his face, counting the dollars.

"Been a few weeks since I seen you, Smurtis. Where you been hiding?"

"The name is Curtis."

"Ok, Smurtis. You're three dollars short."

"Listen, about that. I'm all out of money, but maybe we can work out something else that could be to your benefit."

"Benefit? What you got that would benefit me besides money?"

"I know you're repeating the ninth grade and I thought I could help you with your homework."

"Help me with my homework? Do I look like I need help?"

"We all need help with something. There's nothing bad about asking for help."

"Well, I ain't askin! But, you know what? I got a great idea! I'mma pretty reasonable guy. You can do my homework and only pay me five dollars instead of ten."

"What? I have my own homework to do! That's crazy!"

"Yeah... well, that's life. Either do that or you can take your beat-down right now for not havin' my money. You make the choice since you so smart."

"Treyshawn I hope you're not bothering him," Kelly says sternly as she walks up.

Treyshawn takes a few steps back and feigns innocence. "Me? Nah, you know I wouldn't do that," Treyshawn says mockingly. "Curtis was just offerin' to help me with my homework. We was just workin' out the details. But we can finish this up later."

Treyshawn walks off with his group. He looks back at Curtis before disappearing around the corner, "I'll be talkin' with you later, Smurtis."

"Wow, Curtis," Kelly says, "Treyshawn's going to let you help him with his homework?"

"I offered it to him as a truce, but now he says, instead of helping him, I'll be doing his homework and paying five dollars instead of ten."

"What? That's crazy! Look, I know you wanted to try and reason with him, but that is clearly not working! You really need to talk with my brothers."

"Maybe you're right."

"It's not maybe. I *am* right! Come over after school; they said when you're ready to have them handle it—let them know and it's done."

"Really?"

"Really. If you talk to them tonight, they can have a *few words* with Treyshawn tomorrow. He's usually playing ball at the court on Saturdays. By Monday, you'll be worry free!"

"Are you sure about this?"

"Trust me, you'll feel a whole lot better once you do."

"And what are you doing tomorrow?"

"I've got a dance class in the morning."

"Really? All this time and you never told me you were a dancer."

"You never asked. Besides, I don't tell a lot of people about it."

"Why? Are you shy?"

"No. But, most of my friends don't get the kind of dance I do. Everybody likes hip hop and I do too…but I *love* ballet."

"Where do you go for class?"

"I study at the Alvin Ailey School in Manhattan."

"That's a really good school."

Kelly looks at Curtis with surprise. "What do you know about the school?"

"I've seen performances on television."

"Well, it is a good school. I really like it."

Ding-dong… Curtis stands outside the brownstone on Clay Avenue. He watches with a grin as several kids run past him, playing freeze-tag. The quick, repetitive sound of ropes and sneakers kissing the pavement draws his attention as a group of girls jump double-dutch next to the side of a nearby car. Neighbors sit on their stoops, enjoying the evening breeze, while playing cards and throwing dice. Some of them watch him with raised eyebrows, obviously wondering why he's on their block. He forces a smile, quickly turns back to the door and presses the doorbell again.

Feet shuffle on the other side of the door, followed by the click-clack of multiple locks being released. The door creaks open as a woman stands in the doorway.

"May I help you?" she says with a mix of confidence and caution.

"Yes ma'am. My name is Curtis Powers. I'm one of Kelly's friends from school."

"Did you just call me ma'am?"

"Yeah…"

"Huh. I'm sorry; it's just been a while since a young person called me that. Usually kids come by asking if Kelly's home, as if they own the place?" She says while imitating their expressions.

"I barely get a name from them anymore. It's like pulling teeth. And when I ask, they look at me like *I'm* the one with the problem—and they're standing at my front door!"

Curtis listens to the woman, and smiles slightly. "Are you Kelly's mother?"

"Why, yes I am," she says cheerfully, "and you must be Curtis—well of course you are—you said that already. What I meant was that Kelly said you'd be stopping by. Sorry about giving you an earful a minute ago."

"That's ok, Mrs…"

"Washington. Why don't you come upstairs."

"Thank you."

Curtis enters the brownstone and waits for the locks to be reengaged before following Kelly's mother up the stairs to the next floor.

"You can never be too safe," she says as she nears the top of the stairs. Kelly! Your friend Curtis is here!"

"Ok, Mom!" a voice comes from the back of the apartment.

"Make yourself at home." She leads him to the living room and he sits down on the couch.

"Do you want anything to drink?"

"What do you have?"

"Let's see… we have iced tea, orange juice, milk, apple juice, soda and water."

"Is the orange juice low acid or regular?"

"Regular… I think. Why?"

"I'm sensitive to citric acid."

"Got it," Mrs. Washington says, "I can check for you. If the orange juice is not low acid, what do you want instead?"

"Can I have water?"

"Wow… you just keep surprising me, Curtis. I don't hear many young people asking for water."

"I don't really like water, but my brother says I need eight glasses a day. He works out a lot and I've been drinking a lot of soda."

"That's a smart brother you've got there," she says with a smile. "I'll be right back."

Mrs. Washington walks into the kitchen at the same time that Kelly does.

"What do you think of Curtis, Mom?"

"I like him. He called me ma'am. Do you know the last time one of your friends called me 'ma'am'?"

"I'm sure it's been a while, Mom."

She pours a glass of water. "Here Kelly, take this in with you."

"Who's this for?"

"Curtis," she says with a smile.

"Curtis asked for water?"

"He did."

"Seriously?" Kelly says with raised eyebrows while craning her neck forward.

"That's what I said."

Kelly walks into the living room with a glass of water in each hand.

"Hey, Curtis."

"Hey, Kelly," Curtis says standing up.

"Here's your water."

He takes it and looks at the other glass. "You drink water, too?"

"I *am* a dancer, you know."

"Do you like it?"

"You get used to it after a while. Before I started drinking it, I used to be tired all the time."

"Yeah, me too."

"So, you finally made it," she says while plopping on the couch.

"Yeah," Curtis says while sitting, too. "You know, I like your mom. She's funny."

"She likes you, too. Said you called her ma'am. You made her day."

"Where's your dad?"

"Working. He works for a shipping company." Kelly draws his attention to the photos on the entertainment system.

"That's my dad… and here's me and my brothers—it's not a great picture…"

"Your brothers look similar."

"They get that all the time," she grins.

"What's so funny?"

"Nothing…" she says before moving on. "And here's a picture of my mother and this one's of the whole family."

"Nice. You got any baby photos?"

"Not for *you* to see," she says laughing, "I don't know you like that yet… What about your family? I know you have an older brother."

"Yeah, it's just Omar and me. I would have had an older sister, but my mom lost the baby."

"Oh, I'm sorry…"

"Yeah, it would have been cool. But if my sister was born, I might not have made it."

"Maybe. Or you would've been a surprise."

"Yeah, maybe."

"So… do you think about her often?" Kelly asks.

"My sister?"

"Yeah."

"Every month. Sometimes I wonder what she's doing right now, being in heaven with God… she must be having a good time with my dad."

"Your dad died, too?"

"A few years ago."

"I... I don't know what to say."

"It's Ok. What do you say when something like that happens?"

"I'm sorry..."

"Don't be... It's not your fault. The important thing is that we were close. We did almost everything together!"

"He sounds like a good father..."

"The best."

They both sit for a moment, sipping their water. Curtis strains his neck to look down the hall. "So where are your brothers?"

"In their room."

"What are their names?"

"Kevin and Kelvin?" Kelly says while standing up.

"Wow, their names are similar, too."

She cracks a smile. "You'll see why in a minute." She leads him down the hallway to the last door on the right, knocks and then walks in. Both Kevin and Kelvin are relaxing on their beds.

"He's here," she says to them.

"So Kelly, this is your boy, Curtis?"

"Yep."

"How's it going?" Kelvin asks.

"We've seen you around school," adds Kevin.

"I'm doing alright," Curtis responds as he turns to Kelly and says, "You didn't tell me they were identical twins! How cool is that?" He turns back to the brothers. "How do people tell you two apart?"

They both laugh. "It's subtle."

"Mainly," Kelvin says, "I'm a little bigger than Kevin."

"I play football, while my brother here, plays basketball."

"Oh..."

"Besides that," Kevin says, "we mostly wear the same outfits, but just in different colors."

"I like blue and black." Kelvin says as his brother chimes in, "And I like red and green."

"You got it?" asks Kelly with a big smirk.

"It may take me a couple of days to get it down, but I got it—for the most part."

"Good. Now that we got that out the way, Kelly tells us you're having some problems with Treyshawn."

"Yeah, he says he'll beat me up if I don't give him ten dollars every day he sees me."

"How much have you paid already?"

"Seventeen dollars."

"It helps that Curtis is taking some advanced classes," Kelly adds, "He only has homeroom with Treyshawn."

"He sits right next to me," Curtis says.

"If you have homeroom with him, how come you've only paid seventeen bucks?"

"He hardly ever comes," Curtis replies.

"Sounds like Treyshawn. He's trifling and not about anything; but we hear that you're really smart."

"Me?" Curtis says. "I hear you guys are smart, too, and you're great in sports."

The brothers smile.

"True. We have full scholarships to college already and our grades aren't below a 3.5."

"Wow. I would do sports too, but I've got asthma."

"Hey, don't let that stop you. There's probably a way for you to control your asthma and still do a sport," Kevin says.

"Which sport would you do?" Kelvin asks.

"That one's easy. I'd do track."

"Well, you sure are skinny," Kelvin says, "Your physique seems to be built for speed. I bet you'd cut through the wind real good."

"Do you exercise?" Kevin asks.

"Not really. I figured it would just be a waste of time because of my condition."

"Exercise is never a waste. Start with the basics like jumping jacks, pushups, running in place—anything to help build up your endurance, lung capacity and muscle tone."

"And do specific breathing exercises to help strengthen your lungs."

"If you want we can help you get in better shape."

"That would be great! Thanks."

"No problem, Curtis. If you're a friend of our sister then we're your friends. Now, first things first; we need to have a little talk with Treyshawn."

Saturday afternoon. September 27th. Guys hustle hard in a full court press while others stand waiting for their turn to get their hands on the ball and show off their skills. Treyshawn's first game already ended—his team lost—although not by much. Now he and his boys stand talking about nothing when Kevin and Kelvin approach from across the court.

Both brothers are identical in almost every way—their 6 foot 5 inch frames cast large shadows in the autumn sunlight—and their chiseled good looks draw admiring glances from all around. Girls love to be around them and the young boys idolize them. They're the neighborhood heroes, whose skills on the court and field cannot be denied. Together, they have helped put their school on the map for basketball and football. The whole neighborhood roots for their future.

The game momentarily stops as everyone greets them. Once they pass through, the players continue. Treyshawn's friends see them coming and get a little nervous. "Yo, Trech, look…"

Treyshawn turns to see the twin brothers walking towards him. He's definitely scared, but puts up his bravado face. Even with his tough exterior, he mumbles to himself, "Man, this can't be good. Gotta talk fast."

"What's up Double K's?"

"We need to talk to you, Treyshawn."

"What's going on?"

"We understand that you've got a problem with one of our friends."

"Me? Nah. I ain't got a problem with nobody."

"So, Curtis Powers is nobody?"

"Look, you got it all wrong."

"You calling us liars, Treyshawn?"

"Nah. Nah. I'm just saying you got this all wrong."

"Now you' re calling us ignorant?"

"No way! I ain't callin' you guys ignant!"

"It's IG-NOR-ANT—not ignant. You really need to work on your grammar."

"Listen, we're only going to say this once. You stay away from Curtis and we won't have issues."

"But if you touch him again or even blow hot breath from your big mouth in his direction, then you'll have trouble. You got that?"

"Yeah… I got it."

"We can't hear you."

"I said yeah, I got it!"

"Good. And make sure you give him his money back."

"Nice talking with you."

And with that, the two giants walk off, leaving a tiny, scared and angry Treyshawn in their wake.

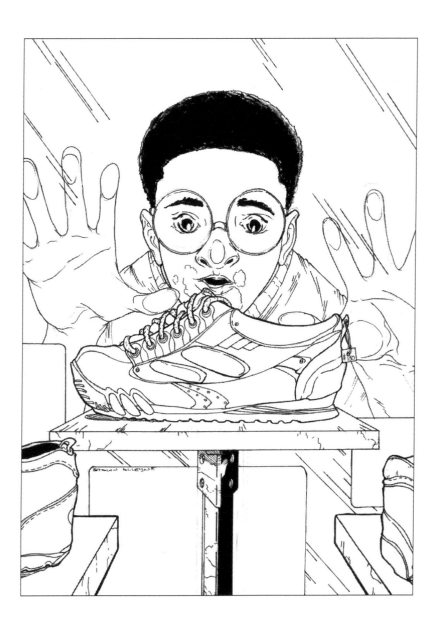

Chapter Four
Initiative

CURTIS CAUTIOUSLY ARRIVES TO SCHOOL MONDAY morning and heads straight to homeroom. As he nears the class, he sees Treyshawn talking to his friends. Their eyes meet, but his nemesis only reacts with a scowl and returns to his conversation.

Curtis smiles—relieved—as he makes his way to class. The bell rings just as Treyshawn enters and takes his seat.

"Hope you had a good weekend, Smurtis," Treyshawn says sarcastically.

"It was ok. What about you?" he responds nervously.

"Don't worry about my weekend," Treyshawn snaps back as he turns to talk to someone else.

Wow! He's actually leaving me alone! I don't know what Kevin and Kelvin did, but it worked!

Curtis grows more relaxed each time he passes Treyshawn in the hall, without incident. He's amazed at the change in the situation. As he stops by his locker—just before his last class—he says a prayer of thanksgiving:

"God, dad often said to give you thanks in the good and bad times. So, thank you. I guess it was a good thing to have Kelly's brothers talk to Treyshawn for me. It looks like things won't be so bad anymore."

He closes his locker, picks up his bag and turns to walk away: SLAM!!! A rough hand crams Curtis' face into his locker! The force of the impact snaps his glasses in two!

"So you had to be a chicken and run to Kelly's brothers for help? You couldn't be man enough to stand up for yourself?"

Curtis cries out in pain as he struggles, but can't break free. Treyshawn's friends form a perimeter around them to keep other students from getting too close.

"You're... hurting... me!" Curtis yells.

"Of course I am! That's what I do! I hurt people who are weaker than me!" Treyshawn punches Curtis in his ribs, causing him to cry out again.

"Quit your cryin! Kelly's brothers told me to stay away from you and I'll do just that! But you gonna wish you hadn't said a word to 'em! And if you tell 'em about this conversation… you gon wish you weren't even born!"

Treyshawn shoves Curtis into the lockers, one last time, and leaves—but not before reaching into his back pocket for a small wad of dollar bills; which he throws at Curtis' face. "See you around, *Smurtis*."

The wad explodes into a melee of bills—flip-flopping through the air—as Treyshawn and his friends disappear into the crowd. Curtis slowly slides to the floor as tears gush without warning and his chest heaves in and out. Panic sets in as he scurries for his inhaler, while his thoughts run through his mind, unchecked: *Why did I have to come to this stupid school? I wish dad were still alive. God, why did you take him from me? I don't know what to do! I wish I could just run away!*

"Phssshh…" The heaving lessens.

"Are you all right?" asks a passing student.

"Just leave me alone!" Curtis blurts out.

"Fine, I'm not the one on the floor crying like a baby!" the girl says as she walks off.

His gaze drops, as he watches his tears burst on the floor's hard surface, and notices that they are mixed with swirls of red. His hand slowly moves up the side of his face to touch his right eyebrow—it stings! A quick look reveals blood.

No one tries to help, but he finally gets tired of feeling sorry for himself, and musters up enough strength to pick up his broken glasses, wipe his face, and stand up. Now begins the long and painful walk to the nurses' office. Looking down at his watch, he realizes that half of his last period is already gone.

Curtis comes home after school, hungry, but doesn't eat. His ribs hurt every time he breathes. He drops his bag and jacket next to his room and makes a beeline for the bathroom mirror, which reflects his slightly swollen jaw and gash above his eye. He pulls up his shirt, revealing a bruise on his left side, right where Treyshawn's fist hit. He had to tell the nurse he slipped and fell, just to keep her from calling his mom. A moment passes before he heads to his room and drops onto his bed. Somehow he forgot that the side of his jaw hurt—that is until his face hit the mattress.

"Ow! I shouldn't have told Kelly's brothers to talk to Treyshawn!" he kicks. "Now things are worse!" He looks over to the clock—it's only 4:30 pm. "Mom's working late tonight… got enough time for a nap before I start my homework."

Curtis easily falls asleep; his mind and body exhausted. As the darkness overtakes him, it slowly gives way to a scene from years earlier.

"Son! Hurry up! You're going to miss it!"

"I'm coming, Dad!" Curtis ran into the spacious living room and plopped down on four large pillows right next to his dad.

"Did I miss anything?"

"No, the race is about to start. Did you wash your hands?"

"Yep!"

Omar sat on the other side of his dad with a large bowl filled with chips. Both sons leaned into their father and watched the giant screen television intently as the 2004 Olympic runners prepared for the 100-meter race.

"Justin Gatlin is gonna win! I bet you he's gonna win!"

Malcolm laughed hard. "You really like him, don't you?"

"Yep! And he's gonna win. You just watch."

The shot fired and the runners launched from the starting blocks with tremendous speed. The crowd cheered as eight men pushed their bodies to the limit for the world to witness. Muscles and tendons, bones and cartilage, lungs and hearts, arms and legs—every part of each runner worked in concert to propel them down the track as fast as humanly possible! But there could only be one first place winner—and that gold medal went to—Justin Gatlin.

"Yeah!" Curtis yelled while jumping up and down on the pillows. His dad and brother looked on while laughing and giving each other high-fives.

"I told you he'd win! I told you he'd win!"

"That's right Curtis! You called it!"

"Dad, when I get older I want to run in the Olympics!"

His dad laughed while Omar was bewildered.

"Curtis? You can't run in the Olympics," Omar said.

"Why not?" Curtis replied.

"Because of your asthma. You know you can't get too excited."

"Of course Curtis can run in the Olympics, Omar," their father replied. He turned to Curtis, who held his head down—saddened by his brother's remark. "Son, you do have to be careful about your asthma, but remember, you can do anything you put your mind to do. If you exercise and find a method that helps you control your asthma… I wouldn't be surprised if one day I was watching you at the Olympics. Anything is possible."

Curtis brightened up with a huge grin. "Thanks, Dad!" he said while hugging his father. Then he looked at his brother and said, "See! I'm going to run in the Olympics."

"No you're not," Omar replied.

"Yes, I am!"

"No, you're not," Omar said with a sheepish smile.

"Yes, I am!"

Omar sat quiet for a moment—as if he'd given up—and then taunted Curtis under his breath, "No, you're not…"

Their dad erupted with a hearty laugh, "Now that's enough you two. Omar stop teasing your little brother."

Almost instantly—as a commercial break began—all three commenced with a friendly wrestling match. They never realized their future would soon change in a tragic and significant way.

Curtis awakens to a darkened room—momentarily confused. He lay on his bed in tears as his eyes scan the quiet space, bit by bit. Slowly, the surroundings regain their familiar feeling as he settles on the clock, with its red digital numbers illuminating the shadows. It was 8:00pm.

The memory seemed so real—he could even smell dad's shirt and feel the hair on his mustache as he hugged him. *Three years since his death… You'd think I'd be beyond this by now,* he thinks to himself. But the memories still come—often at inopportune times: sometimes as a curse, other times as a blessing… like a reminder of sorts. Was this one a blessing or a curse? All he knows is that dad isn't coming back.

In the darkness of the room, Curtis pulls his legs up to his chest and cries uncontrollably. If this was a blessing somehow, it sure didn't feel like it.

Three hours later, Miranda finally arrives home. She struggles through the front door, with multiple bags creasing her arms, along with her class textbook in one hand and her shoes in the other. A sportscast sounds from the living room.

"What's Curtis doing up this time of night?" she says to herself, "he's got school in the morning."

She puts the bags down, makes her way into the living room and immediately stops—taken by what she finds. Only the light from the small television screen illuminates the darkness. The 2004 Olympic games are playing back on the VCR—the cheers of the crowd fill the room. Even so, she can hear the quiet whimpering of her son in the darkness.

"Curtis?" She looks towards the couch where a mound of blankets cover him, leaving only his face revealed, with tears reflecting the television's brightness.

Miranda switches on the lamp and sits next to her son, instinctively peeling away the layers of blankets and gently pulling him to her lap. He embraces her tightly as she begins to weep. She remembers the day this video was recorded: she was there, quietly standing in the doorway—having just given her eldest son a bowl of chips, and making sure her youngest had washed his hands after using the bathroom.

She let Malcolm have his time with the boys; perfectly comfortable with enjoying them from afar. Being with their dad would be a time they would never forget. This would be a time she would never forget.

As she sits and rubs her fingers through her son's hair, she thinks to herself, *he had the dream again…* Tears roll down her cheeks and pool at the bottom of her chin, seemingly frozen in time, before a large, single droplet falls onto Curtis' cheek.

"I know son," she says softly, "I miss him, too."

It's Saturday October 4th. Both Curtis and his mother stand outside the window of the local sneaker store, looking in:

"How much are they?"

"$150.00"

"$150.00! I know you lost your young mind."

"But mom, it's the latest fashion!"

"Latest fashion! First, we don't have the money. Second, do you know how many young people are robbed *or worse* because of the latest fashion?"

"Mom, please."

"Don't 'please' me. We're out here shopping for you, knowing money is tight already and you show me a pair of sneakers for $150.00? You can get a perfectly good pair at the shop down the block."

"I don't want a pair of sneakers from that store!"

"Why not?"

"Everybody knows they're knock-offs of the popular brands."

"Who cares what everyone thinks? If everyone jumped off a bridge would you do it, too?"

"Why do you *always* use that line?"

"Because it works. Curtis, you're smarter than this. Remember what your father told you about accepting peoples' opinions?"

"Mom… a lot of kids are making fun of the way I dress."

"And while they're busy making fun of you, many of them are flunking out of school. Let them laugh! Use their laughter as fuel to drive you to greatness. One day you'll be so well off you won't care if your clothes are name-brand or not. But until then, you need to focus on your schooling."

"Mom, please… Just this once."

"I'm sorry, Curtis. It's just an unwise spending decision for us right now."

Curtis grabs his mother's arm—his eyes pleading with hers. "I'll do extra chores around the apartment to work it off."

She looks at him for a moment before crossing her arms. "I tell you what I'll do. If you still want these sneakers, after answering my questions, then I'll buy them for you."

"OK!" he shouts while standing at the ready.

"Will these sneakers make you run faster?"

"No."

"Will you be able to jump higher?"

"…No."

"Are they bulletproof?"

"Mom…"

"Are they?"

"No."

"Can you fly with them?"

"No…"

"Then why would you want to spend $150.00 for a pair of sneakers that cost some sneaker companies less than $12 to make in a sweat shop on the other side of the world? The conditions are often bad and workers barely make enough to live on. Besides, most sneakers are all form and fashion with no real improvement in function."

The wind is completely sucked out of Curtis' sails. His mom's argument is solid.

"… I guess you're right."

"Curtis, I know it's tough being in a new school, but I also know you are stronger than this. God will get you through; you just watch and see. What he has planned for you is beyond anything you can imagine for yourself. You just need to keep doing what you know you need to do.

"As a matter of fact," she says in a jokingly manner, "you are so smart and good with your hands—you could probably build a better sneaker that would actually be worth $150.00!"

As they continue to walk towards the train station, his mother's mind moves to other concerns while Curtis thinks about her words. It was a joke, but a kernel of truth was contained within it. Was it possible? Could the answer to his problems be that simple? It was a long shot, but what did he have to lose? His mind revved into high gear as they continued to shop; he couldn't wait to get home.

Curtis hangs his new shirts and pants in the closet, before opening the box which contains his new no-name-brand sneakers. He holds them up—looking at them closely from all angles. *At least they're black.*

Miranda puts up the groceries while preparing for dinner. Curtis comes into the kitchen.

"Thanks, Mom... for everything."

"You're welcome, honey. You want something to eat? I was thinking about making beans and franks."

"Sounds good to me."

"Alright, beans and franks it is! What are you going to be doing in the meantime?"

"Oh, I don't know," he says with a grin, "I think I'll get to work on what you said."

"Ok, I'll let you know when the food's ready."

He quickly walks out while his mother wonders, *What did I say?*

Curtis closes the door to his room and sits at his desk. He pulls his journal out of the drawer, opens to a new page, grabs his retractable ballpoint pen and begins to write. His excitement brims to such an extent, that he talks as he writes.

Journal entry 1,135. Saturday, October 4, 2008. New Science Project:

"Mom made a suggestion that just might work. She challenged me to build a better sneaker; something that could actually make me run faster and jump higher. I don't know about being bullet-proof or flying," he laughs to himself, "I'll have to deal with that later.

"But, if I could make a sneaker that would enable me to run faster, then I could outrun Treyshawn. Who knows what else would be possible? What would I need to do this?"

He rotates the pen from his index finger all the way to his pinky and back again; then presses on the push top. Click. Over and over this action continues—causing the ballpoint to engage and release repeatedly—click, click, click, click...The kinesthetic motion of this action always seems to help his mind process information.

"We were just talking about the kinetic energy of moving objects, in physics class," he says to himself as he begins writing down the steps of the Scientific Method:

Step One: Ask a question.

Step Two: Construct a hypothesis.

Step Three: Test the hypothesis.

Step Four: Analyze the data.

Step Five: Communicate Results.

Ok, my question is: how can I make a pair of sneakers that enable me to run faster and maybe even jump higher?

When someone runs, they don't use all of their kinetic energy. Some of it's lost when their feet impact the ground. I need to use the energy that's normally lost.

He turns to his computer, fires it up and connects to the Internet. *Let's see what we can find about kangaroos... Mr. G talked about momentum the other day; kangaroos do a good job using theirs, and could easily outrun a human.*

He discovers something interesting and writes it down: "A kangaroo has strong muscles and long tendons which is one of the secrets to its jumping ability. They can store and redistribute a lot of energy. Their regular speed is between 13 to 25 miles per hour, but they can hop as fast as 44 miles per hour over short distances. And they can jump up to 30 feet!"

Through various links, he stumbles upon several inventions designed to boost human momentum, and writes the relevant information down in his journal. *Now this is cool...*

"Curtis? Food's ready!" his mom calls.

"I'll be there in a minute!"

Minutes turn to hours as Curtis reads page after page of information and watches numerous videos showing various contraptions in action.

Miranda, finishes cleaning the kitchen, looks at the clock and smiles while shaking her head. He's into one of his projects again; food is the last thing on his mind. She wraps his plate in foil, puts it in the oven and goes about preparing her clothes for the next day.

"I never knew there was so much information on this stuff." His excitement turns to slight disappointment. "The concepts make sense, but the designs are too bulky. Treyshawn won't give me time to strap these things on."

Curtis pulls a drawing pad from his desk drawer, flips it to a new page and begins some initial sketches.

"My drawing ability was never that great..." He goes to his closet and pulls out the old pair of sneakers that Omar gave him before leaving for the navy.

"These use special foam technology to store more energy when you move in them." He looks at them for a long time, turning them in his hands and studying them from every angle. *They look better than the ones I got today.* He jumps back on the computer; his fingers streak across the keyboard as he studies information released by all the major sneaker companies.

"Ok. If I'm going to do this, a sneaker won't cut it. It can't store and redirect enough energy."

Curtis leans back in his chair and reviews everything in his mind, while clicking his pen top even faster.

"...long tendons. What can I use? Industrial strength rubber bands?" He goes to his bookshelf and pulls a book on the human body and looks at the color diagrams of the muscular system—specifically the legs. With pen in hand, he writes"

"I need something higher; like a boot. The bottom can be like a sneaker, but the higher part needs to connect to a long, tendon-like structure. And if my foot sits in it, there's going to have to be some kind of up and down motion to absorb the kinetic energy."

Just then, a knock rings from the door.

"Curtis, your food has been waiting for a while."

"Sorry, Mom. I'm not hungry. Can you put it in the fridge and I'll eat it later?"

"All right, but it's getting late. And don't forget we have church in the morning."

"I won't." Curtis looks at the clock again. *I can't believe it's almost eleven. It seemed like it was just five o'clock minutes ago.*

He takes his pen and tries to write in his journal, but the ballpoint is retracted. He doesn't give the action much thought as he presses the pen's top to re-engage the tip. At that very moment, something about the pen draws him. He looks at it closely as he presses the pen's top over and over and over with his thumb... slowly. His eyes open wide, betraying the brilliant idea that forms in his mind; compelling him to quickly make notations in his journal—ending the entry with these words:

"I think I'm on to something."

He closes the log, disengages the pen and steps away from his desk. He takes a moment to rub the circulation back into his legs and arms, as his discomfort is overridden by excitement and physical exhaustion. It's time to rest and continue his research another day.

Chapter Five

Divine Intervention...

THE CHOIR SINGS TO THE LIVELY sounds of the Worship Center music. Praise dancers move throughout the sanctuary in motions of love, adoration and reverence. The congregation listens—some weep, while others stand with their arms stretched upwards. Others clap, while a few silently sway from side to side.

Miranda smiles through her tears as she listens to the words:

"I will never leave you... though you may feel forsaken... My love is with you always... drawing you to me..."

She sings along, almost at a whisper, while trying to put everything in perspective.

Lord, I need you to help me. Things are so heavy. Please, help me. As she worships, an unexplainable peace comes over her—which overshadows the inner turmoil of her circumstances. Even though her husband isn't with her, God has never left her family alone.

Curtis, however, seems almost oblivious to the worship around him. All he can think about is the empty pew a few rows in front of him—the spot where dad used to sit—and the spot next to it—where he usually sat. Before long, he's lost in his thoughts again, journeying back to the past. His surroundings fade away as his mind begins to recount the events of the past few years.

His family started attending this church just after his dad was diagnosed with a rare form of cancer. Before then, they never really attended church—except on Christmas and Easter and the occasional New Year's Eve celebration. They believed in God; after all, they said grace over their food at almost every meal. They even had a bible in the house, which sat on the coffee table. It was big and belonged to grandma—before she died.

Occasionally Curtis saw his dad or mom reading through it, but it mostly gathered dust. They may not have been as close to God as others, but they believed that he created everything and they worked hard to be their best. To the family, that bible was a symbol of God's blessing on their home. Surely the creator of the universe would be pleased about that.

It wasn't until shortly after the 2004 Olympics that Curtis' dad found out about the aggressive cancer. A friend invited him to The Worship Center and the very next Sunday the entire family went, and then the Sunday after that. There wasn't much resistance, even though the commute from New Jersey to the Bronx was forty-five minutes on a good day.

After running extensive tests, the doctors gave Malcolm six months to live, so the family cherished all the time they could get. After a month of attending, Malcolm joined the church. A week later, so did Miranda. Only Curtis and his brother Omar resisted taking the plunge.

"Dad? Why did you join the church?"

Malcolm Powers laughed as he ran his hand through Curtis' hair and drew him close to his side.

"I thought this question would come up. You're very inquisitive, you know."

"Mom said I get it from you."

"She's probably right," he said while hugging his son. "You know there's a scientific principle which basically states, energy is never destroyed, but only transformed."

"Yeah."

"Well, if my body is made up of energy, then what happens to that energy when I die?"

"You mean your soul?"

"Yes, Son. My soul. This cancer has made me wrestle with death: what happens to my soul when I die? Will my consciousness exist in some new form? Will I have to give an account for my life? If heaven is real—is hell real also? And does what I do in this life determine where I go in the next?"

"Wow… those are some deep questions."

"Have you ever thought about them?"

"Not really."

"Do you remember what happened that summer when you were eight? You got caught in that rain storm."

Curtis laughed hard. "Of course I remember, Dad! There's no way I could forget that. I was playing with some friends at the field, a few blocks from the house. Then the storm hit and we were stuck under a tree."

"It was raining real hard," Malcolm said.

"And there was lightning too! We all ran home, as fast as we could, and I fell in a big puddle!"

"And what happened when you got home?"

"Mom wouldn't let me in the house!"

Malcolm laughed at his son's expression. "She had been cleaning all day long, right up to when you came knocking at the door."

"I was covered in mud and soaking wet, but mom wouldn't let me in!"

"You're not coming in here, all dirty, after I just cleaned up the house!" Malcolm said in his *best wife impression.* "What did you say to her?"

"But, I'm your son! Let me in!"

"She told you to strip down to your underwear, right there on the porch!" He said, laughing.

"Dad, it wasn't *that* funny," said Curtis, while trying to keep a straight face.

"Come on! That was classic! You standing outside in your underwear— in the rain! I always wished I had my camera to get that one!"

"Alright. Maybe it was a *little* funny."

"So, then what happened?"

"I took my clothes off while mom got garbage bags and made a path to the bathroom."

"Then she escorted you straight to the tub!"

"And made sure I scrubbed all over! It felt good to be clean."

"I'm sure it did. Mom loved you… but you couldn't just come in to the house any way you wanted. You had to come by the path she made for you. It's the same way with God."

"So…" Curtis said, "…You were like me covered in mud… and God was like mom?"

"Pretty much. You think on that for a while."

Malcolm lived for a whole year before he died. A lot of people prayed for God to heal him… but he never got better; at least not physically. But, a strange thing did happen—his words seemed to carry more weight and he was happier than ever. His body was dying, but there was a twinkle in his eyes that had not been there before—and everybody took notice.

But it was a dark time after his death. Even though the church reached out to the family, Miranda and her two sons dealt with resentment towards God. It just didn't seem to make any sense! Why would a loving God take away a man who was a husband and a father and leave the family all alone? What's the purpose in that?

Struggles came, but giving up on life was not an option. Malcolm's life proved that somehow, God was faithful and the community of faith had become such a part of their lives, even though there were things they didn't understand.

Curtis' attention was drawn back to the pew. The music had stopped and the announcements were being read. There still were things he didn't understand, but he wouldn't think about them now. Something else pressed for his attention: his boots.

The longer things took, the more he began to fidget. He couldn't wait for the service to be over, so he could get home and continue his research. Actually, he had wanted to stay home altogether so he could work on the boots, but his mother was unrelenting in her decision to make service.

As people came to the altar with their tithes and offerings, his thoughts went back to the morning's conversation:

"Mom, do I have to go? Can I miss service just this once? I'll go next week! I promise." Curtis and his mother walked down the six blocks to the church.

"You always want to make sure you honor God with your time. After all, he gave it to you. Your project won't go anywhere. It'll be waiting for you when you get back."

"Yeah, but I'll have less time to work on it. Sometimes service is long; real long and the day will be over before you know it! And please tell me there's no afternoon service."

"There is no afternoon service."

"Thank you God," he says with a rather large breath of relief.

"Listen, if you give God your time… He'll give you his time."

"What's that supposed to mean?"

"You just think about it for a bit and try to pay attention during worship."

As the choir prepared to sing again, Curtis found himself still somewhat agitated. *Lord, help me to give you your time…* His mother's words rang in his ear, so he focused on the one thing he enjoyed most about the church: the pastor. They both enjoyed science and have had several conversations about the latest discoveries. When he gets up to preach, Curtis usually pays attention. Even so, it seemed to take so long to get to the sermon, sometimes, that his mind would wander. Having his project, waiting at home, makes it even harder to keep his mind from wandering! As he fights to keep his focus, the pastor's words catch his attention.

"God has given you a mind, and he wants you to use it. Don't let life bully you! Don't let the devil intimidate you into a corner where you feel like you have no options. Trust God and believe and he will show you how to run and not get weary!

"He will empower you—like he did the prophet Elijah, who was able to outrun the king's chariot. Like David who said, 'For by you I have run through a troop; and by my God have I leaped over a wall.'

"No matter the obstacles in front of you, don't give up! Wait on the LORD! The day is coming when you and I will have to face the things in life that intimidate us.

"Expect God to reveal what you need to do to outrun the enemies that try to overtake you. And then do what he says! He will renew your strength! He will cause you to run—to leap—to soar on wings like those of an eagle!"

As Curtis and his mother walked to the train station, he couldn't help but play the pastor's words over and over in his head.

It was like God was talking right to me, he thought to himself. Like he was encouraging me to keep going with my research. Would God even care about something like this? He's got six billion people and the entire universe to deal with.

His mother could tell he was deep in thought.

"You're quieter than usual. Want to talk about it?"

"Do you think God has time to deal with our concerns when he's got a whole universe to run?"

"Well now… *that's* a big question. I guess we all ask that question in some form or another. Did you know that David, one of the kings of the Jews, from the bible, asked that very same question?"

"Really?"

"That was the lesson for our Sunday school class this morning—Psalm 8. David said to God, 'I think about the universe you have made, and the moon and stars you put in place. Why do you care about us humans? We're so insignificant—why are you even concerned?'"

"He said that?"

"You and King David have something in common, even though he asked the question thousands of years ago."

"Whoa…"

"So, what do you think? Does God have better things to do with his time than to deal with us?"

"Well, it seems far fetched that God would have time to deal with us every day. I mean there are billions of galaxies in the universe! Even if he's got time to deal with us... there's got to be more important people on his list than me."

"*Everyone* is important to God; and don't forget he's the creator of the universe."

"But it just seems so amazing that he would have time to deal with us; there's over six billion people on the planet!"

"Where are all of these questions coming from Curtis?"

"I just... I just felt like pastor was talking right to me. Like he knew what I was going through—exactly what was in my head. But how could he?"

"So what's your conclusion?"

"Maybe he's psychic."

"Curtis!" his mom says laughing. "I definitely didn't expect *that* answer."

"I'm trying to keep an open mind. Pastor could have psychic abilities."

"Or... since you're trying to weigh all the possible options, God could be talking to you through him. God does have things in store for us that stretch beyond our imagination."

Curtis runs to his room, changes out of his church clothes, and sits at his desk while opening his journal to where he left off the night before.

Journal entry number 1,136. Sunday October 5th, 2008.

"God may be trying to talk to me; unless it's just coincidence. I don't really think pastor is a psychic.

"I believe the boots will help me not get tired easily. That means I could run for longer distances and might be able to jump high enough to leap over a wall!

"I just have to keep digging and keep my eyes open for the answers I need. And one more thing: I'm going to have to confront Treyshawn... when I'm ready."

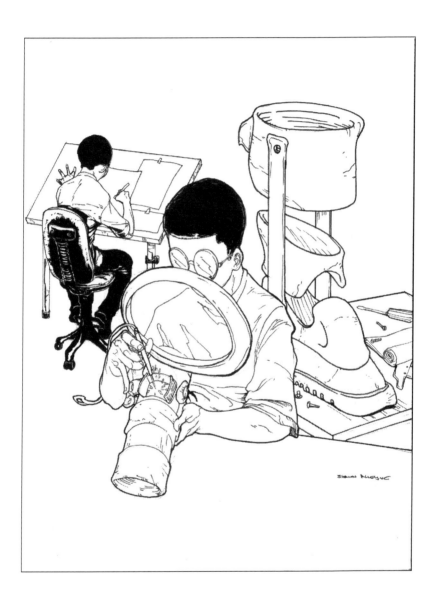

Chapter Six

The Prototype

SATURDAY NOVEMBER 1, 2008. IT'S BEEN almost one month since that Sunday conversation; Curtis has been busy spending most of his time in his room. The phone rings:

"Hey, Kelly, how's it going?"

"Figured I'd give you a call. Haven't seen you outside of school in like a month! You seem distracted. Everything's ok?"

"Things are cool. I've just been busy working on a project."

"Project? What project?"

"Top secret. If I told you, I'd have to kill you."

"That line is so old."

"I still can't tell you."

"I thought we were close."

"We are... it's just..."

"Look, if your project includes another *friend*," Kelly says shyly.

"I don't have another friend."

"It's not like we're going out or anything."

"Kelly."

"I've got friends too, you know."

"Kelly, could you slow down a minute?"

"Even my brothers asked about you."

"Kelly!"

"What?"

"There are no other friends! I didn't tell you because I was afraid you'd laugh."

"Did I laugh when Treyshawn knocked you to the ground the first time?"

"You didn't have to say it like *that*."

"Other kids laughed at you, but I didn't. Besides, even if you tell me and I do laugh, I wouldn't be laughing at you."

"I... like to invent stuff."

"And? I like ballet."

"I never *actually* built any of my inventions yet; I do better taking things apart than putting them together. But, I'm *going to* build this invention. I didn't want to tell you until I actually built it."

"You don't have to keep it a secret from me. You're smart and you like to invent things; I get that. At least I know you're not trying to keep me in the dark on purpose."

"So we're ok?"

"Yeah, we're ok. Any idea how long I have to wait?"

"Not sure. I've got my supply list, process of construction…"

"You're not building a bomb are you?"

"What? No! Are you serious?"

"Hey, I just watched the news where a kid went into his school and shot a bunch of people. You gotta ask nowadays. You see how crazy the world is?"

"Yeah, but I'm not trying to kill anybody; I'm building a way to make me run faster! And when it's done, it'll be *very* cool—if it works."

"See, you can't keep a secret."

"It's better than having you think I'm gonna blow up on somebody! Besides, you don't know any specifics."

"So, I guess you *can* keep a secret. I just wanted to make sure you weren't doing anything crazy."

"Look, you can't tell anybody yet, ok?"

"My lips are sealed, but why you trying to run faster anyway? This isn't about Treyshawn is it? He's supposed to be leaving you alone."

Curtis avoids the question. "I just want to run faster—that's all. It's been a dream of mine for a long time."

Just then Curtis' mother knocks on the door and walks in. "I need to talk with you."

"My mom's here; gotta go."

"Ok, see you Monday."

Curtis hangs up the phone and turns towards his mother, who has a serious look on her face.

"What's wrong, Mom?"

"I'm concerned about you."

"Why?"

"I know you have this secret project; I just want to make sure that it's nothing crazy."

"Kelly just asked me the same thing. What is it with girls?"

"See, I'm not the only one concerned about your behavior. I knew I liked that girl. I mean, I've never met her, but from the way you talk about her... why don't you invite her over for dinner?"

"Why? So you can both interrogate me about my projects?"

"No, so we can talk about your crush on Kelly."

"Mom! I don't have a crush on Kelly!"

"If you say so," she laughs, "right now, just tell me what you're working on and we both can move on with our lives." She cracks a hint of a smile, "Don't worry, your secret is safe with me."

Curtis can't help but break into a smile, himself.

"Just for a few minutes! But you have to promise not to tell anyone."

"I promise." She says while putting her hand over her heart. "Scouts honor."

"Mom... You were never in the scouts."

"I know," she says while feigning an attitude. "I just always wanted to say that."

Curtis takes his mother's hands and pulls her over to the clutter of papers and books on his desk.

"Wow, son... that's a *lot* of paper."

"I know," he says while unearthing his schematics from the large pile.

"You might want to sit down."

She takes her place on the edge of the bed as Curtis hands her his schematics. "Ok, what am I looking at?" For the next twenty minutes, her son—like a mighty rushing wind—explains concepts, methodologies, and his journal entries. He demonstrates how the boots should work and shows what they should look like. By the time he finishes, Curtis falls into his chair exhausted!

His mother sits wide-eyed and speechless for a moment. She's never seen her son so animated. "Wow... this is a lot to take in."

Curtis reaches for his inhaler: "Phsssh..."

"...So what do you think?"

"I think... if your boots do half of what you say they can do it will be amazing. To be honest, I only said you should build your own sneaker, to make my point... For you to do all of this... means you still listen to your mother." She gets up and kisses him on his forehead. He smiles back at her.

"So when will you actually build it?"

"Soon. Maybe by Christmas."

"Well, I'm sure your brother will be able to help once he gets home. Have you told him yet?"

"No, but I will. Hopefully Mr. Grabowski can help, too."

"Your physics teacher? Have you told him about your project?"

"Not yet. I want my plans to be set before I do."

"I'm glad you're able to help him in the lab during your lunch period. That'll help keep you out of trouble," she says playfully.

If you only knew, Curtis thinks to himself.

"When will I meet him?"

"I don't know... Whenever you come by the school, I guess."

"I *am* overdue for a visit." His mom walks to the door. "All right secret agent Curtis Powers—inventor extraordinaire—I'm off to finish making dinner! And don't worry, my lips are sealed."

"That's what Kelly said."

"I can't wait to meet her..." his mother says playfully.

Curtis can't completely hide his smile. "Ok. Maybe I like her a little."

"I thought so!"

They both hug and she heads to the kitchen. *He has such an imagination; who knows where it will lead.*

Curtis gathers and stacks his notes neatly on his desk, "I'm glad I could tell Mom about this, but I can't let her find out why I'm working on these boots—not yet—she'd be worried."

Treyshawn continues to keep his distance, although his friends sometimes seem a little too close for Curtis' comfort. For the most part, he now roams through the school's hallways without thinking about Treyshawn's bullying tactics.

Curtis enjoys all of his classes, but his favorite joy is physics. Every day he comes to school anticipating the possibilities that wait in the physics lab. As soon as the bell rings for lunch, his books are packed, he gets his lunch from his locker, and literally, runs to the lab. In an effort to seem more mature when he gets there, he takes a moment to settle his breathing, and then walks in as if everything's cool.

"So what is your family doing for Thanksgiving, Curtis?"

"My brother's coming home from the navy. Mom will probably cook a big meal."

"That's great! I didn't know your brother was coming home so soon."

"He'll be on leave for a few months before having to ship out again. What are you doing for Thanksgiving?"

"Well, I don't have any plans. I was thinking that perhaps your family could come over for Thanksgiving dinner."

"Really?"

"If you wanted to and your mother agreed, of course."

"I'm sure she would! She's been wanting to meet you!"

"Well, I typed up an official invitation for you to give to your mother. If she agrees, I'd be honored to have you all. I've got this big house in Westchester, but no one to share the holidays with. If she likes, I could cook or we could split up the dishes. My daughter always did like my cooking."

"You have a daughter? How come she's not spending the holiday with you?"

"It's too far for her to travel from the Midwest."

"But families are supposed to be together for Thanksgiving! That's right up there with Christmas—except without the presents."

"Yes, well... things are a little different for us."

"I understand if you don't want to talk about it; some things I don't want to talk about either."

They sit quietly for a moment before Mr. Grabowski speaks up.

"So, you'll ask your mother?"

"Oh yeah! I talk about you a lot, you know," Curtis smiles.

"Good things, I hope," he replies with a smile.

Curtis is quiet for a moment, drawing Mr. Grabowski's concern.

"What is it?"

"It's just that... since my dad died... you're like the only guy to really take time to help me learn things. I mean, I have my brother and some guys at church who I talk to... but you're different." Curtis remains quiet for another moment. Mr. Grabowski just waits for him to continue with his thoughts.

"I know you're not my dad and I'm not asking you to be... I just wish you could have met him. You would have talked about science all day long!" He smiles while holding back tears.

Mr. Grabowski smiles, "If he's anything like you, then I'm sure he was a good man."

The bell rings and Curtis packs up his books.

"Have a great weekend, Mr. G."

"You, too, Curtis. See you on Monday."

"Yeah."

As Curtis walks out the door, he can't help but think about the compliment Mr. Grabowski gave him. It feels good to have someone you admire tell you that you have worth.

Mrs. Powers and her two sons arrive at Mr. Grabowski's house. Curtis and Omar watch television in the living room, while their mother and Mr. Grabowski prep dinner in the kitchen.

"Thanks again for inviting us over for Thanksgiving dinner, Mr. Grabowski."

"You're welcome. Please, call me Jim, Mrs. Powers."

"Miranda."

"Well Miranda, thanks for accepting the invitation. This time of year is usually a quiet affair for me. It's nice to have company for a change."

"This time of year is tough for us, as well. With my husband's death and us losing our home, it's been a struggle. Malcolm's death tends to overshadow everything. He used to make a really big celebration out of the holidays."

"If you don't mind me asking, how did your husband die?"

"He had a rare form of aggressive bone cancer. There wasn't much the doctors could do but tell us to make his last days comfortable. They gave him six months—he lasted a year and a half."

"My wife, Carol, died from cancer about ten years ago. The doctors gave her a year to live—she died three months after their diagnosis. I don't think my daughter and I have ever fully recovered."

"After ten years… I'm sorry."

"Me, too… I'm sorry for your loss. I know what this feels like and I wouldn't wish it on my worst enemy. Life is just too precious."

"Do you see her much?"

"In the face of almost every woman I meet."

"No… I'm sorry… I meant your daughter."

"… That was embarrassing."

"Jim, if I had a dollar for every time I thought I saw Malcolm in a crowd— my family would be well off financially."

They sit quietly relishing their memories.

"My daughter, Catherine, lives in Cincinnati with her husband and my granddaughter, both of whom I've never met. We don't talk much these days; we never quite knew what to talk about after Carol's death. She was our world, literally: the perfect wife and mother—I'm sorry, we're supposed to be celebrating and I'm here talking about my problems."

"No, listening to you is helpful. Most people are so afraid to be transparent, as if that transparency makes them weak or less capable. But it's the transparency that helps us all overcome our issues; so thank you. I needed to hear your story."

"And I needed to hear your story, too."

"But on a slightly different note, my son has taken a liking to you."

"Curtis has me excited about life again."

"Really? How so?"

"I've been a physics teacher, in public school, for over thirty years, and have watched the steady decline in students' love for the sciences. It's easy to become disillusioned after you fight for change and see none: funds are cut; teachers have less resources; parents abdicate their role as positive influencers; the constant media hype urging youth to choose popularity over intellect… my love for physics has been smothered by so many layers."

"I definitely understand; things are a lot different from when we were in high school."

"Very different. Every now and then a student would come through my class with great potential and genuine interest, but I must say your son is simply exceptional! I've never met a ninth grade student who qualified to take physics!"

"Curtis tells me that he comes to your lab almost every day during his lunch period."

"Yes. I extended the invitation and figured maybe he'd come once or twice a week. Surely he'd want to hang out with his friends more than an old, overweight teacher. But he just keeps coming and helps me put class experiments together. He has an innate curiosity about how things work."

"He gets that from his father. That was one of the things that drew me to Malcolm—his desire to understand things."

"Well that's a good trait to have. If Curtis channels it correctly, he could go *very* far."

"Do you really think so?"

"I'd bet my thirty years of experience on it."

"It's taking them a long time in the kitchen. What do you think they're talking about?"

"Probably us. But since we've got time, how's things going at school with the bully—what's his name?"

"Treyshawn. He hasn't bothered me since Kelly's brothers told him to lay off."

"Good."

"But I don't know how long he'll listen to them."

"You want me to talk to him? You know I'd *love* to talk to him," Omar says while pounding his massive fist into his hand.

Curtis smiles at the thought of his older brother giving Treyshawn a taste of his own medicine. "That sounds good, but only if nothing else works."

"So, you got a plan?"

"Yeah. Treyshawn is fast: real fast. I figure if I can outrun him, then maybe he'll back off."

"And how are you going to do that?"

"By building a pair of running boots to increase my speed."

"You think he'll stop just because of that? If you make him look bad in front of everybody, he might come after you more."

"I've got to do *something*. He's going to come after me again and if you or Kelly's brothers aren't around, I'm in trouble."

"What do you mean again?"

"A few weeks back, Kelly's brothers told him to back off—and he did—but not after giving me one last beating."

"He did what!" Omar jumps up from the couch. "How come you didn't tell me?"

"Because he said that if I told anyone, I'd be sorry. Besides, I just wanted him to stop."

Neither of them speaks as Omar paces the room before breaking the silence. "Ok, then. We'll try it your way and build the boots... I hope I don't have to hurt this kid."

"I hope you don't have to hurt him either. Kelly said he's got a lot of issues at home."

"Don't we all?" He sits back down and thinks about Treyshawn. "Maybe we should pray for him."

"Pray? Never thought about that."

"It couldn't hurt."

"Well... I guess you're right; look what it did for *you*."

"Yeah, God is good. So when do we start with these boots?"

"Can you draw the plans for it this weekend? I've got the initial drawings."

"I don't see why not. Are you going to ask Mr. Grabowski to help, too?"

"That's the plan."

"Every night I pray for Curtis and Omar. They've been through a lot, but they have strong minds. Even so, I get scared thinking about the obstacles that they will face. I'm not as worried about Omar, since he's in the navy, but Curtis—I can't be there all the time to protect him. I'm just glad he has you in his life as a mentor."

"It's an honor, Mrs. Powers," Jim says with a knowing smile.

"Mr. Grabowski." Miranda nods in return.

"And on that note, I'm sure your boys are hungry."

"Yes, I'm sure they are."

They pick up the dishes and head towards the dining room—for a night filled with lively conversation, fellowship, and good food.

"Curtis, it was great having you and your family over for Thanksgiving dinner; you made it a day to remember."

"Thanks, Mr. G. We had a good time, you really have a nice house."

"Thanks, it needs a lot of work. Miranda and Omar are very nice."

"Yeah, I don't know where I'd be without them," he says while pulling a folder from his bag.

"What do you have there?"

"It's a project I'm working on."

"Alright, a project!"

"Top secret."

"Even better. What is it?"

Curtis hands Mr. Grabowski the folder. He takes it while putting his glasses on. "Let's see here…" What he sees amazes him. The very first image is a schematic profile drawing of a boot.

"Wow… did you do this?"

"No, Omar drew it for me on Friday."

Mr. Grabowski flips through each page, carefully reading the information.

"Am I reading this correctly? You've designed a way to run faster?"

"Yes. I call them Kinetic Redistribution Boots."

"Impressive. I've seen jumping stilts before, but your design is so much more compact and the way you approach the concept seems unique. What made you come up with the idea?"

"I've always wanted to run fast, but there's this bully named Treyshawn…"

"You're not talking about Treyshawn Jinkins?" Mr. Grabowski closes the folder and stands to his feet. "Why haven't you told me about this before?"

"For the most part, the situation has been handled—a friend of mine has two older brothers who told him to leave me alone. He hasn't bothered me since… well, except one time."

"All the teachers have been warned about him. He's a real hothead who gets into a lot of trouble. Who are these older students?"

"Twelfth grade basketball and football athletes."

"Are you talking about the twins, Kevin and Kelvin Washington? They're in my first period class: smart—both of them."

"I'm friends with their younger sister, Kelly, but I don't think he's going to listen to them forever. Once they graduate, I'll be in trouble all over again. Maybe even sooner than that."

"Have you told your mother?"

"No way! She'd freak out, come down here, talk to the principal and make everything worse!"

"Mmm… you have a point there."

"Omar, Kelly and her brothers know—and now you do too."

"So, in response to this, you designed these boots?"

"I tried to reason with him, but that didn't work. So, I'm trying to outsmart him. He's always saying how much faster and stronger he is; I figured maybe if he couldn't catch me, he'll leave me alone. Can you help me build them?"

Mr. Grabowski is pensive. "I will, but on one condition."

"What's that?"

"We go and explain everything to the principal. If he gives us clearance, then we go through with it. If he doesn't, then we find another way. This way, we're both covered."

"Alright," Curtis says somewhat dejectedly."

"Look," Mr. Grabowski assures, "I like your idea—it's so crazy it might actually work. The issue is I have to follow certain protocols so I don't lose my job and if something goes bad, measures are in place to handle Treyshawn."

"I understand."

"You sure?"

Curtis smiles, "So, if the principal says yes, when do we start?"

"How do your Saturdays look? I have a workshop in my garage.

"This… is very unorthodox," the principal says as he leans forward in his chair, places his elbows on his desk, and clasps his hands together. He looks at the two sitting across from him. "I could just expel him."

"Jack, you know he's a loose cannon," Mr. Grabowski interjects. "If we take direct action, he might target Curtis."

"I see your point, Jim. Lord knows we can't afford to have another fight, stabbing or shooting among our students. Curtis, I read your file *and* reviewed your progress reports. To say you were smart would be an understatement. By the way, I'm sorry to hear about the death of your father, I'm sure he would be proud of all your hard work."

"Thank you sir," Curtis responds.

The principal smiles as he continues, "So, because of your performance, the fact that Mr. Grabowski believes in you, and the issues we already have with Treyshawn—I'm going to allow this... alternative. Quite frankly, I'm interested in seeing if these boots of yours work. Just keep me informed on all major developments and if we have to take tougher action, then we will."

Once outside the office, they quickly walk back to the physics lab while, Mr. Grabowski states the game plan: "Here's the deal, you help me with some upkeep work around the house, and I'll help you with your boots. Ask your mom if she's ok with you coming over, then we can start this Saturday.

Journal Entry 1,170: December 5, 2008.

"Tomorrow's the big day and I can hardly sleep! Wish I could time travel twelve hours ahead. Mom came in twice and told me to go to bed—I won't be any good tomorrow if I don't. Lord, help me to go to sleep. I need to be nice and rested for tomorrow."

The sunlight carves its way through Curtis' window shades as the alarm clock sounds on cue. Three seconds barely pass before Curtis hits the off button, jumps out of bed and runs to the shower. Minutes later, he drips his way back to his room—barely able to contain his excitement—as he dries off, gets dressed, and makes his way to the kitchen.

"I know you're in a hurry, Curtis," his mom says, "but you need to slow down and not gobble your food."

Curtis tries to enjoy the food while repeatedly looking at the clock.

"I make you your favorite meal and you can't slow down enough to enjoy it?" his mom exclaims playfully.

"Sorry, Mom," he says between gulps, "I'm just really excited!"

She chuckles, "I know it's a big day for you; I just want you to enjoy every minute and not miss a thing. Come to think of it, I've never seen you so in a hurry to go clean up someone's house. He must be helping you with your project."

"Yep. I sure hope we can jump right into it."

"Mr. Grabowski's too smart for that."

"What do you mean?"

"You're so excited about this—if you jumped right into it, you wouldn't get any cleaning done. He'll start with the cleaning."

"Aw, man, you think so?"

"Yes, and when he does, I don't want you getting an attitude! You understand?"

"Yes, Mom."

"Good. I know Mr. Grabowski means a lot to you. He's growing on me and your brother, too."

"He's a good teacher."

"According to your guidance counselor, he's one of the best teachers they have."

"When did you speak to Mrs. Fuller?"

"The other day. I've had a meeting set up with her for a while."

"How come you didn't tell me?"

"I didn't think you needed to know. You don't know everything I do; just like I don't know everything you do. But we trust each other to do what's right and to be honest if we mess up. Besides, I may want to surprise you one day."

"While I'm in class? Please, don't do that."

"Maybe I'll give you a heads up—maybe I won't," she says playfully.

"Right now, you need to get going. I don't want you to be late."

Curtis gulps down the last of his milk and rushes to the front door.

"Have a good time and be careful!" she yells.

"I will Mom. Bye Omar!"

"Bye Curtis! I'll meet you at Mr. G's house this afternoon!"

The front door slams as Curtis bolts for the elevator—his footsteps echoing down the hall. Once outside, he heads towards to the train station with a mixture of brisk walking and short sprints; all the while focusing on his breathing—in an effort to keep his asthma from flaring out of control.

The breathing exercises I researched and the ones I learned from Kevin and Kelvin seem to be helping. My chest isn't nearly as tight as it usually is when I run.

Mr. Grabowski waits in his burgundy car, just outside of Rheuman High School's parking lot. He can see his star pupil walking up the block from the train station, and goes to meet him.

"Hey, Curtis! You made it!"

"Yep!"

"Get in."

"Thanks."

"Did you have any problems getting here?"

"Nope!"

"Good, I hope you're ready to get some work done."

At the house, the two prepare for a day of intense work and anticipation:

"Alright. I figured we'd work on the house for about two hours and then grab a bite to eat before starting on your project."

"Sounds good to me."

"If we did it the other way around, we probably would be so engrossed in building your boots that the housework wouldn't get done!"

They both laugh as they head down to the basement.

Mom was right, Curtis thinks to himself. *Man, she's good.*

"Alright, Curtis, I've accumulated so much junk over the years—it usually gets put in this room. We're going to separate and sort everything in here and then throw the *junk* of the junk into these two dumpsters. Rule of thumb—if it's beat up, it gets tossed—unless it's tax information or photos of some kind. Show me those first."

Two hours pass as the monstrosity junk piles slowly begin to decrease. The sound of two shredders ripping through papers becomes almost rhythmic as an occasional paper ball fight interrupts the flow. Before they know it, it's time for lunch.

"How are you feeling, Curtis?" Mr. Grabowski asks as they walk up the stairs.

"A little tired," he says while brushing dust off of his clothes. "You have a lot of stuff down there!"

Mr. Grabowski laughs, "I told you!"

They enter the kitchen, wash their hands and make ham and turkey sandwiches. As they are about to eat, the front door bell rings. Mr. Grabowski goes to investigate and returns with a tall, young man.

"Curtis, there's some guy at the door who says he knows you?"

He looks up, wondering whom it might be. He finds a large person standing behind him. "Omar! You made it!"

"Hey, bro! Yep, I made it."

"As you can see, Omar, we just took our break. I've got ham and turkey in the fridge with all the usual condiments. Feel free to make a sandwich."

"Thanks, Mr. G. I appreciate it."

Soon all three are sitting around the table engaged in jovial conversation.

"...And somehow my belt came loose and my trousers dropped to my ankles! The plane cut across the runway and the thrust from the engines caused me to trip! Imagine a guy, my size, rolling around the flight deck with bright red boxers showing! I'll never live that down."

They all laugh.

"Talk about embarrassing moments!" Mr. Grabowski says, "I think your story wins Omar! I've got to work that story into my physics class—with your permission, of course."

"Hey. No problem Mr. G! If it'll make your class laugh in order to get your point across—I'm glad I could be of service."

"Omar, you're too kind… And on that note, let's get started on the real reason why we're here. Grab your materials and schematics and let's head to the garage!"

Curtis and Omar follow their host into a dark space. At the doorway, Mr. Grabowski turns and looks at them with pride while extending his arms.

"This, gentlemen, is my work lab!" With the flip of a switch, the garage illumination flickers to life, supported by a low electrical undertone hum. The boys are astonished by what they see—a spacious, fully functional, well-lit workstation, with a wide variety of tools and equipment.

"Wow," Omar says, "I work on a naval ship and have every tool that you could imagine at my disposal… so I'm not kidding when I say that this is impressive."

"Yeah!" Curtis adds. "You could build anything with this layout!"

"Actually," he says while laughing, "I spend a lot of time at all the major building superstores. With this equipment and the right parts, you could build furniture, an automobile, or an aircraft, and perhaps a pair of running boots too."

"Wow… So what kind of things do you build?" Curtis says, putting his supplies on the main table.

"I do a lot of craftsmanship work. I've built all of my house furniture with these two hands. I do some other things as well, like building devices to complement the physics experiments I use in class. I also do some metal work.

"You two are the first to see this space. I'm usually pretty private about my work down here. Most people just think that I'm an old, overweight physics teacher, but my life involves more than just teaching high school students."

"Wow, Mr. G, I never would have guessed…"

"Don't get me wrong, for the most part, I enjoy teaching high school students. But sometimes things get hard—you might get a rough class that takes extra effort to impact. So, it helps to come down here and build things. It's cathartic. Now that I think about it, what we're starting today is very similar—we're going to help you build something that will facilitate you dealing with your frustrations, Curtis."

"Thank you, Mr. G. You didn't have to do this."

"Yes, thanks for helping my little brother. I'm gone a lot, so it's good to know that you're here."

"Omar, the navy is helping you so that you can be a real benefit to your brother, mother and countless others."

"I know. It's just tough to be away sometimes. Besides, not many people open up their homes like this. You really didn't have to do this. Thank you."

Mr. Grabowski's eyes begin to tear... "you boys are welcome. You're helping me as well. I think we need each other."

After a moment's pause, and the three of them wiping away a few tears, Mr. Grabowski reaches for Curtis' boot schematics folder.

"Alright... enough crying. Let's get to work."

Parts are laid out, in an organized fashion, on one of the worktables. Their first task is to craft a full-scale foam model, to handle the actual dimensions and determine the practical sizes for each major part. Almost three hours pass—cutting, shaping, drilling, sanding, and connecting—before the foam model is complete.

From that frame of reference, they begin to build the first boot out of the actual metal and plastic materials. They take measurements, trace patterns, cut metal and plastic into shapes, holding them together by screws and clamps.

The three work intently, connecting segments, checking for weight allowances and determining the correct fit around Curtis' feet and legs. Adjustments are made and problems they encounter are overcome by sheer grit and willpower.

"It's nine o'clock, I think we can stop for the day," Mr. Grabowski says. They remove their protective gear and clothing, while admiring what sits before them on the worktable—the framework of the boot, with the initial part of the kinetic leveraging system in place.

"Wow..." Curtis whistles softly, while an angled spotlight captures the boot, causing a glowing silhouette to emanate around its form. "Look at it, actually standing in front of us."

"Just think, Curtis," Omar joins in, "that idea used to be in your head."

"And now," Mr. Grabowski adds, "it's coming together right before our eyes."

"Yeah. It's a little bulky, but it *is* the first prototype."

"The big event is going to see if the boots actually work the way you think they'll work."

"They'll work. I just know they will."

"Alright boys, let me get you home. We'll be back at this again next Saturday."

"Can I take it with me?"

"No need to worry, Curtis, it's safe here. I'll lock it up in my safe."

"No, I'm not worried about that, I just want to look at it during the week... you know, to be inspired."

"By all means then, take it with you. When my students are inspired so am I."

Saturday, December 13, 2008. Journal entry: 1,175.

"We're finally done, at least with the first boot! We worked for another six hours today to get everything working. That's a total of thirteen hours just to build one boot! The only thing missing is the protective covers for certain parts. I'm exhausted, but excited.

"Next week, we start working on the second boot. It shouldn't take us as long since we've done the first one already; I think we've gotten the process down better."

Saturday, December 20, 2008. Journal entry: 1,182.

"No house work today—Mr. G wanted to get more accomplished with the boot. I was hoping that we'd be able to knock out the second boot in one shot, but we didn't. We have to wait another week to finish. It would have been great to have both boots done by Christmas, but that's five days away."

Chapter Seven

Happy Holidays

THURSDAY DECEMBER 25, 2008. CHRISTMAS DAY. A small Christmas tree sits in the living room with only a few presents around it. Curtis wakes up to the smell of his favorite breakfast. It takes a moment before he notices that something is missing from the top of his desk.

"Mom!" Curtis yells as he races down the hall.

"Mom! We've been robbed! As he comes into the kitchen he finds his mom and Omar sitting with Mr. Grabowski, which surprises him for a moment, before he continues talking.

"We've been robbed! Somebody came in the middle of the night and stole the boot!"

"Curtis, why are you yelling?"

"Why am I yelling? It's only the most important invention of my life! When I went to sleep, it was there, but when I woke up, it was gone! We've gotta call the police!" He stands there breathing heavily.

"There's no need for the police," Miranda says.

"Why not?" Curtis asks incredulously.

"Because you're boot wasn't stolen," adds Omar, "it was just borrowed."

"You let someone borrow my boot? It's supposed to be a secret!"

"Calm down, Curtis" Mr. Grabowski chimes in. "We didn't give it to anyone."

"But… you said you let someone borrow it!"

"No," Omar says, "I said that it was *just* borrowed."

"So, what does that mean? Who borrowed it?"

"We did," said Omar.

Curtis looks at all of them. "I don't understand!"

"Go into the living room," Miranda says, "and look behind the tree."

Curtis makes a beeline for the living room; miscalculates the turn, and slams his knee into the wall, while taking a nasty tumble. "Owwww!!!"

When his mother, brother, and Mr. Grabowski rush into the room, they find Curtis holding his leg, while wincing in pain.

"Curtis! Are you alright?" His mother kneels down beside him.

Just then, Curtis peers through the gap between the presents, underneath the tree; and sees part of a boot behind the tree. He pushes through the pain in his knee, stands up and hobbles toward the tree; where he finds both boots fully assembled.

"Hey!" he yells while picking them up. "How did these get here? And the second boot is done?"

Miranda, Omar, and Jim begin to laugh at the top of their lungs as they yell, "Merry Christmas!"

Curtis' eyes practically pop out of his head as he holds the boots close. "How did you...?"

"I told you, they weren't taken, they were just borrowed," Omar interjects.

"Yes," adds Mr. Grabowski, "Omar and I worked on it last night, after you went to sleep."

"And that was tough, considering how late you stay up when you're excited about something."

"But we stayed up all night," Omar adds, "and got it done."

"They just got here about fifteen minutes before you woke up."

"I didn't think we were going to finish by Christmas, but this is great! Thank you!"

"So, you're gonna try them on?" asks Omar.

"I need my sneakers."

"Got them right here." His mother hands them to him.

Curtis quickly puts his sneakers on, then unlatches the straps to the boots and places his feet onto the support plating. His family watches with anticipation as he secures the clamps. He's now a couple of inches taller, but when he presses the release buttons on each boot—activating the spring mechanisms—they expand and boost his height by three more inches.

Curtis walks around and can feel the elastic effect of the springs as they engage the kinetic leveraging system. With each step, he's propelled forward. He jumps lightly as the boots multiply the force of his jump, sending him higher into the air.

Omar and Mr. Grabowski cheer as they watch Curtis. Miranda enjoys his display as well, but still worries for his safety.

"Be careful. I don't want you to lose control."

"Don't worry Mom, I got it."

As soon as the words leave his mouth, Curtis loses his balance, falls backwards, and smashes into the Christmas tree. Presents, ornaments, tinsel and lights explode everywhere!

"Curtis!" His mom yells as Omar and Mr. Grabowski jump to his aid and help him struggle to his feet.

"Are you alright?"

"Yeah… I'm fine."

Omar laughs. "I'm glad you're ok!"

"Stop laughing at your brother!" she says.

"What? I'm only laughing because he's ok, Ma! You have to admit that was pretty funny."

"Sorry, Mom. Are the presents damaged?" Curtis asks. They all laugh.

"Well, Curtis," Mr. Grabowski adds, "You've been inaugurated. You've had your first maiden voyage and lived to tell about it. How did it feel?"

Curtis pauses for a moment…. "It felt like I was walking on air, but it's going to take some getting used to."

"Good, because we've got a lot of testing to do to make sure things work right."

"And when will you start that?" his mother asks.

"Saturday?" Curtis responds.

"How about the Saturday after that?" she says.

"The Saturday after that? That's January 2nd! Why can't we start this Saturday?"

"Curtis, I really wasn't asking…"

"But…"

"No buts, you've worked really hard and made a major breakthrough. Enjoy it; take a break and give Mr. Grabowski a chance to relax. Besides, I miss spending time with you."

"But mom…"

"Listen to your mother," Mr. Grabowski interrupts, "after all, she gave us permission to meet in the first place. You can't blame her for wanting to spend time with you."

"It's just that, I'm so excited."

"That's understandable. We're all excited, but taking a short break, after a major milestone like this can be good: think about how we should test the boots and use the rest of the time to relax. We'll be back in the workstation before you know it."

"If you say so," Curtis says hesitantly.

"Come, give your mother a hug, then get out of those boots and let's open the crumpled presents and go eat breakfast."

"Miranda, thanks for having me over to share Christmas with you. I appreciate it."

"You're very welcome, Jim. Thanks for spending the day with us."

Curtis approaches with his boots in a bag.

"What are you doing?" asks Mr. Grabowski.

"Can you hold onto these for me?"

"You don't have to do this, I'm sure you'll do a great job taking care of them."

"It's not that. I just want you to hold them. If I keep them here, I'll probably try to use them by myself and you saw what happened."

"You do have a point there," he says while chuckling.

"Once I learn how to use them, then I'll take them back." Curtis hands the bag to his teacher. "See you in two weeks?"

"Actually, it's only nine days—a whole lot better than two weeks."

Curtis sits on his bed—bored out of his mind. He looks at the clock: "Ugh! It's only 3:00pm; time's moving so slow!" he yells while going to the window. *I don't know if I can wait six more days. What was I thinking? I could be practicing in my room right now!*

The phone rings. He reaches for the handheld, looks at the caller ID and answers.

"Hey, Kelly."

"Hey, Curtis. How're you doing?"

"Bored out of my mind!"

"You? Every time I call, you're working on something. How can you be bored?"

"There's nothing to do."

"You're always doing something, even if it's just reading. What about the project you were working on?"

"I finished phase one a few days ago."

"You did? When were you going to tell me?"

"I just told you," he says gruffly.

"Ok. *That's* out of character. I don't like it when you're agitated."

"Sorry... I don't like it either. It's no fun."

"If you finished phase one, why are you upset?"

"I gave it to Mr. G for safe keeping."

"Your physics teacher?"

"Yeah. He and Omar have been helping me with the project. We finished it and then decided to take a break for nine days before testing it."

"*Now* can you tell me what 'it' is?"

"A pair of boots that make you run faster."

"Wow! Do they work?"

"Not sure yet. I tried them out on Christmas—they seemed to work—then I lost control and crashed into the Christmas tree."

Kelly laughs hard at the unexpected news. "You crashed into the Christmas tree?"

"That's what I said."

"Oh, I wished I could have seen *that!*"

Curtis starts laughing as well. "It *was* pretty funny. I wish you had been there, too."

Their laughter dies down, followed by an awkward silence. Kelly hesitates to ask a question that's been lingering in the back of her mind for a few months now. Curtis thinks the same. Both know there's *something*, but neither wants to be the first to admit it.

"So," Curtis breaks the silence, "my mom suggested the break. I didn't want to do it, but Mr. G agreed that it was a good idea to regroup and come at things fresh. So I gave him the boots. Now I wish I had kept them so I could practice."

"And risk breaking the furniture or one of your legs? It's definitely not worth it; better to have people around, than trying to do it by yourself."

"Yeah, you're probably right."

"You know, I still haven't met your mom."

"She said she wants to meet you."

"How about this week," Kelly says, "it's not like you're doing anything but sitting around."

"She *is* off tomorrow. I'll ask her."

"Let me know tonight."

"My mom won't be home until around ten."

"Text me."

"Ok," Curtis says with a smile.

"When can I see the boots?"

"When I test them out?"

"Sounds good! So how do you feel?"

Curtis smiles. "I feel a lot better."

"Good. Call me later."

"Ok, bye."

Curtis grins broadly from cheek to cheek after he hangs up the phone. "She wants to meet my mother," he says to himself. "I think she might like me." He looks in the mirror, as a realization hits him: "Aw, man! I need a haircut!"

Omar sits on the couch, and grins, as his brother paces the living room floor. "Keep walking back and forth like that, and you'll burn a hole in the rug."

"I'm nervous," Curtis responds.

"Haven't you known Kelly since the first day of school? That was over three months ago."

"Yeah, but this is different. On the phone yesterday, we hit this point where we didn't speak for like, twenty seconds. It was weird."

"Uh, oh. Has mom had *the talk* with you?"

"Omar!" Curtis says laughing as his brother throws his hands up. "I'm just asking."

"Yes, mom and I had *the talk*."

"You know I'm just messing with you."

"I like her. Do you think she likes me back?"

"Do *you* think she likes you back?"

"Well, she was quiet on the phone, too. That could mean something, right?"

"Yeah. Maybe her phone went dead."

"Omar!"

"Look," Omar laughs, "the important thing is that she's coming over; just focus on tonight. Let mom do most of the talking and you'll be ok."

"If she does like me, she'd be my first girlfriend."

"Don't jump ahead, or you'll miss the beauty of the moment. Enjoy today—cross the *relationship* bridge when you get to it."

The doorbell rings.

Omar gets up and opens the door. Immediately Kelly is dwarfed by his height.

"Wow, you're much bigger than I thought."

"And you must be Kelly."

"Yes. And you're Omar?"

"That's me." They shake hands. "Come on in!"

Kelly enters the living room—Curtis is waiting.

"Hey, Kelly!"

"Curtis! Hey!" They both hug. A smile plays on Omar's face—*I'm proud of my little brother.*

"Thanks for coming."

"Thanks for having me. I can't wait to meet your mother."

"And I can't wait to meet you," Miranda says as she walks into the room.

Kelly stands with a big smile and extends her hand. Mrs. Powers gently swats her hand away and gives her a motherly hug. "Curtis talks about you so much, Kelly. I think we're beyond handshakes."

"It's nice to finally meet you, Mrs. Powers."

"The pleasure is all mine, Kelly. I see you've already met my older son, Omar."

"Yes, ma'am."

"Well, I hope you brought your appetite."

"Yes. I skipped lunch so I'd have room. Curtis says you're a really good cook."

"Both of my boys think I'm a good cook. It'll be good to get a third opinion from a young lady such as yourself."

"I'm sure it'll be good."

"Ok, then. I'm going back into the kitchen to finish dinner."

"Do you need any help? I usually help my mother."

Mrs. Powers smiles. "Well, come on then! There's always something to help with in the kitchen. Curtis, can you and Omar set the table?"

"Sure, Mom," they both say.

Miranda and Kelly head to the kitchen, leaving Curtis and Omar in the living room.

"So what do you think?" Curtis eagerly asks.

"She's cute and well spoken; I can see why you like her."

"Shhhh…. don't say that too loud."

"I think it's obvious."

"That I like her?"

"That she likes you, too."

"How do you know?"

"Trust me, I know what I'm talking about. You sure she's not seeing anyone?"

"As far as I know; seems crazy, right? And why would she be interested in me? I'm a skinny nobody?"

"Hey," Omar counters, "you're a Powers Man—remember that! What you lack in physique you surely make up for in intellect. If she's not seeing anyone, then she's probably waiting for Mr. Right."

"And you think that I'm him?"

"Seems that way."

"So what do I do?"

"Women want a guy who's genuine. If she likes you—and I'm sure she does—it's because of the way you are. Just be yourself; don't try to be anyone else but you."

"Mrs. Powers, Curtis and Omar are right; you are a good cook," Kelly says while getting up from the kitchen table.

"Why thank you Kelly. I'm glad you liked the food."

She prepares to leave and is stopped by Mrs. Powers. "I just wanted to thank you for coming over. You are a delightful young woman, Kelly. And thank you for befriending Curtis and helping him adjust to his new school."

"You're welcome, Mrs. Powers."

"Feel free to come over any time; and hopefully my boys and I can meet the rest of your family."

"That would be great. I'll talk to my parents and see when we all can get together."

"Good." They hug. "Have a good night."

"You have a good night, too, Mrs. Powers. Thanks again for everything."

Curtis is excited by how Kelly and his mom hit it off. "Wow!" he thinks to himself. "They're getting along. This is great!"

With that, Kelly leaves with Curtis and Omar, who walk her to the train station.

Chapter Eight

Brand New Year

SATURDAY JANUARY 3, 2009—THE FRONT door opens to the group of three, as the owner of the house speaks: "Curtis! Omar! Great to see you two again! Happy New Year!"

"Happy New Year to you, too, Mr. G!" they both say amidst a series of hearty handshakes.

"Ah, and you must be Kelly."

"Yes, Mr. Grabowski."

"Please, call me Mr. G. and come on in! No need to stand out in the cold." He holds the screen door wide as they enter and sit in the living room.

"I've heard a lot about you, Kelly," Mr. Grabowski says as he sits in his favorite chair.

"Good, I hope," she says looking at Curtis.

"Oh, yes, definitely good. You know, I have both of your brothers in my physics class."

"They told me."

"Hopefully they told you good things."

"They said you were tough."

"Well then, I'm doing my job," Mr. Grabowski says with a smile. "I like to help develop my students' minds. You can't do that by being soft on them, although I do try to keep things interesting."

"They also said they like your class."

"That's good to know," he smiles. "I like your brothers; they're excellent students. What impresses me the most is that even though they're star athletes, they spend a considerable amount of time on their studies."

"We get that from our parents."

"Really?"

"My dad never went to college, but he reads nonstop: at home, the subway, on lunch breaks…"

"It sounds like he's a life-long learner."

"Both my parents are—we had to read all the Classics when we were growing up and we hated it! It's tough when your friends are outside playing and you're inside writing book reports. Some think you're trying to be better than them.

"Why should my friends put me down because I want to *be* somebody? Anyway, my brothers and I started to love reading. You can learn a lot from books. Now it's like second nature."

"Wow, Kelly. That's an amazing achievement. I wish more students thought like that. What ended up happening with your friends?"

"Some I'm cool with; others I'm not. They still make fun of me and I'm talking like, five years ago this happened."

"And what does your mother do?"

"She's a nurse's aide at a hospital."

"Which one?"

"St. Barnabas."

"Sounds like you all have two hard working parents. They must be proud."

She nods in agreement.

"Well… who knew we were going to get into this type of discussion—all from stating that Kevin and Kelvin are in my physics class!"

"And speaking of physics…" Curtis says with a smile.

"Ah, yes… the reason why we are all here. Now, Kelly, I don't know how much you know…"

"Curtis and Omar filled me in."

"Great. Welcome to the team; let's head downstairs and get to work!"

Mr. Grabowski turns on the lights, at the workroom's entrance—at once they are amazed at the silver boots, sitting on the table before them.

"They look better than I remember, Mr. G!"

"I took the liberty of giving the boots a good shining."

"You did a good job," Omar adds.

"Wow…" Kelly says as she moves closer—speaking almost in a whisper, "so these are the boots." She slowly reaches out and touches them. "Curtis, I can't believe you came up with these."

"I did have help," he says.

"You three are the dream team!" Kelly says while turning around to face them. They all laugh.

"What do you call them, again?"

"Kinetic Redistribution Boots."

"K.R.B.'s, huh? So, when are you going to put them on?"

Curtis looks at Mr. Grabowski, who gives a nod and gestures towards the rest of the workroom. "I've cleared out some of the equipment to make room. I figured we'd test here until I can get us private access to the school gym."

Omar looks up at the ceiling, "It's a good thing you've got a lot of space in here... and a high roof."

"Wouldn't want Curtis to hit his head, now would we?" Mr. Grabowski says with a chuckle.

"Or lose control and smash into something like he did the Christmas tree." They all begin to laugh.

"You guys aren't going to let me live that down are you?"

"No time soon!" Mr. Grabowski says.

"Look at it this way," Omar says, "nothing in here would be as forgiving as the Christmas tree. If you fell in here, you'd be in a lot of pain."

"That's why I got you these." Mr. Grabowski leans behind a table and pulls out a padded vest, elbow and kneepads. "This is what bike racers wear to keep them safe."

"Thanks Mr. G!" Curtis says while putting them on. "This is great!"

"All right people," Mr. Grabowski says clapping his hands together, "let's get to work!"

For the next few hours, they go through a battery of tests and exercises to check the boot's tolerance levels while helping Curtis learn how to efficiently move in the spring-like boots. As a plus, Kelly's dance training proves useful—exposing nuances in posture that lend to a strong sense of balance. Soon, Curtis adapts to a new way of standing and walking while wearing the boots.

Then he does short burst sprints from corner to corner, to measure the force generated by each spring mechanism. By the end of the night, after a few falls, Curtis is confident in the boots and everyone is tired.

"Alright guys," Mr. Grabowski says, "let's call it a night. I think we've done all we can in this environment. I'll check on the gym for next Saturday."

"Sounds like a plan," Curtis says.

"And Kelly… I'm glad you came. Your insight proved invaluable. If I'm still teaching by the time you're ready for physics, I'd love to have you in my class."

"I hope you're around then, Mr. G."

After a few minutes of packing, Mr. Grabowski gives Curtis, Omar, and Kelly a ride home.

"See you all next week."

Curtis heads towards the cafeteria, from his locker, reading a book as he walks down the hall. Most students have already entered their classrooms, but a few stragglers are still making their way; and he's so engrossed in the book that he accidentally bumps into someone.

"Oh, sorry," he says while looking up. "Aw man…" It's Treyshawn.

"Better watch where you walking, Smurtis!"

"Sorry… Treyshawn. Hey, what happened to your face?"

Treyshawn grabs Curtis by his shirt and slams him up against the locker.

"Don't think because I ain't beatin' you up, that you can talk to me like that!"

"Like what? Your face is swollen. I was just …"

"You ain't on my level to be asking me questions!" He throws Curtis to the ground.

"Talk to me again like that and see what I do! You won't be able to hide behind Kelly's brothers forever—then it's me and you." He turns and walks off.

Curtis nurses his arm while picking up his things.

"Curtis! What happened?" Kelly says as she walks up behind him.

"Treyshawn happened."

"Wait till I tell my brothers."

"No. Don't."

"He's supposed to be laying off of you!"

"I know, but something's wrong. The side of his face was swollen. I think he was mad and was taking it out on me."

"He said he got into a fight, but nobody knows anything about it. What I *do* know is his mom's boyfriend stays over sometimes. He's not a nice guy—wouldn't be surprised if something jumped off between them. Did he say anything to you?"

"Yeah. Your brothers won't be around forever. You see… This is why I gotta get the boots ready."

"Is that why you guys made them—because of Treyshawn?"

"You know he *was* chasing me. I need to be able to get away from him."

"What's that gonna prove? So what if you can outrun him. You need to be able to face him!"

"And get my teeth kicked in? Omar told me to use my mind, before having to get violent."

"Easy for him to say."

"*And* he did say if that didn't work, he'd come and talk to Treyshawn himself."

"Your brother's big," says Kelly, "that would be one *good* conversation!" They both laugh.

"I'm glad you can be so cool, Curtis. I don't like seeing you hurt."

"Well, I don't like being hurt."

"So… are you going to Mr. G's classroom now?"

"Yeah. You want to come?"

"I wish I could. I'm supposed to meet some friends for lunch in the cafeteria, but I'll catch up with you after school. Oh, wait—I can't—I have dance class."

"I thought that was Saturday mornings?"

"Usually it is, but our studio is part of a huge performance Saturday afternoon. We're meeting every day now."

"How come you didn't tell me?"

"I didn't think you'd be interested." she says uneasily.

"Your kidding right? Of course I'm interested."

"Well… you'll be working on your project."

"I'll do it in the morning and come see you in the afternoon. Why are you acting so nervous?"

"It's just… I get so self-conscious about my dancing. It's so much easier to do it when family and friends aren't in the crowd."

"Haven't your parents seen you dance before?"

"When I was younger, but we have an agreement now: when I tell them about a performance, they can't say whether or not they'll come. It's easier for me that way."

"So, you don't want me to come?"

Kelly takes a deep breath. "I want you to come—just don't tell me that you're coming."

"Ok. I'll check my schedule," he smiles, "but tell me the time and place just in case."

"It's at Lincoln Center. 3:00pm."

"Wow! Lincoln Center?"

"My first time there—all the more reason why I'm nervous."

"I know you'll be great. How much are the tickets."

"I'll give you one of the family tickets—just in case you can make it. My brothers have a game."

"Can my mom come?"

"I'll give you both tickets—just in case. I've got to get going; my friends are going to kill me."

"I hope not… what would I do without you?"

Kelly smiles, turns away abruptly, and starts walking away.

"I'll talk to you later, Curtis." She says while trying to hide her blushing expression.

Curtis' heart pounds in his chest, as he looks at her. "Did I just say that? I can't believe I just said that," he repeats to himself.

"3, 2, 1—go!" Mr. Grabowski's yell echoes through the empty gymnasium as Curtis runs from the far end of the open space, towards him on the other side—*without* wearing the boots.

"Give it everything you've got, Curtis!" He keeps his eyes on his student and the stopwatch.

"And… time!" His thumb slams down on the stop button as Curtis crosses a pre-set line on the gym floor.

"Twenty three seconds! How are your lungs?"

Curtis nods while walking in a slight circle with his hands on his hips—working to manage his breathing.

"Are the new breathing exercises working?"

Curtis raises both his thumbs before standing still.

"Good. Wait ten minutes—strap on the boots—and do the run again. You need your inhaler?"

Curtis nods as Mr. Grabowski pulls it out of his jacket pocket and gives it to him.

"Phssshh…" A moment passes.

"I didn't have to… use the inhaler as quickly… as I used to."

"Good. The exercise and breathing routines are helping to build your endurance. Even so, I want you to be careful. Asthma is a very serious condition. I don't want you to take things lightly or get reckless with your health. Understand?"

"Yeah. It's just that the only thing the doctor does is give me an inhaler and tells me to take it easy. I don't want to be like this forever."

"And *I* don't want you to have to be restricted either. We just have to be smart about this. And if you feel strained, in any way, you need to tell someone."

"Got it."

"Good. Let's get you strapped in."

A few minutes later, Curtis stands at the starting line as Mr. Grabowski gives the count down from the other side of the gym.

"3,2,1—go!" Curtis breaks into his run, which begins more like a hop as he bounds across the gym with increasing speed. Mr. Grabowski watches in amazement, almost forgetting to hit the stopwatch as Curtis crosses the finish line once again.

"Curtis! That was amazing! It's one thing to do short runs in the work station at the house; it's a completely different thing to see you do it here in the gym!"

"What's my time?"

"You're not going to believe this. Eighteen seconds!"

"Eighteen seconds?"

"Eighteen seconds! Curtis, you were moving!"

"Alright!" They give each other a high five.

"You've really created something here; the first practical running boot that truly augments a person's running ability."

"And this is just the prototype! Imagine what we can do once we make it more efficient!"

Mr. Grabowski looks at the basketball hoop with a sly smile. "Can you dunk a basketball?"

"Are you kidding? I can barely get off the ground!"

"See if you can touch the rim."

Curtis runs for the rim and jumps into the air and easily grasps the rim with both hands.

"This is great!" Mr. Grabowski exclaims.

"Ah... a little help here? I'm afraid of heights!"

Mr. Grabowski runs over and stands just beneath his student. "Ok, let go, but you should be able to land with no problem."

Curtis lets go of the rim and lands with a small, double bounce.

"How was that?"

"It felt like I landed on a mat!"

"Good. Let's get ready to go. I think that's all the excitement I can stand for one day."

"One more time," Curtis says with a smile. After a few more jovial attempts, he un-straps the boots and they prepare to leave.

"So where was Omar today?"

"He had to go to the navy office in Manhattan."

"Everything alright?"

"Yeah. He just has to check in every month and help with some things."

"How long is his leave?"

"He's got a few more months left. It'd be great if they just let him stay... I try not to think about it too much."

They grab their bags, turn out the lights and begin walking towards the building's exit.

"... So what's on your agenda for the rest of the day?" asks Mr. Grabowski.

"I'm supposed to go to Lincoln Center. Kelly's performing there."

"That sounds great. She seems like a nice girl. You really like her don't you?" They walk through the double doors and head towards the parking lot.

"Man, is it that obvious?"

"You get this look in your eyes when you talk about her; a kind of extra excitement. How does she feel?"

"We've never talked about it. I think she likes me too, but I'm not sure. I'm just trying to be a good friend and see where things go."

"Slow is good; kids are moving way too fast nowadays. Back in my day, you generally didn't move that fast. You may have *wanted* to, but you tried not to do it."

"So how old were you when you had your first girlfriend?"

"Honestly," he takes a deep breath, "if I tell you, you may not believe it. My wife was my first girlfriend."

"Are you serious?" Curtis asks in disbelief.

"Yes."

"Wow! When did you meet?"

"We met in college."

"Wait... Your wife was your first girlfriend and you two met in college?"

"Yep."

"You didn't have a girlfriend while you were in high school?"

"No."

"Not even one?" Curtis is shocked.

"Not even one."

"Why not?"

"It's not that I couldn't. There were some girls who were interested in me and who I thought were cute. Quite honestly, I was terrified."

"You're kidding, right?"

"I wish I were." Mr. Grabowski reminisces with an embarrassed laugh.

"I was clearly the nerd who knew a whole lot about math and science and hardly anything about girls. I was also overweight and that didn't do much for my self-esteem. When I would talk to a girl, beyond anything class related, my hands would get sweaty, my mouth felt like it was full of gravel and my words would get slurred. It was terrible! In class I was a genius and outside of class I was a dunce!"

Curtis shakes his head in amazement as they get into the car.

"So, how did you and your wife meet?"

"We met freshman year, in our very first class, 'Intro to Science'.

"All entering freshman had to take it. We were sitting next to each other and I couldn't focus on the professor because I was too busy looking at her out of the corner of my eye. She was so beautiful. Anyway, I didn't hear the professor call on me to answer a question. He called on me two more times and I didn't answer. That's when she looked at me and spoke."

"What did she say?"

"She said... 'The professor's calling on you.'"

Curtis laughs. "And then what happened?"

"I turned towards the professor and began to spout an answer, as if I knew what he was talking about. I was really trying to impress her."

"Was the answer right?"

"It was absolutely wrong!" he says with a laugh. "But after a twenty second rant, the professor stopped me and said, had he been talking about the Periodic Table it would have been perfect. However, he was not talking about that. And if I had been paying attention, instead of looking at the young lady next to me perhaps I would have been able to provide the correct response."

"He said that?" Curtis almost jumps out of his chair with astonishment.

"He said that."

"Aw, man! Then what happened?"

"Everyone started laughing... including her. When the class let out, we got up and she said, 'I like a guy who's smart and can make me laugh.'"

Curtis' breath was almost sucked away by the anticipation. "And what did you say?"

"I was in shock, but I managed to blurt out, 'Actually, the professor was the one who made the joke, not me.' She looked at me for a second and said, 'See, you are funny.' Then she walked out of the class—left me standing there with my mouth hanging open." He starts the car and they drive off.

"Sounds like you had it *bad*." Curtis says while sitting back in the chair and putting his seatbelt on.

"We got married the second semester of our senior year and walked across the stage as Mr. and Mrs. Jim Grabowski!"

"Wow! That sounds like a scene from a movie!"

"Yeah, well… I wish it ended like a movie."

Curtis looks over and sees Mr. Grabowski's eyes tearing up.

"I'm sorry your wife died," he says softly.

"Me too, Curtis; me, too. But we all have to die some time. Some of us just end up leaving sooner than others." He breathes forcibly, wipes his eyes and works up a smile. "At least we had some wonderful years together… some really wonderful years…"

"Thanks for sharing your story with me."

"You're welcome, Curtis. I know how difficult it is for teens nowadays— for people period. Everywhere you look it's 'sex, sex, sex.' Kids are getting into relationships at younger and younger ages and almost everything we see tells us that being in a sexual relationship is the most important thing. Don't be in a hurry.

"Too many teens are dropping out of school because they're having babies or getting sexually transmitted diseases. You've got a good head on your shoulders, so focus on your education. Have some goals you want to accomplish in life. Develop yourself. If the right woman is out there for you… you'll know. Just try and stay focused on what really matters and everything else will work out."

Curtis and his mother arrive just in time to find their seats before the program begins.

"Do you think we'll be able to see her from here?" he asks his mom.

"I hope so, but we are a little ways back."

"We should have brought binoculars."

"You must really like her."

"Mom…"

"I'm just saying…"

"I like her, but I'm going to take things slow."

"That's what every mother wants to hear," she says with a rise in her voice. "Do you think she likes you?"

"I know she likes me as a friend…"

"Well, just focus on being genuine friends first. You can't have a great relationship with someone if you're not friends first."

The music begins as the curtain rises. All chattering ceases as a young man in tights makes his way out on stage—moving as if he's in search of something—or someone. Moments later, a young ballerina gracefully moves onto the stage in a flurry of pirouettes and jumps that seem effortlessly gravity defying.

Soon, more dancers appear, moving in step with each other and in sync with the music. Then Curtis sees her: Kelly bursts onto the stage with such explosive force—each movement displaying poise and control—a flawless performance resulting from grueling rehearsals.

"Wow…" Curtis says under his breath.

"Is that her?" his mother whispers.

"Yeah, that's her."

"My… she's wonderful."

An hour and a half passes, almost unnoticed. Then the theatre erupts in a rolling applause as more than forty dancers end in a kaleidoscope of color, motion, and position. Curtis jumps to his feet, along with his mother and the other concert attendees, cheering and clapping until their hands hurt.

The dancers noisily assemble in the waiting area to meet their family and friends:

"Curtis, you came!" Kelly gives him a big hug, before noticing his mother.

"Mrs. Powers!" They both hug.

"Kelly, you were wonderful! Simply wonderful," she says.

"Thank you."

"The entire production was just wonderful."

Just then, two other voices are heard in unison. "Kelly!" She turns to see her parents coming from across the room.

"Mom? Dad? You made it!" The three hug tightly. "I thought both of you had to work."

"My supervisor needed me to take an evening shift," her mother says.

"And I was able to get some of the guys to cover for me for a few hours so I could come," says her father.

"Mom. Dad. Come meet Curtis and his mother."

"Ah, finally. So you are the young man I've been hearing so much about," says her father as he exchanges a firm handshake with Curtis.

"Good things I hope," Curtis replies somewhat nervously.

"For the most part," Mr. Washington says with a smile and a raise of his eyebrow. They all laugh.

"Mrs. Powers," says Kelly's mom, "It's nice to finally meet you. I'm Stacy Washington."

"And I'm Johnny," says Kelly's father.

As the parents exchange pleasantries, Kelly talks with Curtis for a moment. "I'm really glad you came."

"I had to rearrange like ten appointments—almost didn't make it."

"Uh, huh." Kelly says while nudging him in his ribs. "You are such the busy executive," she laughs.

"You know me, always in demand. I had my personal assistant cancel the afternoon activities."

"You are so funny, Curtis." Kelly says with a sparkle in her eyes.

"And you are so beautiful," Curtis says, before realizing what just came out of his mouth. His eyes register the horror. "What I meant to say was…"

Kelly smiles and shakes her head. "Just what did you mean to say?"

"What I meant to say was…" Curtis speaks very deliberately, "I think that you are funny, too."

"Is that what you meant to say?"

"Yeah…" Curtis can feel his face blush as he looks in every direction other than Kelly's eyes.

"I'm glad you think I'm funny, but I like what you said at first."

"You do?"

"You think you can say it again?"

Curtis takes a deep breath and then speaks. "You… are… so beautiful." He holds her gaze until she looks away. Then she looks back at him.

"You know Curtis, guys say I'm cute like once a week. And I know *why* they do. But it actually means something coming from you, because I know you're not like them. You've got bigger things on your mind… and I like that." She smiles at him softly. "I need to go change. I'll be back out in about twenty minutes."

With that, Kelly runs back to the dressing room, leaving Curtis standing in the midst of a sea of people, caught in a daze as his mother and Kelly's parents enjoy a lively conversation.

Chapter Nine

Be Careful What You Wish For...

ENTRY NUMBER 1, 200. MONDAY FEBRUARY 2, 2009:

"School has been fine for the past month. I've been keeping my distance from Treyshawn, although every time I see him, he looks like he wants to beat me to a pulp! What scares me is that Kevin and Kelvin are leaving in two weeks to visit their top three colleges. If something happens while they're gone, I don't know if I'll be ready.

They'll be gone for about a week, leaving me with no protection. I'll make sure Mr. Grabowski brings the boots to school so I can put them on if there's going to be trouble. At least the weather has been pretty mild—not a whole lot of snow."

Monday February 16, 2009: an unusually warm day, given the time of year. Kelly and Curtis stand in line outside, waiting to enter the school.

"My brothers left this morning. You think Treyshawn is really gonna try something?"

"Not sure," he says, "but I've got this feeling..."

"If your boots don't work, you're going to have to stand up to him."

"Thanks for the vote of confidence."

"What other choice is there? Running may work once or twice, but eventually you're going to have to stand your ground."

"Well, look who it is!" yells a voice from behind them.

"Oh, no..." Curtis says under his breath.

"It's Smurtis!" Treyshawn laughs as he and his friends walk up. "Must be my lucky day."

"His name is Curtis, Treyshawn!" Kelly says while pointing her finger at his face.

"Chill Kelly," he throws up his hands to calm her down, "I know his name. He just *looks* like a Smurtis. No need to act all big. I know your brothers taught you how to fight."

"You remember the scar I gave you back in sixth grade?"

"Hey, you ain't got to remind a brotha. But you know what I see?"

"What?" Kelly says while crossing her arms.

"I see my man, Smurtis... all alone. Your brothers left this morning right?"

"You know what they said, Treyshawn."

"Yeah, I *know* what they said; means I gotta choose. Do I listen when they ain't around or do I have my fun and deal with the consequences later?" Treyshawn turns from Kelly to Curtis. "What you think, Smurtis. What should I do?"

Their eyes lock for a moment—Treyshawn's are rock steady while Curtis' looks away. "I think you should listen to what Kevin and Kelvin told you."

"You tellin' me what to do? I don't like it when people tell me what to do."

"I'm not telling you; you just asked me the question!"

"Oh, *now* you trying to get smart with me? Sounds like you tryin' to start something!" He steps right up into Curtis' personal space.

"You trying to start something, Smurtis?"

"Treyshawn, leave him alone." But he doesn't.

"Huh, Smurtis? You trying to start somethin'? Go ahead... *start* something."

"Treyshawn! I said leave him alone!"

A crowd forms as one of the security guards at the school's entrance begins to make his way over.

"Treyshawn!" she says again—but he snaps back—"Ain't nobody talkin' to you, Kelly! I'm talkin' to my man, Smurtis!"

She walks over and forces her way between them. "Well, *now* you're talking to me!"

"You protectin' your boyfriend, now?"

"He's *not* my boyfriend."

"What you see in him, anyway? He ain't nothin' but a twig with glasses!" The crowd laughs. "He's probably peein' in his pants right now. I know I would be if I was him. Ain't that right, Smurtis?"

Kelly steps to Treyshawn. "Say something else and see what happens!"

Before she can react, Treyshawn pushes her to the ground. The other students start yelling, "Fight! Fight! Fight! Fight!"

"Betta back off girl, it's been a long time since we was in the sixth grade."

The words barely leave Treyshawn's mouth before Curtis' fist plants squarely on his jaw! The crowd goes wild as Treyshawn stumbles back—his face registering his shock.

"Did you…? Did you just *do* what I think you did?"

"Don't you *ever* hit Kelly again!" Curtis says with a fierce tone that surprises everyone.

"Let me get at 'em," one of Treyshawn's friends yells. But Treyshawn stops him, "I *got* this, Hakiim…" He turns to Curtis. "So you wanna be a man now, huh? It's good to see you got some fight in you. You think you can take me?" Treyshawn rushes in and throws a punch—but the security officer grabs his arm.

"That's enough!" yells the officer.

"Get off me!" Treyshawn yells as he pulls out of the officer's grip and tries to rush Curtis again. The officer grabs him again as his friends get ready to jump in, but see several police officers running over; so they scatter.

"Do you know who I am?" yells Treyshawn.

"Do you know who *I* am?" replies the security guard. The officers disperse the students as Curtis helps Kelly up.

"How come you ain't grabbing them?" Treyshawn says while pointing. "Did you see him clock me in my jaw?"

"Yeah, we saw him punch you—*after* you pushed the girl down. Now control yourself or we'll do it for you!"

"But he started it!"

"You think we were born yesterday? You're twice his size, walking around like a thug. Besides, we know who you are, Treyshawn. Let's take a trip to detention."

Another officer speaks to Curtis and Kelly, "We know you didn't start this, but you need to come inside with us, too."

They both begin to walk a few paces behind the two officers restraining Treyshawn.

"You think this is over, Smurtis? This ain't over! We just beginnin'!"

"You the one who's got problems, Treyshawn!" Kelly says. "You just messed up big-time! Wait till my brothers get back!"

"You think I'm afraid of your brothers?"

"I don't think—I *know* you're afraid of them!"

He sucks his teeth. "I'll deal with your brothers when I see 'em!"

"We'll see if you're talking big next week!"

"Oh, I'll be talkin' big. You just watch!"

"Shut your mouth, Treyshawn." One officer interrupts as they practically drag him towards the building. He angrily cocks his head back towards Curtis, with a malicious grin and silently mouths, "This—ain't—over…" He slowly turns back as they ascend the steps in the midst of a multitude of students chanting his name.

"Treyshawn… Treyshawn… Treyshawn…"

Curtis looks at the crowd, but Kelly draws his attention. "Don't worry about them, Curtis."

He looks at her. "Are you alright?"

"More surprised than anything; I wouldn't want to be him when my brothers hear about this."

"I hope I survive long enough for them to hear about this," Curtis says with a nervous laugh.

"What are you talking about? You actually punched him in the jaw! Did you see the look on his face?" Kelly says while laughing hard. "That was priceless! He'll be suspended for sure; maybe even expelled!"

"I am *so* dead…"

"You're like the smartest kid in school. And a guy who's failing every class, but gym, attacked you. He won't be able to touch you."

"Not at school… but they can't do anything once school is over. Oh, man I am so dead."

She stops and looks at him in disbelief. "A few minutes ago, you would have fought Treyshawn!"

"A few minutes ago, you were on the ground!" he snaps back. "I thought you were hurt!"

Kelly smiles. "Were you afraid?"

"Yeah…" Curtis says, with his voice trailing off.

"But you stood up to your nemesis."

He cracks a smile, "…Yeah."

"So even if you're afraid… keep standing. There is a bright side you know."

He looks at her curiously, "What's that?"

She smiles and whispers, "This is what you wanted. If he waits for you after school, you have your boots!"

"Man," Curtis says, "People should be careful what they wish for."

The entire morning and afternoon have been filled with students talking as news spreads through halls, classrooms, and lunchrooms. Several of Treyshawn's friends and associates, quietly, yet intentionally, tell Curtis what awaits him after the last bell rings:

"You're going to get yours after school, Smurtis—If I were you, I'd run home to mommy right now—You gon catch a beat down, little dude."

Each taunt comes with a push or jab, causing him to bump into other students, slam into lockers and fall to the floor.

Other students warn Curtis; sharing any information they might have overheard:

"You need to leave before school ends—You should get a ride with someone—I heard his friends are gonna block all the exits except one… the one Treyshawn wants you to go through."

During his lunch period, Curtis makes a beeline for Mr. Grabowski's classroom.

"Mr. G! Did you bring the boots with you?"

"Locked behind my desk—what's wrong?"

"Remember when I told you Treyshawn was bothering me?"

"Don't tell me that was *you* he got into a fight with this morning."

"He started with me and then knocked Kelly to the ground. Then I punched him in his jaw."

"I overheard my students saying that someone was going to get jumped after school today."

"They're talking about me!"

"Let me notify the principal, so we'll be ready. Come back here right after last period."

"Ok."

"One more thing."

"Yeah?"

"How did it feel—punching Treyshawn?"

"My hand still hurts," he cracks a smile, "but it felt good."

A large crowd of students stand outside waiting for what, they're sure to be, the greatest beat down in recent history. Treyshawn stands ready— He'd been suspended for the week, but has put the word out that 'Curtis is getting his' today.

Curtis realizes there's no way to avoid what's coming. He already called Omar, "You got this, little bro. This is what we've been talking about all along: mind versus muscle. But don't worry, I'll be there if you need me."

All exits are blocked. The time has come. Inside the locked physics lab, Mr. Grabowski and Curtis prepare, while Kelly looks on nervously.

"Are you sure you want to do this?" Mr. Grabowski says. "I could give you a ride home."

"That won't help me in the long run. If he can't get me here, he'll try someplace else." Curtis pulls up the legs of his jeans, steps into his boots and starts securing the latches.

"Maybe we all need to face him and talk about this," Mr. Grabowski continues.

"Already tried talking my way out and that didn't work. If he's going against Kevin and Kelvin, I don't think he'll listen to you. This is all I got. Something's gotta give."

Curtis tightens the last connection. "Sure hope this works," he says while pulling his pants legs down over the top of the boots. "You hardly notice them with the baggy jeans." And with that, he stands and grabs his book bag while Mr. Grabowski unlocks the door.

The three leave the room and head down the corridor to the school's main entrance. As they pass several exits, they see Treyshawn's friends giving updates on their cell phones: "He just passed the gym—He's on his way to the main entrance."

"Don't worry about them," Mr. Grabowski says, "just focus on the task; remember your training."

The clicking of his boots on the floor reassures him. As the three arrive at the main door, they find one of the security guards standing there.

"Mr. Grabowski."

"Mr. Andre."

"The principal filled me in. This should be interesting." He turns to Curtis, "Don't worry, security is on standby just in case things get ugly."

"It's good to know I've got back-up."

"Nurses are on standby, too."

"Hopefully we won't need them," says Mr. Grabowski.

They look out the window. The crowd is in the distance with Treyshawn at the front.

Kelly gives Curtis a tight hug. "Curtis, I changed my mind. I don't want you to do this."

He looks into her eyes and sees her tears.

"I don't want to do this either, but didn't you tell me to stand up to him?"

"He could hurt you. Let security handle him."

Curtis can feel his eyes beginning to moisten as well. "You know you're beautiful, right?"

Kelly cries as she gives Curtis a long kiss on his cheek; then forces a smile. "You said that already."

"And you said I was funny."

"You are—at least to me."

"Well, let's laugh after all of this is over."

Kelly gives a nervous laugh as her tears flow freely down her cheeks. She lets him go and steps back, while wiping them from her eyes.

Mr. Grabowski nods in Curtis' direction. Curtis smiles back at him—turning towards the door.

"Here we go…" he says beneath his breath as he reaches down and presses the release button on each boot. Each spring-lever system engages as his height increases by three inches. His breathing also increases as he feels his chest tightening up. His palms begin to sweat as he pulls out his inhaler. A pressurized burst moves through his lungs, causing his breathing to become less strenuous. As he takes a deep breath, an almost silent prayer is uttered.

"God, it's now or never…"

Suddenly, Curtis pushes the doors open with all his might and quickly takes a few steps! The crowd watches as Treyshawn tenses up, "Finally! This dude is gonna catch it!"

Before everyone's eyes, Curtis leaps down eight stairs like a jackrabbit and rebounds with such speed—they are in awe.

"Did you see that?" Some say among themselves. "Did he just jump…?"

Curtis breaks out into a full run, as Kelly, Mr. Grabowski, and Mr. Andre watch from the top of the stairs. "Run, Curtis, run…!" Mr. Grabowski says in a half whisper-half shout.

Curtis turns to the far side of the parking lot, leaving cars in between him and his nemesis.

"Don't think these cars will save you!" Treyshawn yells while giving chase—attempting to cut Curtis off. But Curtis is already moving too fast, cutting back between the cars—heading straight for the crowd with Treyshawn in tow.

"I thought this kid was supposed to be slow," a student says to another as Curtis whizzes by them, followed a moment later by Treyshawn. "How did he get so fast?" "Go Curtis!" someone shouts, while another exclaims, "Run, Curtis! Run!"

The two boys leave the parking lot in their dust, running along the concrete path through the field, towards the street. The crowd follows; trying to keep up with the action.

Treyshawn pushes himself as hard as he can go, but it is not enough as Curtis increases his stride and begins to spread the distance between them.

If I can get across the street I'll be good, he thinks to himself. *Less than half a block is left before the main intersection.* That's when he sees a strip of loose gravel, just before the sidewalk.

"Uh-oh!" Curtis narrowly leaps over it and just makes the street light as it changes!

Treyshawn, on the other hand, sees it too late and tumbles out of control—slamming into the ground—rolling out into a street filled with oncoming traffic.

Curtis hears the sound of screeching tires, honking horns, and crushing metal as he turns around and sees Treyshawn lying motionless in the street while a large truck barrels around a corner, just over a block away.

Treyshawn struggles to his hands and knees before seeing the large truck, heading straight for him. The driver doesn't even see him because of his preoccupation with his cell phone.

"Treyshawn, get up!" The distance between the truck and Treyshawn closes fast as Curtis realizes, *he's not gonna make it,* and jumps into action!

The sound of the truck's engine overtakes Treyshawn's yell as the driver finally turns his attention back to the road, sees several smashed cars and a terrified boy in front of him. "Jesus!" He slams both feet on the brakes, causing the tires to lock up with a squeal, as the full weight of the large vehicle shifts forward.

"Watch out, kid!!!" The driver yells, knowing the truck won't stop in time. "Oh, God! No!"

Treyshawn's perception of time changes as his life flashes before his eyes and a terror he's never known seizes him. Fear grips him, as the truck's hulking frame is about to swallow him up! The driver blares his horn as Curtis jumps through the air and tackles Treyshawn—mere seconds before the seemingly inevitable impact! They both roll out of danger as the truck roars loudly over the spot where Treyshawn lay just a moment before—the sheer mass being felt through the rumblings of the concrete road. The smell of burnt rubber and diesel fuel penetrate the air as the screeching vehicle comes to a halt a full twenty feet beyond the mark. Clearly, no one would have survived.

"Treyshawn! Are you alright?" Curtis asks.

"Get off me!" he says while trying to stand up.

The driver jumps out of his truck and runs over. "I was sure you were a goner! Are you alright?"

Treyshawn sees the crowd of bystanders and students standing on the sidewalk, astonished that Curtis had saved his life.

"Hey kid, you're a hero!" a bystander yells.

"Yeah!" the truck driver exclaims. "Are you sure you two are alright?"

Curtis looks over at the crowd and sees his brother among them, smiling. He then looks at his nemesis. "Your head is bleeding."

Treyshawn feels the side of his head with his hand and sees the blood. The sound of ambulances and police cars are heard in the distance. He looks at Curtis, somewhat in shock.

"Don't think you're a hero. I didn't need saving." Treyshawn stumbles off, barely able to keep his composure, leaving Curtis standing on the side of the road. Students cheer as he notices their camera phones. Almost everyone captured the entire exchange—from when Curtis bolted down the steps to this very moment.

"Curtis, You did it!" Kelly exclaims while running over and throwing her arms around his neck.

"We did it, Kelly. All four of us."

Omar and Mr. Grabowski stand among the crowd. "We did it," Omar says quietly.

"Everything worked out," Mr. Grabowski adds, "although, I didn't expect the car accidents."

"It looks like everyone's ok," Omar replies.

"That's a good thing," Mr. Grabowski says as the police and paramedics arrive. "We'll have to file a report."

The police report reads:

According to witnesses: two students were running. One—Treyshawn Jinkins—while chasing the other across the street, slipped on loose gravel and tumbled into the intersection. This caused several minor accidents. The other student, who was being chased—Curtis Powers—risked his life to save the first student from an oncoming truck. The first student was seen leaving the scene, refusing medical attention and the truck driver was given a ticket for using his cell phone while driving.

As the crowd disperses, both men know that by Tuesday morning, videos and photographs will have been seen by much of the student body, all because of the social networking and blog sites on the Internet. Curtis will be the talk of the school.

Eyes stare as he approaches the school; and the sounds of voices whispering are evident.

"That's Curtis," one student says to another.

"I thought he'd be bigger," replies another, "Are you sure he's the one who outran Treyshawn?"

The closer he gets to the school, the more students talk, until finally one student gets up enough nerve to approach.

"Hey! You're Curtis, right? My friends said they saw you outrun Treyshawn yesterday. Did you really do that?"

"Yeah."

Another student walks up. "I watched your video last night, like a hundred times! The part where Treyshawn fell... *that* was funny!"

"What are you talking about *my* video?"

"You don't know? A bunch of people caught the whole thing on their cell phones. It's all over the Internet. Don't you go online?"

"Not every night."

A number of other students walk over and soon, Curtis finds himself at the center of attention:

"How did you outrun Treyshawn? He's like one of the fastest guys in the school! —And then you saved him when that truck almost hit him. —Why'd you do that? —Shoot, I would have let him get hit. —Now *that* would have been good! —Yeah, Treyshawn's fun to be around when he's busy beating up on *somebody else*, but he's really a pain." The students laugh as they continue, "You're alright, Curtis. —Yeah, I've never seen anyone outrun that dude before. And how did you jump down all of those stairs? —Do you work out? —But you're so skinny. —You should run track."

Curtis listens silently as the students continue talking. By the time he gets through the security check, he finds Kelly standing next to his locker.

"Curtis! Everybody is talking about what happened yesterday! And I mean *everybody*."

"Yeah, I know."

"People have been coming up to me all morning. You're famous!"

"So this is what that *feels* like, huh? I've got to get to class. Can we talk about this later?"

The first bell rings.

"How can you be so calm?"

"I've never had a whole bunch of people be excited about anything I've done. I think I'm in shock or something. Besides, I didn't do this to be famous; I did this to stay alive! I've got to go." Curtis walks off, leaving Kelly alone.

"I don't understand why he's not excited. I thought he'd be happy."

Curtis gets his lunch from the cafeteria and heads for the physics lab. An older gentleman in full athletic gear, with a clipboard and stopwatch around his neck, stops him. "Are you Curtis Powers?"

"Yes, sir."

"I'm Mr. Cooley, the track coach. I saw the video of you outrunning Treyshawn Jinkins. I've seen you run, in gym class—nothing spectacular—but if you could outrun Treyshawn, then I must have missed something. I'm always looking for good runners."

"Why do you keep comparing me to him?"

"He tried out for the track team last year and qualified. He was fast; blew away almost every runner I put up against him. But I had to let him go because of his attitude."

"I'm sorry, Mr. Cooley, but I'm late for my physics lab."

"But you're on lunch. By the way, I saw your schedule—very impressive— you're only in ninth grade and your taking physics."

"I go to the physics lab during lunch."

"Alright, I'll let you go. But first, just tell me if you're interested in trying out for the track team."

"That would be a dream come true..."

"Great! So I'll see you at tryouts next week!"

"I'm sorry, Mr. Cooley, I can't."

"But you said it would be 'a dream come true?'"

"It would, but I've got too much on my plate."

"Sure you can't make room?"

"I also have asthma."

"Asthma?"

"My doctor says that I'm not supposed to be taking part in any strenuous activities."

"There are a lot of athletes who have asthma."

"Really?"

"Typically, they use their inhaler right before their event. We've had our share of asthmatic athletes in the past five years or so. Still, there were a *few* times when we had some complications."

"What kind of complications?"

"One runner forgot his inhaler and had an attack after his race. He was rushed to the hospital and almost died—but that was the worst encounter. You should talk to the school nurse about your options. We'd love to have a good runner on the team."

"Thanks, but I'm ok."

"Are you sure?"

"Yes, I'm sure. I'm sorry. I really have to go." With that, Curtis heads to the physics lab.

"Word is really spreading around. What did you say to Mr. Cooley?" Mr. Grabowski asks.

"What could I say—I'm slow except when I wear these boots? Besides, it's not like it's legal for me to run track wearing these."

"True."

"Man, I would have loved to run track."

"But like you said, the boots give you an unfair advantage."

"I wish there was a way I could run track with the boots and it be ok."

"That would be great. But in the meantime, what about Treyshawn? You've outrun him, but what happens when he gets off of suspension or you run into him on the street?"

"I don't know, Mr. G. I need to pray for a miracle."

Chapter Ten

Friend or Foe?

FRIDAY FEBRUARY 20, 2009.

"You better get your hands off of me! You're not my father, Melvin!"

"Who you think you talking to, Trey? I'll bust your behind!"

Melvin, clearly larger than the teen, grabs him by his shirt, spins him around and puts him into a headlock. "Boy, I will knock your teeth to the back of your throat!" he growls into Treyshawn's ear—who struggles to break free. "What you gonna do, huh? Nothin! I'm glad I'm not your old man; everybody knows he don't want you! So why don't you go to your room and stay outta grown folks business!" Melvin throws Treyshawn towards the living room doorway.

As Treyshawn turns to leave, he mumbles under his breath, "Don't know why my moms put up with your dumb self."

"What you say, boy?" Melvin grabs Treyshawn and pushes him into the wall. Treyshawn comes back swinging, but he's no match for his mother's boyfriend who pummels him repeatedly.

"Someone needs to teach you a lesson you ain't never going to forget!"

Just then, Treyshawn's mom comes back into the room.

"What's this noise about? I leave for five minutes and you starting trouble again, Trey?"

Melvin lets her son go. "Don't worry, baby. I'm just trying to teach your no-good son some respect. He's always tryin' to put his nose where it don't belong."

"I'm not doin' nothin' to him, Ma!" Treyshawn says, as he gets up, holding the side of his face. "Look what he did to me!" He drops his hand to reveal his bruised eye, cut lip and bloody nose.

"Maybe you had it commin', Treyshawn," Shakira replies.

"How you takin' his side, Ma?"

"You always tryin' to come between me and my happiness—just like your father. Everything's not about you! I'm the one who almost had a singing career until your daddy stole it from me!"

"How many times you gon tell me about that?" Treyshawn yells. "It wasn't my fault!"

"Boy," Melvin interjects, "you betta lower that bass in your voice!"

"Ain't nobody talkin to you, Smelvin!"

Melvin smacks Treyshawn across his face—knocking him to the floor. Tears swell in his eyes as he jumps up and runs for the front door.

"Look at that, baby; he can't even take a hit."

"Shut up!" Treyshawn yells as he tries to keep from crying.

"Go ahead and run, Treyshawn!" his mother says. "Just like your daddy! He got what he deserved and so did you!"

Treyshawn covers his ears, trying to shut out his mother's stinging words. He bursts out the door, leaps down the steps, and breaks into a run while his mother yells out of the living room window.

"Go ahead and run! Just like your no-good daddy!"

His lungs burn for oxygen as his feet pound the pavement. Tears pull from his eyes and blur everything around him as his mother's words echo in his ears. No matter how fast he runs—no matter how far—they chase him. He's not sure where he's running, but any place is better than home.

A honking car skids to a halt as Treyshawn runs across the street, oblivious to his surroundings.

"Are you crazy?" the driver yells while honking his horn before driving away. "Stupid kid!"

Treyshawn runs full speed down the middle of the street. I wish that car had hit me!" he shouts.

After running through several neighborhoods, he comes to a halt, blocks away from where he started; out of breath and out of tears. He always had a tough exterior; but the truth was—inwardly he had always been afraid:

"I *don't* want to be like my father... I don't want to be *like* my father... I don't know *how* to stop being like my father..."

He leans against the side of a building and for the first time in his life he lets go—and cries—not just with his eyes... but also with his soul. Images pass through his mind of his first and only visit to Rikers Island. At four years old his father finally agreed to see him. So his mother brought him, hoping that once his father saw him, he'd want to be a part of his son's life...

and hers as well.

They looked into each other's eyes—father to son—son to father. And the moment lingered almost long enough before he looked away...

"Don't ever come here again." And just like that, he walked back to his cell; leaving them on their own.

That was eleven years ago, but it still felt like yesterday to Treyshawn. "Why didn't he want me?" he yells, "Why!" He picks up a nearby garbage can and hurls it into the street, as the thoughts keep assaulting his mind— causing him to slide down the building wall into a sorry heap on the sidewalk. He has nothing left... but then a familiar voice draws his attention.

"Treyshawn? Is that you?"

He looks up, bewildered, to find Curtis walking towards him.

"Leave me alone..."

"Are you alright?"

Treyshawn doesn't answer.

"And what happened to your eye?" Before Curtis can move, Treyshawn jumps up, grabs him by his shirt and spins him hard into the wall.

"I said leave me alone, Smurtis! And you better not tell anybody about this!" At that moment, Treyshawn sees his reflection in Curtis' horror-filled eyes. He sees himself back in the apartment—pressed between the wall and Melvin's forearm. He feels the full weight of his mother's abusive boyfriend on his throat. He feels his own terror—all through Curtis' fearful expression.

Treyshawn slowly releases his grip from Curtis' shirt as he returns to his slumped position against the wall. "What are you doin' here?"

"I live on this block," Curtis responds as he drops down next to him.

Treyshawn looks and realizes where he is.

"I didn't know I ran this far..."

"What are *you* doing here?" Curtis asks, "You got into a fight?"

"You'd love that, wouldn't you?" Treyshawn snaps back! "You'd like to see my behind get beat."

"Actually, I wouldn't," Curtis responds.

Treyshawn looks at him skeptically. "I don't get you, Smurtis!" he says with a perplexed expression. "I beat you up, take your money, make you look bad in front of everybody—like *every day*—then you save my life and now you tryin' to be my friend? That makes no sense! You're like the dumbest smart kid I've ever seen."

"Look," Curtis says somewhat heatedly, "if you don't want to talk, that's fine. I'll go home; I've got homework to finish, anyway." He gets up and starts walking away; only taking a few steps before Treyshawn starts to speak again.

"I'm just sayin' if somebody was kicking my butt every day, I'd be glad to see him get what was comin' to him."

Curtis stops walking and turns back around. "So you're saying that you're getting what you deserve?"

Treyshawn thinks for a moment, "That's what my mom's said. I guess I walked into that one."

Curtis sits back down. "What if you don't deserve what you're going through?"

"What you mean?" Treyshawn looks at Curtis with wrinkled eyebrows.

Curtis hesitates before saying, "I know a little about your home situation."

"Yeah? What do you know?"

"I know you and your mom don't get along… and you and her boyfriend don't either."

Treyshawn sits quietly.

"What happened to your dad?"

"He was doing some shady stuff and got locked up. He's definitely getting what he deserves. On top of that, he wants nothin' to do with me, and my mom hates me because I look like him. She's always telling me how he took her dream away from her—and that it's my fault."

"Your fault? It's not like you chose to be here."

"That's what I'm saying! She says she wished I was never born…" Treyshawn looks at Curtis, his eyes trembling with emotion, "how does a mother say that to her own kid?"

"I don't know… I'm sorry."

"Before she got pregnant with me, she was gonna be a singer. My dad owned a record label before he got locked up and was takin' her places— meetin' big people. She was about to blow up.

"When she told him she was pregnant, he told her to get an abortion. She wanted to keep me. So he dropped her…just like that. And once he did, all her chances dried up. She's always sayin' if she listened to him, she'd be rich and famous. Instead, she got me and a welfare check."

"That's a lot to deal with."

"Who you telling?"

They sit quietly as a police car drives by, patrolling the neighborhood.

"You can't take a person's dream away. They have to give it up. It sounds like your mom gave up her dream a long time ago; and she's using you as an excuse."

Treyshawn wipes tears from his eyes while Curtis keeps talking. "Maybe underneath, your mom is *really* afraid. It seemed like everything was working and then it all dried up and she didn't know what do. That's a scary place to be."

"Yeah..." Treyshawn says.

"But she's gotta make a choice... just like you do."

"What you mean *me*?"

"You've had it tough your *whole* life and you didn't *ask* for the family drama. But, you can choose... do nothing, act crazy or do something positive." Curtis hesitates—not sure if he wants to say his next words. "And if we choose to do nothing positive... then honestly, we deserve every bad thing that comes our way."

"So what you saying," Treyshawn says in a slightly agitated tone, "is that where I am is my fault because of my choices."

"I'm saying that you can choose: be the victim or do something different."

"That's easy for you—you from the 'burbs."

"...At least your dad is *still* alive..."

They look at each other without saying a word—two boys—both without fathers... even if for very different reasons.

"...I've got a lot weighing down on me," Treyshawn finally says. "You don't *know* my life."

"So? But, I know what kind of life you *could* be living. What about your dreams? What do you want to be when you grow up?"

"I don't think I'll be anything. All I know how to do is run the streets."

"The track coach said you're one of the fastest guys in the school."

"I don't want to run track no more."

"Why?"

"I only wanted to do it to get girls and make a name for myself. Besides, the track team is whack. People was always givin' me problems. That's why

I quit."

"The coach said he kicked you out."

"Quit—kicked out—same difference."

"Ok… Well, forget about track, then. What else do you like to do… besides beating people up?"

"You got jokes now, huh?"

"Gotta do something to pass the time."

"I like to draw. It's the only thing I do besides runnin' and ball. I'm really good at ball, but so are a lot of other guys—like Kelly's brother. Nobody can touch him on the court. Let him go for the NBA. Maybe I'll focus on drawing."

"My drawings look like stick figures."

"I've got some tags on the side of some buildings not far from here. Guys from my block say it's hot."

"How long have you been drawing?"

"As far back as I remember."

"You ever entered any contests?"

"Contests? Nah… I don't know if I'm good enough to win anything. I just draw for myself. Besides the graffiti, nobody sees my stuff."

"Well, if you like to draw, you could think about being a graphic artist or an illustrator."

"You mean like draw comics and stuff?"

"You could do that or draw other things, too, but I like comics, myself."

"You like comics?" Treyshawn asks.

"Yeah." Curtis responds excitedly. "I like Icon, Static…"

"Wait! *You* like Milestone Comics? I get down on *all* of their stuff! Blood Syndicate and Hardware are my favorites."

"I like some DC and Marvel stuff too, like Batman, Iron Man and Superman."

"Yeah, those are cool, too," Treyshawn adds, "but give me the Black characters any day! Like Benoist from Soulfire. You know that one, done by Aspen comics? Michael Turner's art is crazy!"

"How about Demetrius Veasy? His art is serious!"

"Yeah? What does he do?"

"The Lions 12 series. I could let you borrow them, if you want." Curtis pauses as he gets an idea. "Listen, how about we make a deal? You teach me to draw and I'll help you with your school work."

"School again... I can't get *that* stuff."

"You seem pretty smart. Besides, if you can read Icon and Static, you can read anything! You know they use some pretty big words in there."

"Yeah, they do," Treyshawn laughs. "Sometimes I got to get a dictionary!"

"Maybe you just need to focus. I can help you learn some studying techniques."

"I already have to do summer school again. I'm failing everything but gym."

"Never too late to change," Curtis smiles.

"Easy for you. You're the nerd—I mean the smart guy."

"Believe it or not, I did have to have some serious help in math a couple years back. I almost failed, but my mom forced me to get extra help."

"Really?"

"I like science, but I can do without math. I had to work real hard and learn techniques to help me compensate. Now math isn't too bad."

"I never would have guessed *you* had problems with school. You really think I could get better?"

"If you put your mind to it."

"And you'd help me?"

"Sure."

"I still don't get you," Treyshawn says, "Why you even takin' time to help me?"

"Why not?"

Both sit silent for a moment.

"Alright, I'll give it a shot; but nobody at school can know you're my tutor. My friends wouldn't get me."

"Yeah. I know how tough it is to fit in."

"About that—me beating you up and stuff—I'm... sorry."

"No problem; that's behind us now."

"But I'm still gonna call you Smurtis," Treyshawn says with a sly smile.

"I'm used to it, now," Curtis responds with a big smile of his own. "If it ever bothers me, I'll let you know." His smile slowly diminishes as he realizes a sobering fact.

"You know… Kevin and Kelvin will be back in a couple of days."

"Yeah, I was trippin'." Treyshawn chuckles before getting serious. "I know they're comin' to see me, but it's alright. I'll Man-up and take the punches. Whatever happens—happens."

"Maybe I can put a good word in for you."

"You ain't got to do that," Treyshawn turns and smiles at Curtis, "but I won't stop you if you decide to speak up for me." They both laugh. "But do you think Kelly will forgive me?"

"I don't know. I can't speak for her."

"Man, I really messed up. I've known that girl since 3rd grade. She's a good person…tells you what she thinks. She's never backed down when I was actin' stupid; gets that from her brothers."

"Yeah. She *is* pretty strong."

"Don't tell her I told you that. But since you and me are cool now… I gotta ask you something?"

"Yeah?"

"I'm one of the fastest dudes at the school. How'd you beat me the other day? You were *always* slower than me."

Curtis looks at Treyshawn, trying to figure out what to say. "Come over for dinner and I'll tell you."

Later that night…

"Are you serious?" Kelly asks loudly, as Curtis pulls the phone away from his ear. "You're kidding, right?"

"I'm serious," he responds while lying on his bed. "Treyshawn and I are cool now."

"How did that happen?"

"Remember when you told me that he had a lot going on at home?"

"Yeah?"

"He got into a really big fight with his mom's boyfriend. And then she sided against him."

"Oh, wow…"

"I saw him on my block and we started talking."

"Just like that?"

"I think it's because he's dealing with a lot."

"So you guys are cool now?"

"Looks that way. I even invited him over for dinner."

Kelly drops the phone, shocked at what she just heard. Curtis hears the commotion as she fumbles to bring the receiver back to her ear.

"Kelly? You there?"

"I'm here... So he's coming?"

Curtis laughs hard. "I wish I could see your face right now. It takes a lot to make you speechless!"

"Well, you did just tell me that you and your nemesis are cool now; and you invited him over for dinner! But you didn't answer my question: Is he coming?"

"He said he would."

"Wow. You guys are friends. I can't believe it."

"I'm not sure if we're friends yet. It's probably more like... associates."

"Well whatever you guys are... friends, associates; you know this isn't going to change much."

"What do you mean?"

"When Kevin and Kelvin get back, they're going to do the big brother thing. Treyshawn is going to catch a serious beat down."

"Even if you tell them not to?"

"They're not going to let *that* go."

"Even if I tell them not to?"

"If we both tell them, they may go easy on him, but he's gonna catch something. Did he say anything about it?"

"He wanted to know if you'd forgive him. And he told me if there was a beat down; he'd take it. He knows he messed up."

"Well, we'll just see what happens."

Sunday February 22, 2009.

"Well, Treyshawn, you are the second friend Curtis has had over for dinner," Mrs. Powers says as they start eating. "I'm glad you could make it."

"Thanks."

"Do you have any siblings?"

"Siblings?"

"Do you have any *brothers* or *sisters?*"

"Oh. No, it's just me. Sometimes I'd wonder what it'd be like to have a brother, though," Treyshawn says, "but it's just me."

"Well, Curtis' older brother, Omar, should be home shortly."

"You got an older brother?" he says to Curtis.

"Yeah, he's on leave from the navy."

"So how long have you two been friends?" Mrs. Powers asks. Curtis and Treyshawn look at each other, trying to hide their uneasiness.

"We... met the first day of school," Curtis sputters.

"Do you two have any classes together?"

"Homeroom," Treyshawn says quickly.

"So what do you want to be when you grow up, Treyshawn?"

They look at each other again, this time with a smile.

"I dunno. Maybe a graphic artist or illustrator."

"Oh, you like to draw?"

"Mom, he can really draw!" Curtis exclaims.

"I do alright," Treyshawn says bashfully.

Just then the front door opens as Omar enters the apartment. "Hey, everybody!" He drops three very large bags on the floor next to the door.

"Omar!" Curtis yells.

Treyshawn watches with trepidation as Omar enters the kitchen, kisses his mother and hugs Curtis.

"You guys started eating without me?"

"We *just* started," his mom says while tapping his stomach, "don't worry, there's enough for you."

"How's it going little brother? Haven't seen you all day."

"I'm good."

"So who's your friend?"

"I'll let him introduce himself," Curtis says with a slight smile. Omar approaches, as Treyshawn's eyes grow wider by the second.

"I'm Omar," he says while extending his hand.

"You are huge," is Treyshawn's only response.

Omar laughs. "Thanks."

"What are you, like six-three?"

"I'm six foot four. And if your eyes get any bigger, they're going to pop out of your head."

"Sorry," he laughs. "My name is Treyshawn."

Omar cuts his brother a surprised look before turning back to face the young houseguest. "Hey, Treyshawn, I've heard a lot about you." He gives a *firm* handshake, causing Treyshawn to grimace in pain while chuckling nervously.

Miranda speaks. "They've been friends since the first day of school."

"Really?" Omar tries not to sound too surprised as he lets go of Treyshawn's hand. "It's good to know my brother has people looking out for him; keeps *me* from having to come down to the school. You know how some folks can be."

Treyshawn nods and smiles as he rubs his sore hand, "Yeah... Some people just act crazy."

"Omar, do you want meatloaf or chicken?"

"Can I have both, Mom? I'm starving. Hey Curt, help me take my bags to the room."

"Be right back," Curtis says as he gets up from the table. It takes almost all of his strength just to move a single bag, but Omar picks up two as if they're nothing.

They walk into the room as Curtis finally drops the bag in the corner. "Sorry I didn't get a chance to give you the update."

"Are you two really friends or did you just say that for Mom?"

"No. We're friends now. Well, really associates, but we're moving towards friends."

Omar smiles slightly. "So, how'd *this* happen?"

Curtis shares the events from a few nights earlier. By the time he finished, Omar is clearly pleased. "I told you bullies intimidate others to cover up their own weaknesses? I'm proud of you. You used your mind to deal with the situation and things worked out. But if Treyshawn gets out of hand, let me know." Omar cuts his brother a big grin.

"You got it," Curtis laughs.

"Alright, tell mom, I'm coming, I just want to change out of my uniform."

Curtis comes back to the kitchen, as Treyshawn asks about the bathroom. As Treyshawn walks down the hall, he notices a cracked door and slows just enough to see Omar taking off his shirt. To his surprise, Omar has five noticeable scars on his back.

"Whoa..." he whispers as he peeks through the door. "I wonder what happened to him?" Omar turns as Treyshawn quickly jumps up, heads to the bathroom and then back to the kitchen.

Later... in Curtis' room.

"Those are the coolest things I've ever seen," Treyshawn says as he looks at Curtis' boots sitting on the desk. "You built these yourself?"

"I had help from my brother and my physics teacher. My brother's a mechanical engineer."

"Wow. I don't know if I could ever do something like that. Can I try them on?"

"If you can fit a size 9 and a half."

"Man, I'm a size 11."

"Sorry. These are built custom for my shoe size. I'll see what I can do with the next model."

Curtis opens the desk drawer and pulls out the first set of drawings of the boots and hands them to Treyshawn.

"Wow, I see what you mean; your drawing skills do need some work."

"I want to learn how to draw for myself. I can see what I want in my mind, but when I draw it, it comes out looking like this."

"Can you rotate the image around in your head?" Treyshawn asks.

"You can do that?" Curtis asked amazed.

"Yeah. You can't?"

"No. Can you show me?"

"It takes lots of practice, but I can show you."

"Did you take a special class to learn how?"

"Nah... just practiced on my own. It's always been kind of like, something I could do."

"Do you think you could help me with the drawings for these designs?"

"You sure you want *my* help?"

"Why? You can't do it?"

"Oh, I can do it—no problem."

"Ok, then. I trust you. Just keep it a secret."

"I can do that. You keep my secret about the tutoring thing and I'll keep yours about the boots."

"Listen. Me, my brother, and Mr. Grabowski are going to the PA Relays in a couple of weeks. You want to go?"

"PA Relays? What's that?" Treyshawn says as he sits on the edge of the bed.

"One of the largest Track and Field events in the country—held every year in Pennsylvania."

"You into track?"

"Yeah, but my asthma acts up. So I can really only watch it."

"So when I was tellin' you about me not wanting to run track..."

"Hey. That's how *you* felt. I'm cool. Kelly's brothers are helping me improve my endurance."

"How's your asthma when you're in the boots?"

"Not as bad. The boots allow me to cover more ground while using less energy."

"Now, that's hot."

"So do you want to come?"

"Yeah. Sounds like a plan."

"Great. I'll talk to Omar about an extra ticket."

"Speakin' of your brother. Can I ask you something?"

"Yeah."

"I passed by his room, on the way to the bathroom, and saw the scars on his back. What happened?"

"Why don't you ask him? He tells the story better than I do."

"I don't know..."

"Omar's pretty open about it. Ask him while we're at the Relays. I'm sure he'll tell you."

Wednesday February 25, 2009.

Treyshawn's body hits the fence hard! His face—creased by the metal links—as Kevin presses the back of his head even harder. "We know you lost your mind!"

"You think you were going to get away after hitting our sister?" Kelvin says as he punches Treyshawn in his ribs!

"Then you go after Curtis?" Three punches follow which drop Treyshawn to his knees—holding his stomach, gasping for air.

"I'm... sorry..." he sputters.

"Oh, you sorry alright!" Kevin shouts.

"And you're going to be even more sorry when we get done!" adds Kelvin.

"I want... to apologize to... to Kelly." Treyshawn coughs.

"Don't worry, when we're done, you'll apologize!" Kevin yells as he gives a well-placed kick to Treyshawn's chest. "And you don't have to go far, because Kelly's walking up right now."

Treyshawn looks and sees Kelly approaching. Her expression says it all—she enjoys seeing him catching his beat down. But as their eyes meet, the more her emotions soften.

"Guys... lighten up," she says to her brothers. "I think he's learned his lesson."

"How do we know he's learned his lesson?" Kevin asks, "Have you learned your lesson?"

Treyshawn nods his head as Kelvin bends down and yells in his face, "We can't hear you! You need to speak up!" He hits him hard with a back fist—causing blood to spew from his mouth.

Treyshawn yells out with a gurgled cry. "I... learned... my... lesson..."

"Alright, guys! Cut it out!" Kelly says as she steps in between them and Treyshawn.

"We'll tell you when we're done, Kelly."

"Come on, he *only* pushed me down. This is way more than what he did to me!"

"Treyshawn needs to learn what happens when he disrespects us, you, and Curtis."

"I think he learned his lesson," a voice says from behind them. They turn and find Curtis standing there.

"Guys... I think he's learned his lesson."

They all look at Treyshawn lying on the ground—his face swollen and bloody.

"Treyshawn wants to change," Curtis says as he walks over to Kelly.

"Change? He *can't* change," Kelvin says.

"You guys *know* what's going on at his house," Kelly says. "I'm not trying to make an excuse, but you know it's tough. If he and Curtis are friends, then give him another chance."

"Is that true Curtis?" asks Kelvin."

"When Kelly told us, we didn't believe it," adds Kevin.

Curtis locks eyes with Treyshawn as he says, "Yeah, it's true. We're cool now."

"Alright then..." Kelvin says. "Treyshawn, if they vouch for you, then you get a second chance. But break our trust and you won't like the consequences."

"If you really *want* to change," Kevin says, "then you better do it." The twin brothers turn and walk off. "We'll see you at home, Kelly. Talk to you later, Curtis."

A few moments later, Curtis and Kelly try to pick Treyshawn up, but he stops them. "Thanks guys..." he says while spitting out blood, "I got it."

"You need help." Kelly says with sadness in her eyes.

"Nah, you told your brothers to back off. Trust me... *that's* help enough... I'll be ok."

"You need us to do anything?" Curtis asks.

"You guys just go... I'll talk to you later."

"Alright..." they say as they walk off, leaving Treyshawn by himself. He forces his body up and leans against the fence—holding his side with one hand and wiping his face with his sleeve. He struggles to keep his balance as he considers his life and all that's happened.

If you really want to change, then you better do it.

Chapter Eleven

Revelations

THE PA RELAYS: APRIL 23-25, 2009.

Thousands descend upon the track and field stadium. The atmosphere is filled with excitement as teams from over sixty countries prepare to compete for international recognition. Coaches give constant reminders as their athletes visualize each event. News crews and sports networks provide moment-by-moment coverage and commentary, as each leg of the massive competition unfolds.

Several events happen over the weekend: the Long Jump; Pole Vault; Javelin Throw; Shot Put, Discus… but what has everybody's complete attention are the multitude of track races.

Curtis, Omar, Treyshawn, and Mr. Grabowski quickly take their seats.

"Can you believe that we're here?" Curtis asks his brother.

"Yeah! This is nice," Omar replies.

"Nice? This is great!" Curtis says as he turns to Treyshawn, "How do you like it?"

"This is pretty cool. I've never been outside the Bronx before."

"You've never been outside the Bronx?" Mr. Grabowski asks in surprise.

"Nah… never. City streets is all I know."

"Well, Treyshawn, we're glad you could make it. The more the merrier!"

Hours pass as they watch the events—Curtis captures everything with his video camera—thinking how he can improve his boot design.

"How's the camera, little brother?"

"It's great," he says while thinking back to when he first got it.

Three days before...

"Curtis! Come here! You gotta see this!"

Curtis runs into the living room to find a Track and Field segment on the cable sports channel.

"Wow!" He plops down in front of the television as several news personalities recount the events from the previous year's PA Relays. Curtis is glued to the screen and doesn't even notice the gift-wrapped box next to him. The segment ends and Curtis jumps up—extremely excited.

"I can't believe we'll be at the Relays this weekend! I wonder if we'll meet any famous athletes there? Imagine what I can learn from watching the runners—maybe even figure out a way to improve the boots."

Curtis stops when he sees Omar's growing smile. "What?"

Omar laughs. "For such a smart kid, sometimes you're so unobservant."

Curtis looks around the room and finally sees the box on the floor next to his feet. "Where did this come from?" He kneels down; rips open the wrapping and then stops. He barely speaks, "Is that a video camera?" Then he starts yelling at the top of his lungs. "It's a video camera!"

Omar laughs as he watches his younger brother. "I know how analytical you'll be at the Relays this weekend. I figured this would help you gather data for your boots."

"Thanks, Omar! You're the greatest!"

"God's the greatest," he counters.

"Yeah, well, he gave me the best brother ever!"

They both hug. "I'm proud of you, Curtis. You're going to do great things with your life. Don't let anyone tell you different. You just keep running towards your goals."

The present...

As one of the main events nears, a nearby coach reminds his runners: "You're not out there to show off. You're not even out there to make another runner look bad. You're out there to do your best. Remember, time is your opponent. So, stay focused and run towards your goal. Don't worry about the other runners because they'll try to get you to run their race and not yours. If you do your best, then you'll be a winner—even if someone else crosses the finish line before you do."

The race is about to begin as the athletes take their mark. Curtis sits at the ready—his video camera already recording. The pistol fires into the air and the runners burst out of the starting blocks!

The crowds cheer, many jumping to their feet, as the runners make their way around the track for the first lap. Curtis follows the runners closely with his camera; then notices something in the viewfinder—an action he'd seen a thousand times before, but never paid attention to.

Several of the runners fall into a close line as they continue around the track. "That's drafting!" he says as an idea begins to take shape in his mind.

"Each runner deals with wind resistance, but when they get close to each other, the first guy gets the brunt of it—making it easier for the others behind him. What if there was a way for a runner to use the oncoming air to his advantage?"

He quickly hands the camera to Treyshawn. "Here! Keep recording the race." Curtis breaks out his notebook and pen while Treyshawn fumbles to keep the camera on the runners. Mr. Grabowski and Omar notice Curtis' actions and look at each other with a humorous expression. *There he goes again.*

The crowd's roar rattles everything but Curtis' mind where only his internal voice is heard. His hand writes quickly, trying to keep up with his thoughts. Once again he goes through the steps of the scientific method: Ask a question. Construct a hypothesis. Test the hypothesis. Analyze the data. Communicate results.

How can a runner make the oncoming air work for him? It takes more energy for the first runner, but less for those behind him. Curtis recalls a time when he ran in the same direction as the wind. He actually was able to run faster as the wind propelled him forward. By the end of the race, he has a complete concept. "This idea should work," he says to himself. "I'll test this first—then tell the guys."

The boys sat in the back of the car while Omar sat up front with Mr. Grabowski. The three-hour car ride back to New York was a much-needed break for them—having been surrounded by thousands of screaming fans for the past few days.

Mr. Grabowski focused on the road as Omar took a light nap. Curtis was consumed with his notes and camera footage—oblivious to Treyshawn—who was about to ask a question that had long been on his mind:

"Hey Omar…" he calls from the back seat.

Omar opens his eyes and turns his head towards him. "What's up Treyshawn?"

"I've been meaning to ask you… that time I came over for dinner, I passed by your room and saw the scars on your back. Were those bullet wounds?" Curtis looks up from his work—shocked that Treyshawn had finally asked the question.

Mr. Grabowski turns towards Omar in surprise. "You were shot?"

"Yeah," Omar says, "before I joined the navy."

"If you don't mind me askin'," Treyshawn continues, "how did it happen?"

"You've been smoking marijuana again!" Miranda said to her eldest son as he entered the house after being out all night. "I told you to stop hanging out with those boys!"

"And?" he says defiantly.

"And?" she repeats. "Omar, I need you here."

"Who cares what you need, Ma! What about me? What about what *I* need?"

"Your father's sick."

"I know that! *I* was at the doctor's with him, while *you* were at work! I'm outta here."

"So, that's it? You're just going to run?"

"Why not, Ma? Better than going to church with you to worship a God who's letting dad die."

"People think I'm strong because I'm big, but my dad's sickness hit harder than any punch or kick. He was always so strong, but seeing his body wasting away like that... I couldn't take it."

"Omar, we talked about this," Malcolm says in a weak voice, "I'm not mad at God."

"Well, maybe you should be!" His son's voice trembles.

"I'm not saying I never was mad, but I'm not anymore. The doctors said there was no hope. All I have is God and my family. How does being mad at the world help anything—except make my cancer flare even more out of control? Son, you're stronger than this."

"That's just it, Dad... I'm not."

They all sit quietly—only the sound of the engine is heard as the car speeds down the highway. Omar can barely fight back the tears.

"I wasn't even there when he died. I thought dealing with his cancer was too much—but the guilt of not being there when he died was unbearable. I didn't know how I could ever come back to my mom or Curtis. So, I just ran the streets.

"One night a drug deal went bad and a friend and I were caught in a hail of bullets. He didn't make it and I almost bled to death. It was like God was trying to get my attention. I pulled through and *everything* changed after that.

"Since joining the navy, I've been to five continents, trained as a mechanical engineer, and worked on fighter jets. And the navy will pay for college after my tour is up. That's what happened."

"Man... that's serious," Treyshawn says.

"Yeah, God is good."

Monday April 27, 2009. Entry number 1,246.

"We got in real late last night—too late. And Mr. Grabowski had a meeting during lunch, so I couldn't go to the lab. I've got all these ideas in my head; I'm just glad school's almost over. I can't wait to get home and start testing."

Curtis rushed home after the last bell, eager to begin his new project. He skipped his usual ritual—heading straight for the refrigerator—and went straight to his room. This was all he could think about... and now the time was here.

All of the supplies are laid out on his desk: fan, cardboard, fabric, tape, paper, scissors, and a full bottle of mouthwash. He drops his bag next to his bed and quickly sits at his desk. Next to the desk, sits the tripod and video camera—at the ready. He powers it up, presses 'record' and gets to work.

An hour passes as he assembles the materials into a singular unit—all while providing copious commentary about the construction process and its purpose. Satisfied, Curtis turns to the camera and smiles. Before stopping the recording, he says, "The first phase of this idea is complete."

A somewhat crude-looking wind tunnel sits before him, with the mouthwash bottle placed at its exit vent. Fabric strips are taped to the back of the bottle—in a numerical sequence. He looks at a picture on his wall of the first wind tunnel built by the Wright Brothers, and smiles as he hits 'record' again: "April 27, 2009. Preliminary test for what I am calling... the Slipstream Concept."

As the fan powers up, the air rushes past the bottle. The strips on its edge begin to move, but the ones directly behind the center mass of the bottle are undisturbed. Curtis takes a sheet of paper, folds it in half and curves it around the bottle. As the paper enters the airflow and approaches the side of the bottle, the fabric strips, at its center, begin to move. After a few moments of trial and error, he focuses the camera on the fabric strips—all are now being affected by the oncoming wind.

He speaks for the camera, "I think I've found a way to make the oncoming air work for me."

Tuesday April 28, 2009. During fourth period, Curtis shows Mr. Grabowski the videotape.

"Sounds like an interesting premise."

"I just need to test this out on a larger scale. I've been researching the work major sneaker companies do to develop aerodynamic sneakers and tracksuits. They have access to wind tunnels; too bad we couldn't visit one of theirs."

"That would be difficult, especially if we're trying to maintain a level of secrecy until we finish developing your inventions. But tell you what... we'll break this into two stages. Take your slipstream concept and attach larger strips to a tank top. See if Treyshawn will run around the track with it while you videotape. Then analyze the data. In a few weeks, we'll get supplies to construct a larger wind tunnel in my garage—one big enough for a full-size person. When school is over we'll build it and do some serious experimenting."

"You'd help me do that?"

"Why not? It shouldn't cost much. We can get most of the supplies at the hardware store. You've already proven your premise for the boots; I'd be crazy *not* to help. But if your concept works on a full-size person, what will you do with it?"

"Well... if I can use this new concept to reduce wind resistance and channel the oncoming air so it works for me instead of against me; then with my boots, I could run even faster. I'm not sure about the optimal design yet; this is where Treyshawn's drawing skills come into play. I'll tell him what I'm thinking and see what he comes up with."

"Why Treyshawn and not your brother?"

"Omar would do it, but Treyshawn isn't confident about his drawing skills. I figured maybe helping me, will help him. Besides, Omar likes to get his hands dirty building stuff. He won't mind if Treyshawn picks up the artistic stuff for a while."

"Speaking of Treyshawn, I'm glad he had a good time this weekend."

"Yeah, he did."

"I hear his grades are starting to pick up."

"We've been studying together a few nights a week."

Mr. Grabowski chuckles to himself. "His teachers don't quite know what to make of his improvement. With this being his second time in the ninth grade, they're so used to him failing. When I'm in the teachers' lounge, I just sit back and listen, and try not to smile. That's a good thing you're doing—helping him. Who would have thought that the guy who bullied you would end up becoming your friend."

Weeks pass as Curtis and Treyshawn work hard on their schoolwork; practice study tips, do drawing exercises and run track to gather data. Things have changed so much between them that Curtis goes to his guidance counselor to make a request.

"Mrs. Fuller, I have a friend who needs help and I want you to be his guidance counselor."

"Really? And who might this young man be?" she says with a smile.

"Treyshawn Jinkins."

Her smile quickly disappears. "Yes. I know of him. No ambition. He's a troublemaker who is repeating the ninth grade—although," she says with a rise, "I *have* heard that his grades have started to improve." She eyes him curiously as she swivels slightly in her chair. "I wonder why?"

"I know he's done some bad things, but he's different—once you get to know him."

"So you *have* been tutoring him!"

"Yes."

"Are you sure you haven't been *doing* his work?"

Curtis laughs while waving his hands, "I've only helped with his reading and study skills."

"Ok. So, what's wrong with *his* counselor?"

"He already messed up *that* relationship. He needs a fresh start, and I know you work hard to help your students be the best they can be."

"Are you flattering me, Curtis?" she says flashing a smile, "Because if you are, it's working."

He smiles back. "I'm just stating the obvious."

"Alright. Based on *your* recommendation, I'll consider it. Tell Treyshawn to stop by my office tomorrow so we can have a nice little talk."

Tuesday June 2, 2009.

Treyshawn sits in front of Mrs. Fuller's desk. She doesn't say anything for the first few moments—just looks at him. He looks around nervously, trying to avoid her eyes as she reaches into a pile and hands him a typed sheet. "Here. I want you to read this out loud."

Treyshawn takes it, somewhat reluctantly and looks at it. "What is it?"

"It's a poem by an author I like. Although his writings are not prolific; they are sagacious for a person his age."

"Wow," he shakes his head slightly, "Those are two words I don't know."

She raises her eyebrow in surprise. "You know, it takes a smart young man to do what you just did."

"What did I just do?" he says shrugging his shoulders.

She smiles. "You admitted you didn't know something. That was probably the smartest thing you could have said so far."

"Why's that?"

"Most students, when they don't know certain things, never admit it. What you did means you're teachable. Are you teachable, Treyshawn?" She looks into his eyes for a few moments—searching out his soul. "Take out a pen and your notebook and write down what I'm about to tell you."

Treyshawn opens his bag, pulls them out and flips open to a blank page—poised with pen in hand. She smiles slightly and begins to speak.

"The word 'prolific.' Can you spell that?"

"No."

"P-R-O-L-I-F-I-C. Prolific. It means to have a lot of; an abundance. Do you understand?"

Treyshawn writes quickly while nodding his head. "I got it."

"Good. 'Sagacious.' S-A-G-A-C-I-O-U-S. Sagacious. This word means to have acute mental discernment and keen practical sense."

"What does acute mean?"

"Acute… can mean a few slightly different things. But it basically means sharp… focused."

"Ok. How do you spell that other word with a 'D'?

"Discernment?"

"Yeah… that word."

"D-I-S-C-E-R-N-M-E-N-T"

"Ok. What does that mean?"

"Discernment means judgment, which means the ability to form sound opinions and make sensible decisions or reliable guesses."

"What does *sound* got to do with opinions?" Treyshawn asks with a bewildered look.

Mrs. Fuller tries hard not to chuckle.

"What's so funny?" Treyshawn asks, feeling a little uncomfortable.

"I'm sorry, Treyshawn. I'm not laughing at you. It's just that you're like a child learning for the first time."

Treyshawn drops the sheet of paper, grabs his things and quickly stands up. "I come to you for help and now you disrespectin' me?"

"Treyshawn," Mrs. Fuller says, standing too, "I would *never* disrespect you."

"Well, that's what you doin'!" Treyshawn fires back as he heads for the door, "I ain't no child! I'mma man!"

Mrs. Fuller moves to cut him off. "Treyshawn, wait! Let me explain."

"There's nuthin' to explain!"

"I'm sorry, I thought you *wanted* help," Mrs. Fuller says while standing in front of the door with her arms crossed.

"Get out of the way or I'll move you."

"Oh, now you're going to disrespect me?"

"You started!"

"Treyshawn, this isn't elementary school."

"Well, you said I'm actin' like a child!"

"Yes, like a child who's *excited* about learning something new. I was laughing because your response made me happy. Can you get that through that skull of yours, Treyshawn? I was delighted at your response!"

Treyshawn stops in his tracks and tries to bring himself under control. "So... you weren't trying to disrespect me?"

"Honey, I wouldn't waste my time trying to disrespect anybody. I've got *way* too much to do than waste my time trying to put somebody down."

He slowly looks Mrs. Fuller in her eyes, but says nothing.

"Don't leave yet, alright?" She says softly while laying her hand on his shoulder. "This could be a great opportunity for you."

Treyshawn looks down at her hand on his shoulder and then slowly moves back to his chair. Mrs. Fuller breathes a sigh of relief and sits down as well. "You're not use to people being nice to you, are you?"

He looks at her before lowering his gaze to the floor. "No..."

"You know, Curtis asked me to talk with you because he believes you want to change and do something positive with your life."

"I do," he says before going silent, "...but it's hard." Mrs. Fuller waits for him to continue. "But I want to change."

"If you want to change, the first thing it takes is a willing mind. As *hard* as everything else is, once you are determined to be willing—everything else becomes easier." She searches his blank expression for any indication of understanding. "What are you thinking about, Treyshawn?"

He looks up and begins to smile as he asks the question, "What does inquisitive mean?"

She leans back in her chair with a smile. "When someone is inquisitive, it means they are eager for knowledge. Does that sound like you, Treyshawn?"

"Maybe," he says while sitting up in his chair.

"Good. Now read. I want to see what you pick up from this poem."

"I'm not... a good reader."

"It's just like exercise. The more you do it, the stronger you become.

Don't worry about speed. Read as slow or as fast as you like. Just concentrate on the words and their meaning."

He picks the paper up from the carpeted floor. After staring at it, he swallows hard before reading in a slow, somewhat choppy and labored voice.

"What about your dreams? Don't you ever think about the future that's filled with... possibilities?"

"That's good," Mrs. Fuller encourages, "keep going."

Treyshawn looks up and smiles at her before continuing. "Have you ever pictured in your mind, the coming day's light? The day's light shines on your dreams: the light of recognition—the light of realization. What about your dreams? Do you choose not to dream to avoid the off-chance that it might not come true? Are you afraid of broken promises? Is this what you do? What about your dreams? Is it stupid to dream of a future when you're trying to make it through today? When you're just trying to overcome the struggles you must face. With no dream for tomorrow can you really survive? Something within you slowly dies... With no joy in the morning will tonight draw you away? What about your dreams?"

Mrs. Fuller waits for the words to sink in as Treyshawn looks at the page.

"See, that wasn't so bad. So, tell me, what does the poem say to you?"

"... The first line got my attention."

"Why? What about it?" Now she sits on the edge of her seat—arms crossed on the table—fully engaged as he continues.

"Well... I've never really had any dreams for my life..."

"Ok..."

"I never really *had* anything to live for. And at home—my mom's always downing me."

"Go on..."

"It's like the author gets me when he says, 'Is it stupid to dream of a future when you're trying to make it through today? When you're just trying to overcome the struggles you must face.' That was me—just hanging out in the streets—trying to survive."

"And what about your dreams now?"

"... I think I've got dreams now... Maybe."

"What changed? How did you go from 'just trying to survive' to having a dream?"

Treyshawn smiles confidently as he answers.

"Curtis."

Chapter Twelve

Summer Time

THE SCHOOL YEAR ENDS AND SUMMER BEGINS: Kelly's off to dance camp and Treyshawn gears up for summer school. Meanwhile, Curtis, Mr. Grabowski, and Omar start building their wind tunnel.

For the first seven days of July, the three work several hours each afternoon to complete the project. Three large fans connect to hoses, which feed into the main, central chamber. This chamber is made of PVC pipe over which large sections of transparent plastic are stretched to form a seal. When fully assembled, the wind tunnel occupies a large portion of the room.

Treyshawn finally visits Mr. Grabowski's house, before the testing begins.

"Well, look who it is!" Mr. Grabowski says as he opens the side door, "Glad you could finally make it."

"Thanks for having me."

"Come on in. Curtis and Omar are in the next room."

Treyshawn stops in the doorway to the next room—amazed at what he sees. "It's like a big lab down here! Where's Tony Stark and the robot arms?" They all laugh as he walks around, examining things, before stopping right in front of the wind tunnel.

"So what do you think?" Curtis says.

"Can I touch it?"

"Go ahead."

Treyshawn reaches out and places his hands on its wall. "It's like you can put a person in there!"

"Yep!" Omar says. "You can."

"And you're gonna get inside that thing?"

"That's the plan."

"To test the boots?"

"No," Mr. Grabowski interjects. "We're going to use this to test a design for a new component."

"It's the vest idea I was telling you about," Curtis says excitedly.

"So when do we get started?" Treyshawn asks.

"Tomorrow," Mr. Grabowski says before changing subjects. "How'd the first week of summer school go?"

"Intense. But I'm on top of things. Mrs. Fuller set me up with extra help."

"Right... Curtis told me about your assessment results."

"You know what's funny? I just thought I was dumb and figured, why even try in school? But if Curtis didn't help me get Mrs. Fuller—I never knew I had dyslexia. The special after-school program is teaching me a lot about how my brain works. I even got my textbooks downloaded to my mp3 player! It really helps to listen *and* read."

"I'm glad to hear you are improving, Treyshawn."

"Yeah, me, too. Now if things got better with my moms... then everything would be good."

"What's going on with your mother?"

"Can we talk about that later?"

"No problem. We'll just focus on the plan. If we work on the project at least a few hours a day, we could have a workable prototype vest in a month. You got your supplies, ready?"

Treyshawn opens his backpack and pulls out his pad and a pencil. "I'm ready to get drawing."

The next leg of the journey continues as the group meets almost every day for four weeks of wind tunnel testing, vest research, and design. Tracksuits are purchased—different types of fabric, examined and ways of integrating them with composite materials are discovered.

By the end of July, Treyshawn has drawn more sketches than any other time in his life; but the result was worth it: the slipstream vest prototype was complete and ready for its first real-world test on the track field.

Data from the wind tunnel experiments is promising—yielding a positive airflow that significantly reduces passive drag and generates a "boost" effect for the wearer.

By August 7, the group celebrates before finalizing preparations for the vest to be field-tested.

"It's hard to believe that summer's almost over," Treyshawn says.

"Yeah," Curtis replies. "I can't believe August is already here."

"And look at all the things we've been able to do," Mr. Grabowski reminds them. "The four of us have been able to create something that's never been done before."

"We wouldn't have been able to do it without you, Mr. G," Curtis says.

"Yeah," Treyshawn says. "Thanks for letting me be a part of this. If it wasn't for you, Omar, and Curtis, I'd be in a very different place right now."

"And if it wasn't for you," Omar says as he crosses the room, "so would we."

The four reflect on that last statement before Mr. Grabowski breaks in. "My summer would have been pretty boring without you guys."

They all laugh as Omar says in toast-like fashion, "To a successful run!"

"To a successful run!" The others reply.

Later that night… Curtis yawns as he lies in bed. "I'm glad you made it back, Kelly. It seemed like you were at dance camp for a long time."

"You sound tired. We could talk tomorrow," she says while lazily flipping through a dance magazine.

"Let's talk for a few minutes. Hearing your voice is better than sending text messages."

"You better not fall asleep on me."

"I won't," he yawns. "When did you get back?"

"About an hour ago," she jumps on her bed and gets comfortable, "I'm pretty tired myself."

"Yeah… I'm exhausted. We've been working on the project for like a month straight."

"How's it coming?" she says excitedly. "Your text said you got some new ideas?"

"Wait till you see what we've done. It's going to blow your mind. Are you free tomorrow?"

"I've got a couple of days free before I go back to regular dance classes. Why?"

"We're doing a test tomorrow at an outdoor track in New Rochelle."

"What time?"

"Early. Like sunrise."

"Sunrise? That's before six o'clock!"

"Yeah, I know. We have to leave about four."

"Why so early?"

"The track is public. We don't want to test when everybody's out."

"How are you guys getting there?"

"Mr. G's meeting us at the train station. Me and Omar can come get you."

"I have to ask my parents. I already know they're gonna flip."

"What are your brothers doing?"

"I don't know."

"Maybe, if they come, your parents will say yes."

"Maybe. Let me talk to them and call you back."

An hour later...

"Are you going to videotape your experiment?"

"Yeah. Why?"

"I'll just have to watch the tape."

"They said no?"

"No would be an understatement."

"Did they flip?"

"Forwards and backwards."

"Aw man... now they hate me."

"They don't hate you. They know you're a good guy. I could have gone if your test was later in the day. But, it didn't help that I couldn't tell them what you were working on. Mom kept saying, 'what kind of experiment? He's not going to blow something up is he?'"

Curtis laughs. "How come everybody thinks I'm gonna blow something up?"

Kelly laughs, too. "Then mom said you sounded like Steve Urkel, from the show *Family Matters*. You remember that show?"

"Yeah, I remember!" Curtis says in laughable disbelief. "Sometimes you can catch the re-runs. Steve was a *real* nerd!"

"He was always building stuff that blew up. I can't believe she compared me to Steve Urkel! But I'm not clumsy like he was."

"You're like in between Steve and his alter ego, Stefan," Kelly says with a bit of excitement. "Now he was the cool one! Besides, he ended up with the girl in the end."

"That sounds like a good place to be," Curtis says with a smile.

"It's not bad," Kelly says as if she didn't care either way. "Listen, I better let you go. You've got to get up in a few hours. Me, on the other hand, I'm going to enjoy sleeping in."

"Make sure you get some sleep for me, too."

"You make sure you don't forget the video. Can you bring it over this weekend?"

"Yeah, maybe tomorrow. I'll let you know."

"When you come over, I can show you some footage from my dance camp."

"Cool."

"Have a good night, Curtis."

"You too, Kelly."

Saturday August 8, 2009. 4:00am. The subway train rocks back and forth—speeding down the track, as three young men sit, barely awake. Curtis tries desperately to keep his eyes open, and pulls out his journal to write.

"Note to self: try and do experiments late at night instead of early in the morning. Me and Omar had to get up at 3:30am! Treyshawn met us at the train station and now the three of us are headed to meet Mr. G. I wonder if he's awake?"

The train arrives at their stop and they drudge themselves to the rendezvous point. Their adult mentor stands waiting—fully awake. "I can't believe you guys are so tired! How can you sleep at a time like this?" Mr. Grabowski says, puzzled as he watches the three slowly approach from the train station.

"How can you be so awake?" mutters Treyshawn. "The sun's not even up yet?"

The four of them get in the car and drive away.

"What time did you go to bed?" asks Omar.

Mr. Grabowski's response pierces through their sleepiness. "I didn't."

"You mean to tell me you stayed up all night?" Curtis asks.

"Sometimes I get like that. When I'm excited about something it can be difficult for me to go to sleep. What we're doing is like a physicist's dream. I think I'm running on pure adrenalin!"

"Well, can we have some of *your* energy, then?" Treyshawn asks.

"Don't worry, once we get to the track and start setting up, you'll be just as awake as I am."

The group arrives at the high school track. They disembark from the car and notice that the sun itself is just peeking over the horizon, shaking off its own slumber. They grab the equipment from the car and take it to the track. Mr. Grabowski was right—the adrenalin is kicking in.

"Treyshawn, you set up the camera and tripod," Mr. Grabowski says, spitting orders rapidly. "Me, Curtis, and Omar will check the vest and boots. After you get the camera set up start stretching because you're going to do the first run with the vest."

"Are you serious?" His eyes widen. "You're going to let me do a run?"

"Why not?" Curtis says.

"But the vest is for you."

"We've already decided you've earned it," says Omar.

"Besides," Mr. Grabowski says. "You helped design it."

"Yeah," Curtis adds. "How the vest works may be *my* idea, but how it looks is *all* you."

"Now that's hot. Thanks, guys."

"After you run," Curtis says, "we'll look at the data and then I'll run."

Once everything is set up, they begin. At Omar's signal, Treyshawn runs an entire lap without the vest. Mr. Grabowski keeps time as Curtis works the video camera.

"Man, he's fast," says Omar. "I can see why you needed the boots to beat him, Curtis."

Treyshawn comes down the final stretch to the finish line as Mr. Grabowski slams his thumb down on the stopwatch. "Time! Treyshawn, that was fast!" says Mr. Grabowski.

"What's my time?" he says while pacing slowly.

"You ran the lap in just under fifty seconds! If you're this fast already, I can't wait to see what you can do in the vest. How do you feel?"

"I'm out of shape," he says while breathing heavily. They all laugh.

"Take a few minutes to relax while we look at the data. Then we'll get you in the vest."

Fifteen minutes later, Treyshawn zooms around the track again. This time clocking even faster than before!

"Amazing! You shaved off a full seven seconds! How did it feel?"

"Just like you guys said it would feel! It was way easier to run—like less resistance in front, and more force pushing me! This thing actually works!"

After reviewing the data again, Curtis suits up with the vest and the boots. When he starts to run, the results are even more encouraging. Not only does he beat Treyshawn's fastest time, but also he runs faster with the vest, than when using the boots alone. The faster Curtis moves the more air the Slipstream vest puts to work.

Around 7:30am, the sunlight beams brightly, as more people are seen walking near the school.

"Alright, we need to get out of here," Mr. Grabowski says. "Don't want anyone getting too good a look at us."

They break down; repack the gear and head to the house for a homemade breakfast of grits, eggs, sausage, bacon and waffles. As they eat and review footage in the living room, Curtis suddenly gets another idea. "Hey, guys! What would happen if we added a jet to the back of the vest?"

The guys look at each other in stunned silence.

Mr. Grabowski shakes his head as he laughs. "A jet? We just finished the prototype vest and you're already thinking about a new add-on? Your mind never slows down, does it?"

"Not really..." Curtis replies.

"I don't think his mind *can* slow down," Omar says with a grin. "The ideas just keep coming."

"A jet sounds cool to me," adds Treyshawn. "How would it work?"

"I'm not sure, but if we could strap it to my back it could move more air through the vest, and produce thrust—a lot of thrust."

"Now you want to be the Flash?" Treyshawn asks.

"I'm just saying...it sounds crazy, but it could work."

"There's a lot of physics you'd have to work out Curtis," Mr. Grabowski says. "Control, power supply, braking system, and that's the short list."

"Well it's a good thing that we've got you here, huh?" They all laugh.

"If you're talking about running significantly faster," says Omar; "you're going to need a padded body suit to help protect you against impacts."

"Cool...then he can look like he has some real muscles," jokes Treyshawn. "I've always liked drawing superheroes."

"Is that what we're doing?" Mr. Grabowski says in surprise. "Are we building... a superhero suit?" He cuts himself off and shuts his eyes tight while waving his hands. "Wait—don't answer that."

"My mom took me to the Superhero and Fashion exhibit at the museum last summer for my birthday. Each display talked about how superhero science fiction and reality were coming together through technology.

"A lot of companies are spending millions on stuff like what we're doing. But, from what I can tell, no one's coming at things like we are. We're like the Wright brothers—going up against the big companies and figuring out how to fly... first."

"Well said, Curtis," Mr. Grabowski adds, "We've come this far... we might as well see where this will take us."

"And who knows," Treyshawn says while stuffing a huge forkful of waffles into his mouth, "maybe we can set a world record or something."

Omar, Curtis, and Mr. Grabowski look at each other and then at Treyshawn, who tries hard not to choke on his food. "What you guys looking at?"

"Treyshawn," Mr. Grabowski says, "you're a genius!"

Curtis finishes the thought. "We can set the record for the world's fastest running man."

"Yeah?" Treyshawn swallows some more waffles. "I was just saying..."

"That could work." Omar says. "Like the guy last year, who flew—what's his name, Curtis?"

"Fusion Man, a.k.a. Yves Rossy. He set the world record for flying across the English Channel on a wing and jets that he created and built himself. He's from Switzerland."

"Yeah, that's the guy. We could do what he did; set a world record—just on land. If we can do that, we can get exposure, but more importantly, the exposure will lead to more resources."

"We'd be famous..." Treyshawn says—his eyes glistening.

"We would," Mr. Grabowski says, "but it's more about what we *do* with that fame that counts. What do you think, Curtis?"

"Well... we didn't start this for fame. But doing something big—people will find out anyway—and that could mean more resources. Then we wouldn't have to spend all your money, Mr. G."

Mr. Grabowski laughs heartily. "My money's not endless, but we're in no danger of me going broke. If you want to go for the world record, then I say we go for it."

Sunday August 9, 2009. Kelly's house...

"I can't believe you guys were up so early in the morning," Kelly says as they sit on the couch and the footage begins to play.

"I can't believe it either," Curtis responds, "Mr. G stayed up the whole night—said he gets like that when he's really excited." The picture flashes on the television screen. "Ok, there's Treyshawn running with the vest."

"How can you tell he's faster in the vest?"

"We timed him running—with and without the vest. The vest, kind of pushes you from behind, and causes less resistance in front. If the wind blows against you; you really feel it."

Kelly points at the screen in excitement, "There you are!"

"That's me."

"You've got the boots and the vest on. Were you faster than when you outran Treyshawn?"

"Yeah, a lot faster." They watch as he launches himself down the track and quickly picks up speed.

"Wow, it's so amazing that you came up with the idea of the boots in the first place."

"I wish you could have been there."

"Me, too. But I'm glad you were able to share this with me."

Their eyes lock for a moment, before Curtis breaks the gaze. "Uh, speaking of footage, where's *yours* from summer dance camp?"

"Oh, you don't want to see that."

"Yes, I do."

"But your video is so much more exciting!"

"Stop stalling. I'm sure it's great." He unplugs his video camera from the DVD player. "We don't have all day," he smiles.

"All right, but you promise not to laugh?"

"At you? Never... unless you trip or fall."

"Hey!" Kelly punches Curtis in his arm as he laughs while throwing his hands up in mock defense, "I'm just kidding!"

A few moments later, Kelly's video is playing on the television screen. The well lit, mirrored dance studio is filled with girls of various heights and sizes standing at long horizontal bars, each slowly raising their legs up and down.

"Wow..." Curtis says. "That's *a lot* of control. I'd probably fall over. Where are you?"

"Fourth one from the front on the right side," she says while trying not to look nervous. As if on cue, the camera zooms in on Kelly's position.

"There you are!"

"There I am."

"Who's working the camera?"

"One of my friends from camp. Her session started after mine."

The class lines up on one side as each dancer runs and leaps into the air! Kelly's form is practically flawless.

"Wow! Can you rewind that?"

"Why?" She says while rewinding the clip.

"That was amazing!" Curtis exclaims. "Your leap—it was like you were gliding through the air!"

The scene plays again as he sits in awe looking at his friend.

"I do need to work on it," she says.

"What are you talking about? That looked perfect to me? What did your teacher say?"

Before she can answer, the teacher speaks.

"That was beautiful, Kelly. Wonderful extension. Excellent height! Placement and landing are exquisite. Class, you need to pay attention to Kelly. Many of you will do well to follow her lead."

Kelly jumps up and stops the video. "That's enough of that."

"Why? You did great and the teacher liked it!"

"I know. *That's* the problem." She stands by the television—her arms crossed and head down.

"What? You're a great dancer; why are you putting yourself down like that? Are you ashamed?"

"No."

"Well what is it? Why are you so afraid?"

"It's just," she plops down on the floor, "I love ballet. I really love it. And I work hard at it. But when the teachers are always telling the other students to watch me... it's so much pressure!" She throws herself to the floor, in a huff, and stares at the ceiling.

Curtis crawls over and lies next to her. "You're afraid you'll mess up?"

"...Yeah..."

"And what happens if you do?"

"You heard my teacher. I'm exquisite, wonderful... marvelous!"

"She didn't say you were marvelous."

Kelly stops for a second, and then slaps Curtis in his stomach.

He gasps for air, "Hey! You're heavy handed!"

She laughs. "And you always got something smart to say or you *try* to be funny."

"I'm glad to know it still works. You know, I never paid attention to your ceiling before."

"Curtis, this is serious."

He puts on his best serious expression.

"Curtis…!"

"What?" he laughs, "you said this is serious, so I'm being serious!"

"No, you're not!" Kelly says giggling. "You're *acting* serious. Actually, overacting is what you're doing."

"Alright, alright. I'm for real now… seriously."

Kelly laughs, crossing her hands behind her head. "Why are you so silly?"

"Because it makes you laugh."

"Usually, but sometimes you're corny."

"Hey, we can't all be perfect." As soon as the word 'perfect' leaves his lips, he instantly wishes he could take it back, as Kelly becomes depressed all over again.

"That's what I'm getting at, Curtis! Everybody expects me to be perfect. It's like I'm on this pedestal and I didn't ask to be there."

"So quit," he says abruptly.

"What?" She turns and looks at him—partially confused.

"If you feel you can't handle the pressure, then quit," he says while looking straight in her eyes.

Kelly looks away and sits up. Her lips quiver as she tries to summon her response. "How… how can you… say that?" She looks back at him. "You *know* I love ballet."

The hurt in her eyes is almost unbearable to him, but he doesn't back down. "I know… but why do you love it?"

"Because… because I'm *free* when I'm dancing. Nothing can touch me. The only things that matter are the music and the movements."

"What's another reason?"

"I don't know… I'm *good* at it."

"From the first time you ever danced ballet?"

"No!" She says with a slight giggle while remembering when she was little. "I was six when I had my first class at a small dance studio near Southern Boulevard." She lets out a huge laugh. "I was horrible!"

"Really?" Curtis asks while trying to keep a straight face.

"I was so uncoordinated and a little… *chunkier* back then."

"You used to be… big boned?"

Kelly laughs. "Something like that. The first few months were terrible. According to the teacher, I couldn't do anything right. She said I was hopeless and that ballet wasn't for me. My mom was going to pull me out, but I told her I loved the class. So she decided to keep me in."

"Even though the teacher said you couldn't do it? Wow…"

"I think part of keeping me there was to get back at the teacher," Kelly says with a laugh as she lies back down.

"But *why* did you love it?" Curtis presses.

"Because it was so fun! And I thought I looked so beautiful in my leotard and ruffled skirt. I would stare at myself in those large mirrors… and imagine that I was a *princess.*"

"Really?"

Kelly looks away embarrassed. "I can't believe I'm telling you all this! I know you must think it's so dumb!"

Curtis jumps to his feet. "Hey, you're talking to a guy who used to tie a towel around his neck and stand in front of the mirror pretending to be a superhero."

Kelly laughs as she sits up and watches Curtis act out his story.

"I'd run around the house making 'whooshing' sounds, while leaping onto the couch or jumping down the stairs!"

Kelly laughs again and stumbles over to the couch as Curtis plops down next to her. "We both did the same thing… just different. You wanted to be beautiful—I wanted to be strong."

They sit quietly for a moment, looking up at the ceiling, before Kelly speaks.

"When my mom let me go back, I started getting better. I'd practice for hours, and my teacher started to notice."

"So you were determined."

"I guess so. I slowly worked my way from the back of the class all the way to the front. And by the time I got there, I was a whole lot thinner and one of the best dancers in the school."

"Wow. Then what happened?"

"My mom took me out; I auditioned at Alvin Ailey and got accepted into their dance program. I've been with them for three years and danced in some pretty big productions. I even spend two weekends a month helping my old teacher with her girls."

"So do you still love dancing?"

"Yeah."

"Do you want to quit?"

"No. But that still doesn't change how I feel."

"Sure it does. Dance because you love to dance! If you make a mistake—you make a mistake. Only God is perfect."

"But you don't understand…"

"What's to understand? If you focus on the pressure, you'll stop loving dance. If you stop loving it, you'll start hating it and eventually quit. You don't have to be flawless. Just do your best."

Kelly looks at Curtis in amazement. "How did you get so smart?"

"I'm not that smart. I just had a good dad. We talked about everything; and he would tell me to do my best, so the miraculous could happen. I'm just telling you what he would probably say."

Chapter Thirteen

Crash

HAVE YOU EVER LOOKED AT A CATERPILLAR? It doesn't seem like much; not very attractive while it crawls around in the dirt. But there comes a time, if it lives long enough, when it creates a cocoon and cuts itself off from the outside world. Inside of that space—a transformation takes place—while outside, it's difficult to see the change. And when you don't see… and don't understand, you try to disrupt the transformation.

Tuesday September 8, 2009. Tenth grade: Day 1

Treyshawn stands in the middle of the hallway; at the center of a confrontation; outnumbered by those he called his friends—although that's presently up for debate at the moment.

"The whole summer goes by and we hardly see you."

"I told you, Hakiim, I was busy."

"Now you think you betta than us?"

"I didn't say that."

"You didn't have to. We know what you been busy doin'—getting a tutor and extra help. So, you tryin' to act White now?"

"What are you talking about?"

"You think we're stupid? You know what we talkin' about, Trey. Kuamane overheard some teachers talking about how you improved and all that. You even talking 'bout college? College ain't for Black people."

"Why is being smart trying to act White?"

"See. You even talkin' more like 'em. What's really messed up is you hanging out with the same kid you used to beat up! Everything we been through and you disrespect us like that?"

"It's not like that. But, you still didn't answer my question. Why's being smart trying to act White?"

"The only smarts you need is how to run the streets. We make more money in a week than most people make in a month!"

"We also have to keep watching out backs, too."

"That's the way it is out here! You think actin' White is gonna get you outta that?"

"I'm not tryin' to act White."

"So what you tryin' to do, huh?"

Treyshawn stands in front of seven guys he's known since he was four years old. They all live on the same block—got in trouble together and never hesitated to fight for each other. They survived shootings and swore to die for each other. They called each other brothers.

The pressures of life in the 'hood forced them into a mold—into a pact of sorts. Now that pact had been broken, like a newly-created butterfly trying to press its way out of a cocoon. A choice had to be made. Would Treyshawn turn his back on all he knew in favor of an unseen future? Or would he refuse the possibility that stood before him—the possibility for genuine freedom?

It was then that he realized, he had already made the choice... and had been walking in it for the past few months. So he didn't have to make that choice again. He only needed to understand it and follow it through. At this moment, contrary to how things looked, there really was no pressure. And so, he speaks.

"You all know me. You know I don't back down easy from a fight. That's not how I get down. I'm not better than *any* of you. I only want something better than what I've got right now.

"I'll tell you what's messed up. I gave up on school because I could hardly read. I thought I was dumb. But then I found out I'm not dumb—I'm dyslexic. And now I'm getting help from tutors. If it wasn't for Curtis I would have gone my whole life thinking I was dumb.

"Now I'm in the biggest fight of my life—to become somebody other than the guy who gets locked up—like my father. I ain't gonna lie; I've been trying to hide from you—afraid that you'd find out. But now you know; so

I'm not backing down. You know me. I'd fight for you in a second... Now I'm fighting for me.

"I'm not gonna choose between you guys or Curtis. I'mma choose me. If you want to go where I'm going then come on. If not—then respect that. You can do you. I'mma do me. I ain't better than you. I just want better."

The brothers look at each other in silence—weighing Treyshawn's words. Then one of them speaks.

"You've always been the one out front. It takes a lot of guts to do what you just did. I was hopin' you wasn't goin' soft. We can respect that."

"So you guys coming with me?"

"...Nah Trey. That ain't us. But you go and handle your business. We know where you live."

The brothers embrace and then separate. As they walk away, one of them stops as the others turn the corner. "Aye yo, Trey... If you make it, then we'll know it's possible."

They swore to die for each other. Now, one of them chose to live. Treyshawn had broken through the cocoon's shell and was no longer a caterpillar. He was beginning to spread his wings... and fly.

Later that night, at Treyshawn's apartment.

Cars drive down the block setting off automobile alarms, with their bass-infused music, while people hang on corners and in front of buildings. Even at 7:00pm, as the sun sets, a fire hydrant spews cool water to kids and adults alike, while those inside leave windows open and fans set to maximum.

Treyshawn looks out of his bedroom window, watching the girls jump double-dutch as the boys play football between parked cars. He listens to snippets of people's conversations—slightly amused by their yelling and laughing; while a few sit with their make-shift grills on the sidewalk—burning up some ribs and curry goat.

"I used to be the first one outside," he says to himself as he sees his friends standing on the corner, spouting their favorite lyrics. *Me and my boys used to be out till three in the morning, hustling for money.*

Treyshawn scans the block one last time before saying, "Time to get back to work." He pulls himself inside and walks to his desk, which is only a piece of wood on top of four crates. He can't remember where he scavenged the desk lamp from, but it illuminates the open books and papers that await his return. He'd been working for two hours already, but didn't mind. He was learning new things and actually beginning to see how they connected to the world around him.

"Now I got a *new* hustle." He sits down and takes a deep breath and reengages with the textbooks. Just as he resumes, he hears singing from the other room. *Mom's watching her show again.*

He picks up his pencil and ruler and continues to read, line by line, marking off important concepts and circling words he doesn't know. Within twenty minutes, he's so fully engrossed in the assignment that all surrounding noises fade away and only the words on the page remain.

Shakira sits in the living room, laughing loudly at the television set. "She can't sing! How'd they let *her* on the show?" The singing woman's voice is off key, as she plows through her song roughly. "She actually thinks she's *doing* something! I need to get on this so people can hear some *real* singing!"

As the show ends, she looks around for Treyshawn. "Treyshawn! Bring me a soda!" A few minutes pass with no response. "Treyshawn!! I'm calling you boy!"

Treyshawn sits, deep in thought, listening to one of his textbooks on his mp3 player. As he removes his headphones, he hears his mother calling him.

"Treyshawn Jinkins!!! You betta answer me, boy!"

He gets up from his desk and walks into the living room. "Yeah, Ma?"

"Don't 'Yeah Ma' me! Didn't you hear me calling you? I called you three times, boy! What you doin' back there?"

"I was doing my homework."

"Homework?" she says shocked. "You don't *do* homework. You've *never* done homework!"

Treyshawn fights to keep his cool. "I do now."

"Since when?"

"Since I got a tutor."

"A tutor?"

"Ma, I've got dyslexia."

"Dys—what? That better not be contagious!"

"It's not contagious, Ma! It's a learning disability."

"See, I knew you was dumb!"

"I'm not dumb!" he yells. "I was *never* dumb. I just learn differently than most—why am I even explainin' this to you?"

"That's right. I don't want to hear it anyway. Just get me my soda," she says while turning back towards the television.

Treyshawn stands there, motionless, just looking at her. "If you care more about your stupid soda than me—then get it yourself."

She turns back, "What you say, boy?"

He disregards her question. "A *friend* has been tutoring me."

"Back to *this* again? You ain't got no friends smart enough to tutor you!"

"I do now, Ma! Why you trippin'?"

"Why am I trippin'? Look at you! So you tryin' to change your life, huh?"

"What if I am?"

Shakira jumps up from the couch and steps to her son.

"So, you tryin' to 'man up' now and handle your responsibilities?"

"I *am* a man!" Treyshawn yells.

Shakira hauls her hand back. SLAP!!! "Who you yelling at? Don't talk to me like I'm one of your little friends. I am your mother!"

Treyshawn grits his teeth while the side of his face stings. "Well start acting like a *real* mother and don't talk to me like I'm stupid!"

Shakira grabs her son's arm so tight that her nails dig into his skin.

"You think you betta than me, Trey? You think you betta than me? You ain't never gon be anything other than like your sorry daddy! You ain't *never* gon change! And I ain't gon be nothin but your sorry mama—collectin' a welfare check!"

"No!!!" Treyshawn yells while pulling free from his mother's grip. Tears slowly form in his eyes as he paces back and forth, trying not to punch a hole in the wall. And then he faces her. "That's just it, Ma! You ain't got to stay that way! You can change! You can choose… and then walk it out—every day!"

"Who are you to be tellin' me what I need to do?" She tries to leave the room, but is stopped.

"No, Ma! This is my time to talk! *You* listen! For so long I thought I was dumb 'cause I could hardly read! And you never cared enough to help me! On top of that I got your stinkin' voice in my head tellin' me I'mma be like the man who don't even want me!!!" His tears flow freely now, and he does nothing to stop them. They are his badge of honor—his sign of freedom. He takes his mother's arms in his grasp and looks straight into her eyes.

"You keep sayin' I'mma be like the man that stole your dream and broke your heart. But I'm *not* him!"

Shakira begins to cry as well and tries to pull away, but her son won't let her. She tries to turn her face away from his, but he shakes her.

"No! Look at me, Ma. Look at me!"

"Noooo!" she yells as she resists one last time, but her son is too strong for her.

"I'm not letting go until you look at me!"

Shakira finally stops pulling away and slowly turns towards her son. She sees all of his hurt… and she knows he can see hers as well—and it's painful to suddenly be transparent.

"I'm your son, Ma! *Your* son! I used to wish I was dead… Do you hear me? I used to wish *I was dead* because of how you treated me… you made me so afraid, Ma! I wished I was dead *just* so I could get back at you for all the things you did to me… I hated you… I hated my life… But I don't any more… And I'm *not* gonna take the blame for *your* fears and mistakes."

They look at each other in silence, locked in a gaze neither can break. She notices her son's dried tears—like etched lines down his face.

"Ma… I didn't ask to be here… but I'm here, part dad—part you—all me. I can't change who I am… but I can change who I become."

He lets her go and slowly backs away. "I got homework to do…"

Shakira's body shakes as she watches her son walk out of the room. Overcome by the swell of emotions inside her, she slumps to the floor and cries. Her son's outburst broke through years of resentment like a sledgehammer bursting through a brick wall. As she cries, she hears his footsteps coming back to the doorway.

"Ma," he says while looking at her somewhat softly, "if dad stole your dream, then take it back… or get a new one. But don't blame me because you're afraid to try."

"It's tight," Curtis says while Omar zips up the back of the suit.

"What did you expect from a form-fitting bodysuit? This has just enough padding to give you *some* protection from collisions—but not much. It was the best I could get on short notice."

"Divers actually wear these?"

"Yeah, I got this one from a friend in my unit, whose parents run a diving shop. Once we finalize the backpack design, we can figure out how to integrate it with the vest and boots. This is temporary until we can fabricate a custom-made suit, designed to work with the entire system."

"I'm hot in here."

"Add that to the list. We need some kind of cooling system in the suit—maybe a group of small tubing that cold water can be pumped through."

Omar steps back, with a surprised look. "Have you gotten taller? I think you had a growth spurt."

"I'm trying to be as tall as you."

"Don't get your hopes up. But if you ever make it, just remember I'm stronger than you and we won't have any problems."

"How can I forget? Your biceps are like the size of my head!" They both laugh.

"Speaking of biceps," Omar squeezes Curtis' arms, "I noticed lately that you seem… a little more solid. Have you been working out?"

"Yeah, with Kelly's brothers, twice a week since August. They said it would build up my endurance so I could be more active in sports."

"You told them about the suit?"

"No."

"Did Kelly?"

"No. She's waiting on me to tell them. They would've known had they been at the track."

"Speaking of running, you do realize what you're trying to do here? If you *are* able to run significantly faster—it could be dangerous."

"I know there are some control issues to work out: maintaining thrust, turning, power, traction."

"Traction is crucial," Omar interjects. "You'll need to stop *very* quickly."

"Nothing to worry about, big brother! We'll figure it all out."

"If we don't, you could get hurt—seriously hurt."

"Don't tell me you're afraid."

"I'm not afraid. But if you get hurt, mom will kill us both!"

"You are *so* right about that one!"

"Maybe you should have a parachute that shoots out from your back to slow you down, like a drag racing car," Omar says with a smile.

"Are you kidding? Where would I put it with everything else? And then I'd have to repack it after every time I use it."

"Hey, it's just a suggestion, but I really was just kidding."

"Although… you may be on to something."

"Another idea, huh? Add it to the list."

A knock at the door breaks their conversation, as their mom enters the room.

"Dinner is ready…" Miranda stops in mid sentence as she curiously looks at her son. "Curtis, what are you wearing?"

"It's a diving suit."

"Are you going diving? You don't know how to swim!"

"Nobody's going diving, Mom."

"Then why are you wearing it? Are you trying to get a head start on Halloween?" She starts laughing.

"Ma…."

Omar explains, "I'm helping with his boot project, Mom. I was showing him the basic kind of diving suit we use in the navy."

"So is this going to be your super suit?"

"Mom…!" Curtis exclaims.

"What? You have boots that make you run faster and a form fitting suit—by the way, when am I going to get to see you run in them?"

"Soon, Mom. Still some things to finish."

"I can't wait. And don't think I forgot about our trip to the museum," she says, "I had to tear you from those superhero exhibits." She makes a crazy face while pointing at his diving suit. "Just don't go splashing around in the tub before dinner."

Omar laughs, "Now *that* was funny!"

"Yeah," Curtis says sarcastically, "I didn't know you were a comedian."

"Oh, you didn't, huh?" she replies. "All the problems with the economy and everything else going on in the world; you have to laugh just to keep your sanity. Anyway, *Mr. Diver*, dinner is ready."

"Ok, we're coming," Omar, says.

"Carry on then," she says while doing an about-face and walking out of the room in her best military swagger. As she heads down the hall, she offers a short prayer of thanksgiving, "Thank you, Lord. My boys are going to be all right."

Omar begins to help Curtis remove the diving suit. "Have you thought about a fuel source for the jet? We'll have to figure out where you'll store the gas; not to mention the exhaust is going to be hot."

"I don't want to use anything combustible. I'm thinking electric."

"That could work. We don't want to cook someone who stood to close. So, you're basically going to strap a big fan to your back. We'll need a high performance, light weight, electric motor."

"That's the idea... a custom turbofan design with intake ducts that work with the vest. It can't be too big, but it should move a lot of air and provide *a lot* of thrust."

A few passing hours leaves Treyshawn asleep at his desk—exhausted from studying—his head facing away from the door to his room. As he sleeps, his mother slowly opens the door—her eyes red from crying. She wants to speak, but doesn't know what to say or where to begin.

She stands at the door—motionless—slowly growing in tune with the rhythm of her son's breathing. He stirs and turns his head towards the door without waking. Her gaze drifts to his face and she simply looks at him. As seconds stretch into minutes, she begins to notice what was once hidden from her: in Treyshawn's face, she sees less of his father and more of her own. At that moment, a glimmer of hope kindles in her heart as her son's words replay in her mind:

"I didn't ask to be here... but I'm here. Part dad—part you—all me... if dad stole your dream, then take it back... or get a new one."

The next morning...

Treyshawn awakes at his desk to the smell of food cooking. He slowly rises, walks to the window, and looks outside. The block is empty and quiet. As he pulls away from the window he glances at the clock. It's 7:00am.

"I'm starving," he says to himself, "and someone's cooking breakfast. But it can't be here, cause mom never cooks."

He slowly walks down the hall, in his wrinkled clothes, and to his surprise the smell of bacon and eggs increases and the sound of a fork scraping the inside of a frying pan becomes evident. He enters the kitchen, astonished to find his mother standing at the stove cooking, and the table set with a plate, plastic ware, and a cup of orange juice.

"Ma?" he says in disbelief.

Shakira turns around, her eyes still bloodshot from crying all night, "Hey, Trey..."

He almost doesn't know what to say. "What... what are you doing?"

"I thought... I thought you might be hungry; so I was makin' breakfast. But if you're not..."

"I'm hungry, Ma... thanks." He slowly takes his seat as his mother smiles, turns back around and finishes up the eggs.

"They're a little burnt—the eggs and bacon."

"That's ok. Nothing ketchup can't take care of. Do we *have* ketchup?"

"I'll check the drawers." She fixes his plate, rinses the skillet and checks the drawers. A moment later, she puts a few packets on the table next to his plate, "This is all we got," and starts to leave.

"Ma! Wait... you're... not going to eat with me?"

"Not today... I've got some things to do. Maybe tomorrow. But I left something for you."

Treyshawn looks down and sees a folded piece of paper in the middle of the small table. His mother watches with nervous eyes and a faint smile.

"I'm going to take a shower."

She walks out, leaving Treyshawn alone at the table. The steam rises up from his breakfast as he stares at that piece of paper for what seems like hours. Finally, he picks it up. On the page are two words.

"I'm sorry..."

Treyshawn cries as he holds the note tightly in his hand. This was the first time his mother ever told him she was sorry—for anything. By the time he pulls himself together, his food is cold, but he picks up the plastic fork and starts eating—without the ketchup. The eggs and bacon never tasted so good.

Later that day...

"What you mean we're *finished?*" Melvin yells.

"Just what I said! We're... finished." Shakira shoots back.

"You breaking up with me?"

"No. I *just* broke up with you."

"Now you think you betta than me, Shakira? You just gon leave me? Just like that?"

"No. You're gonna leave. I put your things by the door."

"If I leave, who gon pay your bills, huh? You ain't got a job. You can't make it without me!"

"Just go back to your other women, Melvin. I know I'm not the only one."

"That's what this is about?" he lightens up and smiles. "You know you're my favorite."

"Melvin!" Shakira says with a half laugh, "this is *not* about your other women."

"Well, if you know, then why you breakin' up with me?"

"I need to do something with my life and you need to give me my keys back."

"Why you little..." Melvin hauls off and slaps Shakira across her face, knocking her to the ground.

"You must be crazy!" Treyshawn yells as he runs down the hall. "I'mma kill you!"

"Come bring it, Trey!" Melvin yells back as he prepares for a fight.

Shakira jumps up and stands between them, keeping her son back.

"Treyshawn! Stop!!"

"But he hit you, Ma! I ain't letting no punk slap you around like that!"

"What you gon do about it, *little* Treacherous?" Melvin says mockingly. "Oh, you *little* alright!"

Treyshawn tries to lunge at Melvin, but his mother stops him again.

"Treyshawn!" She takes his head in her hands and forces his gaze. A tear runs down his left cheek as he sees the bruise on his mother's face. "Ma…"

"I got this, baby," she wipes his tear away. "You're my Son," she smiles, "I got this… We can *choose*, remember?"

"Aw, this is sweet; a mother and son reunion!"

Shakira turns back towards Melvin, puts one hand on her hip and stretches out her hand.

"I want my keys—*now*."

"Or what, Shakira?"

"Or the cops gonna arrest you for domestic violence." She pulls her cell phone out of her pocket. As she raises it near Melvin's face, he can see that 911 has been dialed and can hear the operator, *Ma'am hang tight, the police are a couple of blocks away from you.*

Sirens are heard in the distance as Melvin's bravado quickly gives way to nervousness.

"I called them just before you got here, after you cursed me out on the phone."

"Listen, baby. Let's talk about this. I don't want to go back to jail."

"Oh, now you wanna talk? Ok—let's talk! Let's talk about you giving me *my* keys, taking *your* junk and leaving *us* alone! Then *maybe*, I won't press charges."

He pulls the keys out of his pocket and tosses them to her, as the police cars pull up outside. A moment later there's a hard knock at the door.

"NYPD!"

"So?" Shakira stands with Treyshawn.

"Ok," Melvin says, "I'll leave you alone."

"And *my* son?"

"*And* your son."

"Forever!"

178

"Yeah, you got my word—forever."

The police officers knock harder. "NYPD! Open up!"

Shakira walks down the steps to the front door and opens it. The two officers, one male the other female, see Shakira's bleeding lip and noticeable bruise across her cheek.

"Ma'am, we got a call about a domestic disturbance."

"Yeah, I made the call."

Footsteps can be heard as Melvin walks down the stairs with a big box and a couple of bags in his arms. The officers place their hands on their guns and step back as he nervously walks up behind Shakira.

"This is the man who beat me and my son. I broke up with him and told him to leave us alone."

"Would you like to press charges, ma'am?"

"He promised to leave us alone, so I'm not going to do that."

"That's your prerogative," one officer replies. The other adds, "I recommend you at least fill out a report so you can have this on file for future use if necessary."

"You mean," Shakira says, "like if Melvin decides to break his promise to me and comes back around here?"

"Yes, ma'am."

"Now, that sounds like a great idea!" She turns to her former boyfriend, "What you think, Melvin?"

He stands quiet before speaking. "Whatever you want to do, Shakira."

"Whatever *I* want to do, huh?" She turns back to the officers—taking pleasure in the moment. "He's so *nice*, isn't he?" she says sarcastically.

"Do it, Ma," Treyshawn says as he comes down the stairs, "file the report."

"Officers, this is my son, Treyshawn. He's gon be somebody someday. You watch and see."

"That's nice, ma'am," the officers smile. "So what do you want to do?"

"Let's file that report."

"All right," the male officer takes the lead, "sir—Melvin is it? Step over here towards the car, please. And keep your hands where we can see them."

"Ma'am you can come with us too." the female officer says.

Treyshawn watches his mother from the top of the steps. He knows she's not perfect, but he's grateful that she's making a choice that's different from every other choice she's ever made: she's choosing to live.

Chapter Fourteen

Oxymoron

FRIDAY OCTOBER 9, 2009. 8:00PM. A closed track.

"How did you find this track Mr. G?" Curtis asks.

"Six degrees of separation. It's amazing what you can get when you ask around. In my case I know the head track coach who works here at the college."

"Wow! That's cool!"

"I guess it is. And since we're using his track, he'll be here—for insurance purposes. But he can be trusted not to let the 'cat out of the bag.' He and I have known each other a long time."

Mr. Grabowski, Curtis, Omar, and Treyshawn begin wheeling in several cases from the van. Once all of the equipment has been brought in, they begin assembling the components.

Treyshawn sets up the camcorder while Curtis gets into the suit and boots. Omar and Mr. Grabowski set up the monitoring equipment.

"Hey, Smurtis?"

"Yeah?"

"You're not scared?"

"Why should I be?"

"This is the first test with all the different parts together. What if something goes wrong?"

"Ok, maybe I'm a little scared. But don't worry; nothing's going to go wrong. Besides, I'm familiar with everything, so if something *does* go wrong, I can make the necessary adjustments."

"By the way, where's Kelly tonight?" asks Mr. Grabowski.

"She had a dance recital. You know, she's really in demand."

"Make sure you tell her hello, for me."

"You got it, Mr. G. She said when we're ready to set the world record, then she'll definitely be there—no matter what."

About twenty minutes later, Curtis stands—fully clad in the first prototype of the Speedsuit. "How do I look?"

"A bit bulky," Omar says, "but you look good. Remember, we've cobbled these pieces together, they're not all designed to be an exact fit."

"I know," Curtis smiles. "This is the first step. We're gonna need a name. Something cool."

"We're making history," Treyshawn says.

"We are," adds Mr. Grabowski, barely able to contain his excitement. "I never would have thought that when Curtis walked into my class, it would be the beginning of a life-changing experience that would lead to this."

"Mr. G, you're like a kid in a candy store," Omar says.

"Isn't it fun!" Mr. Grabowski laughs heartily. "All right… I think I've gotten the giggles out of my system. Let's focus and make sure we have a successful run."

Just then, the double doors to the indoor track open and a figure stands in the doorway.

"What are you guys doing over there?" a voice booms.

"Paul!" Mr. Grabowski shouts from across the track.

"Ahh, you got me, Jim!"

"No matter how you disguise your voice, I can always tell when it's you!"

Paul Leonard walks over as Mr. Grabowski meets him halfway.

"Paul, it's good to see you!"

"Good to see *you*, Jim! It's been a long time."

The two men shake hands and embrace.

"Thanks again for helping us out with this."

"How could I say 'no' to my old college roommate? Glad I could help. I'm dying to see what you guys have cooked up!"

"Come on over. I'll introduce you to the team."

As they approach, Paul gets his first glimpse at the Speedsuit. "Now, what do we have here?" he asks inquisitively.

"Pretty interesting, isn't it?" Jim says excitedly.

"Paul Leonard, this is Curtis and Omar Powers and Treyshawn Jinkins. Guys, this is Paul Leonard."

"Nice to meet you," the three say in unison.

"Nice to meet you guys, too," Paul replies.

"Wow," he says while looking at Curtis.

"You're looking at the Speedsuit," Jim says. "And Curtis is the brainchild."

"You made this, Curtis?" Paul says astounded.

"I dreamed it, but these guys helped build it."

"So how fast does it go?"

"We're about to find out."

"I'm looking forward to seeing *this*," Paul says.

After more small talk, they quickly focus on the task at hand and double-check the equipment before the first test commences.

"Everything looks good," Omar says, "power system is fully charged. It's now or never."

"Is the camera ready?" Curtis asks.

"Yeah," Treyshawn responds, "just remember to take it out easy."

Omar reaches into his pocket and pulls out Curtis' inhaler. "Do you need this?"

"My chest *does* feel a little tight. Probably from the excitement." Curtis takes a puff. "Phsssh…"

"All right, then. Gentlemen," Mr. Grabowski says, "let's make history."

Treyshawn hits record. "Camera's rolling."

Curtis gives the thumbs up, turns towards the camera, takes a deep breath and starts talking.

"Curtis Powers—here with Mr. Grabowski, Omar, Treyshawn, and Mr. Paul Leonard. It's October 9th, 2009 and this is the first test of the fully assembled Speedsuit prototype—version one.

"I'll run with the Kinetic Redistribution Boots, for the first quarter of the track, before engaging the Vortex Thrust Pack, which works in conjunction with the Slipstream Vest. So here we go."

Curtis takes his mark on the track and hits the release levers on his boots, which engage the spring-mechanisms. Mr. Grabowski monitors the sensor inputs added to the inner lining of the suit; which measure temperature, speed, pressure and heartbeat. Treyshawn keeps the camera trained on Curtis as Omar prepares to give the countdown.

"Just for the record," Curtis adds, "we haven't added the internal climate control system yet, so it's getting a little hot in here."

"We'll have it ready for next time," Omar interjects. "Take your mark! Here we go in 5... 4... 3... 2... 1... Go!"

Curtis takes off down the track! The steady pounding of the boots on the pavement can be heard like clockwork as his strides begin to increase.

"10 miles... 15 miles... 20 miles per hour... 25 miles... 30 miles per hour!"

"Is he at 30 miles?" Paul asks in shock, "That's already faster than the fastest Olympic runner!"

"I know," Jim grins, "and Curtis isn't even warmed up yet. Watch what comes next."

"Ok," Curtis says, "I'm starting the Vortex in 3... 2... 1..." Curtis presses the button on his glove and the Vortex pack roars to life! Whoosh!!! He immediately feels the increase in speed and struggles to maintain his stride.

"Ugh! Didn't take this into account!" he says. "It's already different running in the boots, now the added thrust makes it harder to keep my balance."

For a moment, Curtis' speed actually decreases as he reduces the throttle. But it only takes seconds for him to regain control, as his foot placement and balance become more deliberate.

"I have to remember what Kelly said about balance. I wish she was here."

Curtis mashes on the throttle and lurches forward as the thrust kicks in.

"...35... 40... 45...," Omar yells out. "He's getting the hang of it!"

"Man, this feels great," Curtis says to himself, but his excitement is momentarily cut short as his chest tightens. *Got to remember what Kelvin and Kevin taught me. I can do this.* After a few deep breaths, the pressure in his chest starts to diminish.

All the men celebrate as Curtis makes his way around the track multiple times! "He's holding at 50 miles per hour!"

Paul stands with his mouth wide open. "I don't believe it!" he says half laughing, "I see it, but I don't believe it. This is simply amazing!"

At 50 miles per hour, Curtis can feel the strain on his knees, hips and neck as he takes the turns.

"Note to self: need to reinforce the suit's neck support joints."

Just then, a loud snap is heard from one of the boots—followed by clanging metal—and ending with a clunk! Curtis suddenly finds himself hurtling uncontrollably through the air! To him, everything *seems* to move in slow motion, but to the rest of the group, it all happens in an instant! He lands hard and tumbles multiple times before skidding to a stop on the far side of the track.

"Curtis!!!" Omar drops one of the monitors and bolts across the track, followed by Paul, Treyshawn, and Jim.

"Curtis! He's not moving!" Omar starts to pick him up.

"Don't pick him up!" Jim yells.

"But he's hurt!" shouts Omar.

"And you could make it worse by moving him!" Jim counters. "What if his neck is broken?"

"Let me take a look at him," Paul says.

"You call 911, Omar!" says Jim, "Paul and I will take care of Curtis."

"What do you want *me* to do?" Treyshawn asks.

"Pray," Mr. Grabowski responds, "and keep recording."

As Omar calls the paramedics, Paul and Jim assess Curtis' condition.

"He's still breathing. Multiple fractures in his legs and arm. Thank God, his neck doesn't *feel* broken, but he'll need x-rays to be sure."

Curtis regains consciousness, "Ahhh... it hurts!" He looks around, "What... happened...?"

"Not sure yet," Mr. Grabowski says. "Something went wrong with the suit!"

"You think...?" he says sarcastically.

"Good. Your sense of humor's still intact. Try to stay calm."

"Everything hurts..."

"Don't try to move. The ambulance is on its way."

"You have to... take... the suit off..."

"Curtis, that's crazy. You're pretty messed up. If we move you, it's gonna hurt."

"I don't want... anyone... to see the suit..."

Omar runs back over to the group. "The paramedics are on the way!"

He looks down to see Curtis looking up at him.

"Hey, little bro… you're going to be ok."

"Omar," Jim says, "we need to remove the suit."

"What?"

"Your brother doesn't want it to be found."

"You sure, Curt?" Omar asks.

"Do it…"

Paul stands up and heads for the exit. "You guys do that while I lead the paramedics here!"

"All right, Curtis. I hope you're ready for this."

"We'll lift him up on three: 1… 2… 3!"

Curtis yells in pain as they force him up. A few minutes pass as they remove all of the gear, and the body suit—leaving Curtis in his shorts and t-shirt.

"We gotta pack this stuff up!" Omar says, "Treyshawn, stay with Curtis!"

"So… what did you… think?"

"What did I think?" Treyshawn says, trying not to sound too alarmed. "You were hot—before you crashed and burned of course."

Curtis laughs, but stops because of the pain. "*Ow*… it hurts to laugh. *Don't* make me laugh."

"Ok, Smurtis. I won't make you laugh."

Curtis starts laughing again. "Ow! I told you… not to make… me laugh!"

Treyshawn laughs. "What'd I do?"

Omar and Mr. Grabowski pack up the last of the gear as the paramedics run in with a stretcher. They rush Curtis to the hospital, with Omar riding in the back of the ambulance and Mr. Grabowski and Treyshawn following in the car. Mr. Leonard stays behind to deal with the necessary legal matters.

The ambulance zooms through the streets—weaving in and out of traffic with sirens blaring!

"I was doing it…" Curtis says.

"You were, little bro." Omar says with tears in his eyes.

"How fast was I going?"

"You were holding at 50."

"What was he driving at 50 miles per hour?" the paramedic asks.

The two brothers look at each other and exchange grins before Omar speaks. "You know what I have to do when we get to the hospital?"

"Man, mom is gonna flip! I'll try to make sure she doesn't kill you."

"And I'll try to keep her from killing you after you get better."

"We're both in trouble aren't we?"

"Uh, huh."

The emergency room doors slide open as the click clacking of Miranda Powers shoes heralds her entrance. She quickly passes a long line of persons waiting to speak to the attendant at the front desk.

"Can you tell me where Curtis Powers is?"

"Hey, there's a line here!" someone shouts from behind her. She ignores them.

"Ma'am there *is* a line…" begins the attendant before being cut off by Miranda's stern voice.

"When a mother's oldest son calls to say that her *youngest* son is in the emergency room and it takes the mother over an hour to get to the hospital because of traffic, the most important thing you can do when she walks in, is answer her question!"

The attendant looks at Mrs. Powers and then at the people in line as someone leans out and says, "I'd answer her question, if I were you."

The attendant turns back to Mrs. Powers.

"What's your son's name?"

Moments later, Miranda rushes into the room and pulls the curtain back. She gasps at the sight as Omar, Jim, and Treyshawn move back to give her a full view of her son—who is swaddled in bandages.

"Curtis!" She bursts into tears as she hugs him.

"Ow!" he yells, "take it easy, Mom!"

"I'm glad you can still talk," she says while wiping her tears, "now tell me what happened."

"Mom…" Omar says before being cut off.

"Omar, right now I'm *talking* to your brother. I will deal with *you* in a minute, and then you can tell me how you allowed this to happen to my baby!"

She turns back to Curtis and motions for him to start explaining.

"We were… testing out the boots."

"I thought you tested them already. What were you trying to do, *jump* to the moon?"

"I… came up with a way to run even faster by strapping a jet to my back."

"A jet? Lord Jesus, help me. Now you're trying to fly? Honey, you are *not* Superman! And you are not that other guy you like—what's his name?"

"Iron Man. But, I wasn't trying to fly, Mom. I was running and one of the boots broke."

"Curtis… it's by the *mercy* of God that you're still alive. I don't know if I could take another death in our family."

"I know…"

"Do you really?" She breathes deeply and shakes her head while trying not to smile. "Oh, if I don't laugh, I'll go insane! You both have that same adventurous spirit—just like your father… Just how fast *were* you running?"

"Fifty miles per hour."

"Fifty miles per hour? As in 5-0—*that* fifty? Is that even possible?"

"It is now," he says with a wide grin just as the doctor comes in.

"I'm Dr. Montgomery. Are you the boy's mother?"

"Yes, doctor. How's my baby?"

"We've done all the necessary tests, Mrs. Powers, and for the most part, Curtis is fine. Besides having multiple fractures in both legs and his right arm, and a slight concussion, he's in good condition. There's no internal bleeding, but he does have quite a few bruises. I'm told this was the result of a running accident?"

"Yes… from what I understand, my son was trying out a new pair of running shoes, got a little over zealous, tripped and took a really bad tumble."

"He must be very fast to have gotten banged up like this. I'll tell you, if I didn't treat numerous kids with a wide range of injuries, this would surprise me. You'd be amazed the amount of crazy stunts people pull nowadays.

"He's going to have to be off his feet for a while, and he'll need to stay home for a bit. Can his schoolwork be brought to him?"

"Yes," she says while looking at Treyshawn, "That won't be a problem."

"After a few weeks recuperating he'll go to physical therapy to regain his strength. It could be three to four months before he runs again. We're preparing the casts for his arm and legs now. The nurse outside will provide you with all the particulars."

"I'm just glad my son is all right. Thank you, Dr. Montgomery."

"Not a problem, Mrs. Powers. Just doing my job. You all have a great night. And Curtis..."

"Yeah?"

"Try not to take anymore bad tumbles." Dr. Montgomery leaves as Mrs. Powers motions for Omar and Mr. Grabowski to come into the hallway.

"Miranda... I'm *so* sorry..."

"No need to apologize, Jim. I know this wasn't intentional. I also know how Curtis can get. When Malcolm was alive, he'd encourage Curtis and told me not to stifle his creativity. So, I just try to channel him into positive directions. But an accident like this has never happened before; and that's my baby. What if this *jet* had exploded?"

"It's not flammable, Mom. Curtis didn't want to use anything combustible. It's basically a very efficient, specially designed, electric fan."

"Well, that helps a little... I knew you all were working on the boots and the vest, but I didn't know about all of this! Why didn't you just tell me?"

"Curtis wanted to surprise you when everything was complete. Besides, he didn't want you to worry about him strapping into a machine that could provide some serious acceleration. And, we were careful to follow all of our checklists and make sure things were as safe as possible."

"If I've learned anything from life," Miranda says, "it's that you can't plan for everything. No matter how much you try, there's always some unknown variable that rears its ugly head."

"Miranda. Again... I'm sorry that this happened."

"I know Jim." She takes a deep breath and runs her hands through her hair. "Fifty miles per hour... We'll talk more about this later. All I ask is to be kept informed. *Fully* informed. No more secrets. If *you* know it—I know it. If you can do that, then this adventure can continue. If you can't, then I pull the *mother card* and everything stops now."

"I don't see any reason why we can't keep you informed on all of our developments," Jim says.

"Speaking of developments," Miranda adds, "this seems pretty significant if he has the three of you so heavily involved."

"It's more than significant," Omar says. "Mom. I think we're making history."

"Well just don't make me have to make you two... history." With that, Miranda leaves them in the hallway as she walks back into her son's room.

February 23, 2010. Entry number 1, 450.

"I never thought lying in a bed could take so much out of you. Days go by slowly when you can't walk. But my schoolwork has helped to keep me busy. The last couple of months have been the coldest on record! November wasn't that bad, but I thought December and January were ridiculous!

"The last part of January was brutal, and the building manager even turned the heat off because he didn't want to pay for the extra oil! People were so mad, I just knew someone was gonna get shot! People picketed, got the news involved and filed lawsuits. It didn't take long before he turned the heat back on.

"Anyway, I didn't realize just how many students and teachers cared. Kelly told as many people as she could, and when they heard the news about me being in an accident, students got together and made a huge 'get well' card and had everyone else sign it!

"Of course, I hurried through my homework so I could continue researching the Speedsuit.

"A quick diagnostic of my right boot revealed that one of the springs snapped completely in half, got caught in the machinery, and caused everything to seize up! The resulting imbalance caused me to lose control.

"I keep thinking about an oxymoron: two contradictory terms that don't seem to go together. Terms like 'same difference,' or 'pretty ugly' and 'freezer burn.' That's what happened with my boots. Who would have thought that something so small could cause a problem so big? Omar and Mr. G examined the spring and the boot and came to two possible conclusions: 1. The spring itself was bad—or 2. Shock from the high-speed repetition stressed the connections beyond their tolerance. I think it was just a bad spring, but we're going to test everything again, making sure we take into account the higher speeds achieved with the Vortex Thrust Pack—which got banged up really bad in the crash.

"I knew springs were the easiest option for building the first set of boots, but they may not be the most efficient. I've been toying around with the idea of using electromagnetic repulsion instead, but that gets really complicated. I'll *definitely* need to talk with Omar and Mr. Grabowski about it. Another much easier *option two* would be to use a compressed gas cylinder.

"Back to my legs. The casts finally came off and then the hard part really began! Physical therapy is gruesome; twice a week for an hour each time. The pain seemed unbearable at first. I never realized how much I took walking for granted. Everybody was very supportive though, especially mom. She always makes sure I have everything I need, even with her busy schedule. Kelly and Treyshawn have been great, too. She comes with me to therapy whenever she's not in dance class, and he stops by the apartment to check on me.

"But I guess what pushed me the most was the anticipation of running in the Speedsuit again! My dream to run is coming true right before my eyes… with every step I take! The time came and went; and we made a lot of improvements to the overall design—considering all the free time I had.

"I finally got back in school—and went from a wheelchair to crutches, to a cane and finally to walking completely on my own again! Treyshawn and I even jogged a couple of blocks the other day. But it'll be a little while longer before I run again. But hey, who knows what the future holds."

Chapter Fifteen

World Record

FRIDAY FEBRUARY 26, 2010. CURTIS COMES into his room, drops his bag next to his desk and kicks off his sneakers before diving onto his bed. Within a few moments, he's completely comfortable, lazily stretched out on his stomach with a magazine in his hands. "Man, it is so good to be home from school," he says to himself. "I have the whole weekend ahead of me."

Omar quickly walks into the room.

"I thought I heard you come in."

"Hey, I didn't even know you were here."

"I was doing paperwork in my room. Listen, I've got some 'ok' news and some 'great' news."

Curtis hesitates, but finally speaks. "Give me the 'ok' news first."

"I got my shipping orders this morning."

Curtis drops his magazine to the floor and sits up. "When do you leave?"

"In two months. I'll have to spend a few weekends down at the naval base for prep though."

"I don't want you to go."

"I don't want to go either, but duty calls."

"But who's going to help me with my experiments?"

"Don't forget, all the help I've been is because of what I've learned in the navy. Imagine what else I can learn if I go back. Besides, you got Mr. G, Treyshawn, and Kelly."

"I know. But that doesn't mean I've got to like you not being here. It's great having you around."

"Don't worry, we've got our routine."

"Yeah, we do."

"So I'll still be around—by phone, email and text message."

"So what's the 'great' news?"

Omar reaches into his back pocket and pulls out a paperback book. "Take a look at this." He tosses it to his brother.

"The Book of World Records?"

"I was thinking. What if we set the record for the fastest running man before the PA Relays this year? Maybe you'll get enough publicity for them to have you do an exhibition run."

"Man, that would be a dream!" Curtis says with excitement, "and maybe this could lead to a run at the 2012 Olympics!"

"Anything is possible," Omar says. "Running in the Olympics has always been your dream…"

"That would be sweet!" Curtis says. "We're going to need to get the suit patented before we break out onto the world."

"I was thinking the same thing," says Omar. "So what do you think about the world record?"

"I think we've got just about a month to do it!"

Saturday March 20, 2010.

The sliding door opens on a large white van with tinted windows. Video and digital cameras capture the moment as Curtis exits the vehicle wearing the Speedsuit—Version 2.0—still rather nondescript in its design: basic black, nothing flashy, although it has had several upgrades.

Kelly weaves through the group with the video camera, capturing close-ups of everyone. "This is going to be good, guys."

"Make sure you get my good side," Treyshawn says while laughing.

"Honestly," Curtis says, "it feels funny wearing this suit in public."

"Don't worry," Kelly counters, "you look heroic!"

"After we do this," Curtis says to Treyshawn, "we seriously need to talk color scheme."

"Way ahead of you…" Treyshawn pulls out his drawing pad and shows Curtis some initial color ideas he's been working on.

"I was so excited last night, I couldn't sleep. Just like Mr. G, huh?" Curtis takes a quick look at the sketches.

"Not bad Treyshawn! These designs are definitely cool. That's going to look great with the official name for the suit."

"Yeah. I'm really feeling *this* design right here," he says while pointing to the page, "and the name is hot! Your brother did a good job with that."

"Guess it pays to work on jet planes for a living. But I can't wait to see the color schemes on a mocked-up sketch of the suit."

"There'll be plenty of time to get flashy later," says Mr. Grabowski, as he walks from the other side of the van. "Why am I *always* the one to tell you two to focus?" he says with a laugh.

"We balance each other out," Curtis says.

"Yeah," adds Treyshawn. "You help us focus and we help you loosen up."

"You might have a point there," Mr. Grabowski says with a grin. "We can celebrate later because the World Record Group is just about finished with their setup. They'll be tracking the data independently, with their own equipment, to verify the results. And the TV news crew just got here, so look busy."

"I'm Katie Tourie, from The News Channel, standing here, in the Bronx, NY, on a half mile-long stretch of pavement where the team, you see behind me, is preparing to attempt a record for the world's fastest running man. The man doing the running is in fact, 15-year-old, Curtis Powers.

"The three other men, and young lady, are Curtis' teammates: his brother, Omar Powers of the U.S. Navy; his physics teacher, Mr. Jim Grabowski; and two of his best friends and fellow high school students, Treyshawn Jinkins and Kelly Washington.

"Now, what makes this world record setting attempt so interesting is that *here*, science fiction and reality meet. Under Curtis' vision, the team has built a suit, which enables its wearer to run significantly faster than an average person. And they have formally named their creation the Mach-1 Speedsuit.

"Now just to give you some context; an average person runs somewhere between 10-15 miles per hour. A trained Olympic athlete can run between 25-30 miles per hour. Just how fast will the Mach-1 go? This group isn't saying, but what they have divulged is that right now, it's

somewhere between Usain Bolt—the 2008 Olympic Track champion—
and a cheetah—which is the world's fastest land animal—clocked at up to
80 miles per hour.

"By the way… don't bother asking how the suit works. The team is
rather quiet on that one as well. However, if this attempt is successful, I'm
sure more information will be forthcoming.

"Just remember you saw it here first. I'm Katie Tourie, of The News
Channel, here in the Bronx."

A small crowd gathers, as the five-person team springs into action,
finalizing the Mach-1's start up protocols.

"Power levels at 100%."

"Vortex Thrust Pack is operational."

"Kinetic Redistribution Boot diagnostics are green."

"Slipstream Vest intake connections are clear."

"Internal climate control system is active. How's it feel in there, Curtis?"

"Nice and cool…"

"That's pretty good considering it's almost eighty degrees and sunny
today—kind of warm for this time of year. I'm sweating already!"

"Kelly, are you getting all of this?"

"It looks great Mr. G. I've got nice shots of everything. By the way, my
brothers should be here in a couple of minutes."

"Good."

"Breaking system is online."

"Communications array is active."

"Vitals look good."

"We are good to go!"

Mr. Grabowski keeps his eyes on the monitors. He, Omar, and Treyshawn
are patched into the suit's communication system, but the honor is given to
Treyshawn to give Curtis the necessary updates.

"Can you guys hear me?" Curtis says while tapping on his earpiece.

The three look at each other and nod as Treyshawn responds, "Loud
and clear."

"Now remember, Curtis," says Mr. Grabowski, "we have multiple
cameras covering you: one at the starting line, one at the finishing line, as

well as your helmet-cam. Kelly will have your camera in the chase car with Kevin and Kelvin and they'll be following you the whole way. And don't forget that The News Channel and the World Record Group have their cameras rolling as well. So all you have to do is focus on running. You got it?"

"I got it," Curtis says while scanning through the growing crowd. "Hey Omar, did you check the boots?" he says with a laugh.

"We've triple-checked the boots. Everything's solid."

"Good." He continues to look through the crowd with a concerned expression. "When is mom supposed to get here? We can't start without her."

"She said she'd be here," Omar replies just as a car screeches to a stop behind the crowd. A door opens and quickly slams shut.

"Wait! Curtis! I'm here! Omar! Jim! Don't start yet!" The group smiles as they see Miranda pressing through the growing crowd. As she breaks through and sees her youngest son, she stops in her tracks, amazed, having never seen the entire suit at one time.

"Wow, Curtis, you look fast just standing there! Sorry I'm late. Last minute things at work."

"I'm just glad you made it, Mom." Curtis says. "I told them we couldn't start until you got here."

"Well, she's here," Treyshawn says energetically, "so let's get this thing going!"

The crowd cheers as Curtis takes his mark.

"Here we go!" Mr. Grabowski shouts.

Miranda says a quiet prayer as they get ready, "Lord Jesus, this is my baby... Please don't let him get hurt again."

"Recording equipment and sensors are ready. The World Record Group is ready. Kelly and her brothers are ready. Curtis, we are ready when you are."

"I'm ready!" he says as he assumes his stance.

"Here we go! In 5... 4... 3... 2... 1... go!"

Curtis launches himself down the stretch of pavement. The re-designed boots have a marked improvement in response time and within seconds he reaches the boots' top speed.

"Alright, Curtis," Treyshawn says, "you're at 35 miles per hour. How you holding up?"

"Great! Everything's smooth. We ready for stage two?"

"Ready when you are!"

"Activating Vortex thruster in 3... 2... 1... now!"

Curtis hammers the control switch on his glove and the thruster roars to life! This time Curtis is prepared for the sudden burst of speed and moves accordingly. Omar relays the rate of acceleration to Treyshawn, who communicates it to Curtis.

"40... 45... 50... 55... 60... 65... 67... 68... 69... Curtis, you're holding at 69 miles per hour!"

Mr. Grabowski verifies the data with the World Record Group before relaying instructions.

"It's confirmed Curtis! 69 miles per hour! You just set a world record! Congratulations! Time to brake and bring it home!"

"Got it! Activating braking system now!" With the press of another button, Curtis braces himself as several small braking flaps extend from the Vortex Pack while the motor revs down, reverses rotation and powers back up: providing negative thrust. These two systems, combined with the positive traction soles on his boots, quickly bring Curtis to a halt. With another press of the button, the Vortex Pack powers down.

"Just so you know," Treyshawn says, "your total run time took just over 60 seconds."

"That's all? Seemed like longer."

The chase car comes to a stop next to him. "I don't believe what I just saw!" Kevin yells.

Kelvin adds, "Curtis, you're the man! Whew!"

Kelly exclaims, "That's the absolute coolest thing I've ever seen!"

He smiles, as they jump out of the car to congratulate him. After a moment, he looks at them and says, "Race you back?"

Curtis arrives back at the starting point to thunderous applause from the crowd. The validation team from the World Record Group approaches.

"All I can say is... amazing. Simply amazing."

"And we've seen some pretty amazing things. But Curtis Powers... you are officially the world's fastest running man!"

News coverage quickly swells by dinnertime, as several reporters call the apartment, hoping to get exclusive interviews.

The News Channel clip airs by 6pm as Omar edits the team's camera footage into a 3-minute clip and uploads it to the Internet.

By Sunday morning, the video has already been viewed over two thousand times. By Monday morning, as Curtis prepares to leave for school, the views have climbed even higher, as several media outlets pick up the story.

"Curtis, I've been thinking," his mother says as she walks into his room; finding both her sons focused on the computer screen.

"Mom!" Omar says excitedly, "the video's up to seven thousand views!"

"Seven thousand!" She says, impressed, "it hasn't even been a week yet!"

"I know!" says Curtis. "Can you believe it?"

"Boys, listen," Miranda says while sitting on the bed, "that's why I came in here. I'm worried about all of this attention."

"No worries, Mom," Omar says. "I'm going to go with Curtis to school to make sure he gets there."

"Good. That makes me feel a little better."

"And," Curtis says, "we've called in reinforcements." She gives them a curious look as the door buzzer rings. "Can you get the door, Mom? We're going to finish up here."

"I take it you know who's at the door."

"Yep," Curtis says with a smile.

When she opens the door, familiar faces greet her while speaking in unison.

"Good morning Mrs. Powers."

"Now this is a pleasant surprise. Good morning, Kelly and Treyshawn. And you two young gentlemen behind them... I still can't tell you apart." she says with a laugh.

"We get that a lot," they both say in unison.

"Now which one of you is Kelvin and which one is Kevin?"

After a few seconds of determining the twin brother's identities, the conversation continues.

"We figured with all the hype that's going on, Curtis might need an escort to the school," Kelvin says.

"Your sons called us this morning," adds Kelly.

"Now this puts me at ease. Please, come on in. My boys are just about ready to leave."

Minutes later, the whole group is ready to walk out the door. "Now you all listen," says Mrs. Powers sternly, "go straight to school and make sure you go *straight inside*. Don't stop and talk to anyone—not even reporters. School first and fame second. Got it?"

News crews, from several major outlets, are already waiting at the school. As they see the group approach they begin to scramble.

"Is that him?"

"Here he comes."

"Camera's rolling?"

"Let's do it."

"Curtis! Curtis Powers! Can we have a minute of your time?"

As the reporters rush over, Treyshawn, Kevin, Kelvin and Omar stonewall them.

"You reporters need to back up!"

"Ain't nothin' to see here!"

"I'm sorry," says Omar as he takes the lead position, "but we have strict instructions to head straight into the school. So, you'll have to wait until later."

The group pushes past the reporters and enter the school, as word spreads through the entire student body that Curtis is in the building. His fame is practically instant as he walks through the halls and is greeted by others. The first to greet him are a few guys from the football team.

"What's up 'Speedsuit' Powers?"

"Are you talking to me?" Curtis responds with a surprised look.

"Yeah," replies the first guy. "That's your new name—your new handle."

The other speaks up. "That's what you call it, right? A Speedsuit?"

"Yeah," Curtis says with a smile.

"So, there you go!" A third person says. "Curtis 'Speedsuit' Powers. By the end of the day everyone's going to know your name. Everybody!"

By fourth period, everyone is talking about the world record, forcing the principal to call a school-wide assembly for the afternoon.

By sixth period, the auditorium is filled to capacity as Principal Jack Riley approaches the podium.

"Students and colleagues, by third period, I realized that it would be terribly difficult for you to focus on your class work until this incredible situation was dealt with. I've spent the better part of the morning fielding questions from the media.

"I've seen the remarkable video that has been circulating its way through the school's hallways. I'm embarrassed to say that I'm not incredibly advanced when it comes to using these Internet social networking sites. And I didn't watch television this past weekend, so I've been a little out of the loop, but four gentlemen, and a young lady—four of whom are affiliated with this school—three students and one of our physics teachers, have made history by setting a world record for the fastest running man!"

The students cheer.

"By doing this, they have helped put our school and our district on the map for something positive, uplifting, and innovative! Who says that nothing good ever comes out of the Bronx?"

The students cheer again and begin to chant at the top of their lungs: "Rheuman! Rheuman! Rheuman! Rheuman!"

After they quiet down, Mr. Riley continues.

"I've called this assembly to give you a chance to ask questions, since you're all wondering about the world record. After your time, the news reporters will be given an opportunity to ask their questions as well. Each of you was told to write your question down on a slip of paper. Each class was to have gone through their questions and picked the one asked most frequently. Your teachers have turned in each class question and those questions have been sorted. The top five, most frequently asked and relevant questions have been chosen. So now, without further delay, I bring to the stage Curtis 'Speedsuit' Powers, Treyshawn Jinkins, Kelly Washington, Mr. Grabowski, and Curtis' brother, Petty Officer Second Class Omar Powers of the United States Navy!"

The students erupt into a deafening applause as the five come out onto the stage.

By the end of the week, the story has spread through the international community and the record setting video has been viewed over one million times. In light of this, the group meets to discuss the latest turn of events.

"We didn't plan for this." Omar says.

"No, we didn't." adds Treyshawn.

Curtis and Kelly sit silent.

"In all of our calculating," Mr. Grabowski asks, "how did we not plan for this?" The phone rings. "Hello? Yes, this is Mr. Grabowski... Really? That sounds great! Yes, I have a pen..." He writes down the information. "Thank you very much! Yes, I'll look for your email tomorrow. We look forward to seeing you there. Have a good night. I will... bye."

"Who was that?" Curtis asks.

Mr. Grabowski tries to hide his enthusiasm, but it clearly isn't working as he starts smiling while looking at them silently.

"Mr. G, who was that?" Kelly asks.

"Do you want to run at the PA Relays?"

"No way!" Curtis jumps up. "Are you kidding?"

"That was the PA Relays. They want us to come!"

Curtis sits back down, speechless, as everyone shouts in celebration before growing quiet again.

"Curtis? Curtis, are you ok? Say something."

"Just a year ago... we went to the Relays, for the first time, as spectators. Now we're being *asked* to come as participants. This is unbelievable!" He leans back in his chair for a moment as everything slowly begins to sink in.

Then he jumps up with his hands above his head. "This is a dream come true!"

The group spends the rest of the evening in celebration, grateful for this incredible opportunity. They only have about two weeks left to come up with a color scheme for the suit and a heroic 'stage' name for Curtis as the word spreads quickly that the Mach-1 Speedsuit will be showcased at this year's PA Relays.

Thursday April 22, 2010. The PA Relays.

The stadium is filled to capacity, as attendance is the highest it's ever been in recent history. Everyone's excited about the entire occasion, but even more so about the showcase event.

"Ladies and gentlemen, boys and girls," the announcer's voice booms across the arena, "the PA Relays is proud to present a special showcase event! You know him from the media as Curtis 'Speedsuit' Powers, the young genius sensation from New York who set the world speed record with the Mach-1 Speedsuit. We present this young man to you today as… Jetstream!!!"

People cheer as Curtis and the team walk out onto the field and take their positions. Once there, the announcer continues.

"Of course, no man is an island to himself. Standing with Jestream are his friends, Treyshawn Jinkins and Kelly Washington, his brother, Petty Officer Second Class Omar Powers, and his physics teacher, Mr. Jim Grabowski!"

The crowd cheers again as the team waves and then prepares to carry out the task at hand.

"You've seen the video footage on television and the internet! Now see the phenomenon with your own eyes!" The crowd gives a roar of applause again as the announcer continues.

"One lucky visitor has been randomly selected to help with this exhibition run. *That* visitor will run 100 meters, as fast as they can. If you look down to the end of the track, you will see that we have a Pennsylvania State Trooper standing at the ready with his radar gun. He will clock the visitor's speed. Our track coach, here at the starting line, will clock the visitor's running time. Once the visitor has finished, one of the pre-selected PA Relay athletes will run the same 100 meters as fast as they can—having their time and speed measured! Once the athlete has finished, Jetstream will do the same run—and he *may* get a ticket if he breaks the speed limit."

Laughter breaks throughout the stands as the announcer continues. "So let us begin!"

While the crowd cheers, the chosen visitor runs out onto the field and takes her mark on the starting line. She shakes Jetstream's hand before taking her position. The announcer signals her start and she runs the 100 meters in 22.5 seconds, a speed of 9.94 miles per hour.

Next the athlete runs the 100 meters and finishes in just over 11 seconds—moving at 20.34 miles per hour.

Jetstream then takes his position at the starting line. When the announcer gives the signal, he launches down the track in 6 seconds, to a myriad of camera flashes, moving at 37.28 miles per hour!

The crowd erupts into thunderous applause as the demonstration participants stand together for group photos; followed by a meeting with several PA Relay officials, who congratulate the team.

"That was remarkable! Absolutely inspiring! You all should think about doing demonstrations for different schools around the country. You could, quite possibly, single handedly inspire this entire generation to do better in school and in life."

Another adds, "We've already discussed it and if you are interested, we'll utilize our international network of high schools, colleges, and universities to help provide you with a solid platform."

"We also have contacts with the Olympic board and would love to see you do a similar exhibition run at the 2012 Olympics in London."

Curtis is completely astounded. *Is this a dream*, he thinks to himself, as his mind summons a familiar quote his father used to say before he died:

"Remember Curtis, your gifts will make room for you and bring you before important people. Even if it takes a long time and you have to go through a lot of obstacles—just do your best. The extraordinary can happen only if you do your best."

"Curtis?" The official says, "Do you hear me?"

"I'm sorry sir. This seems like one big dream! I zoned out for a second."

"I can see you are in a state of shock," the man says with a robust laugh. "So, do you think you would be interested in this kind of opportunity?"

"Yes," Curtis replies, "this would be a great opportunity. Thank you! Thank you very much!"

"You and your team have got great potential! Keep up the good work and you will go far."

The next few weeks were a flurry of activity as Curtis, Omar, Kelly, Treyshawn, and Mr. Grabowski find themselves swamped with interviews for television shows, radio stations, newspapers, and magazines:

"Hello and welcome to Wake Up America. This morning, on our show, we have Curtis 'Speedsuit' Powers..."

Late night talk shows immediately include his story into their opening banter.

"Welcome to The Night Show with Ray Spano. Have you heard about the world's fastest man? Apparently he's not a man at all. He's a fifteen-year-old kid! He's not even old enough to drive, but he can *literally* outrun almost any car on the road! So here's my question; if a cop stops him for speeding—how awkward is that? Doesn't he actually have to be driving a vehicle in order to get a ticket? I can see it now. 'Officer, I was only out for a jog!' Ladies and gentlemen, Curtis 'Speedsuit' Powers is with us tonight!"

As the few weeks come to an end, it's finally time for Omar to leave. After a somber celebration with his family and friends, he packs, dons his uniform, and prepares to depart.

"Omar," Curtis says as he enters his room, "I don't want you to leave."

"I know. It's even harder now that things have really picked up."

"How am I supposed to do these runs without you? I can't do it."

"Sure you can, Curt. Even though I may not be with you, I am *with* you. I'll be praying for each run, that everything goes well. Besides, you still got everybody here, who's supporting you. The time's going to fly by and I'll be back home before you know it."

The brothers embrace as Omar struggles to keep his tears back. "I'm proud of you, Curtis—real proud. And I know dad would be proud of you too. Just keep running forward."

Months pass as Curtis, Treyshawn, Mr. Grabowski, Mrs. Powers, and Kelly work to balance their personal and public lives—carving out time for home, school and a bi-weekly speaking circuit. They also learn how to manage coming from relative obscurity to being members of a national platform where many seek to hear their views on various topics.

While at Mrs. Powers' for a group dinner, Mr. Grabowski shares some news.

"I received a phone call last night."

"From who?" asks Curtis.

"From my daughter." Mr. Grabowski beams with excitement.

"That's great, Jim! What did she say?" asks Miranda.

"She saw all of the news coverage about Curtis and thought it was great that I was helping him. She told me that a lot of people were talking about what we're doing and she got great joy out of telling them that the 'physics teacher' was her father…" Mr. Grabowski begins to cry.

They all look on in quiet concern as Curtis' mom puts her arm around him. "It's ok, Jim."

"I'm just overwhelmed with joy! It's been a long time since we've talked and even longer since she's called me her father."

"Group hug," Kelly yells out as they all come together for an embrace.

"There's more," Mr. Grabowski continues, "she wants to bring her husband and daughter out here to visit me."

"That's wonderful!" Miranda exclaims.

"Yeah, that's really good news," adds Treyshawn.

"It is," adds Mr. Grabowski, "especially since I've never met them. I'm excited and terrified at the same time!"

"But you *are* going to meet them, right?" Treyshawn asks. "You're not gonna chicken out?"

"You bet I'm not, Treyshawn!"

A moment of laughter and small talk pass as they eat.

"Treyshawn?"

"Yeah, Mr. G?"

"Thanks."

"For what?"

"What you just said about chickening out. You tell things like it is, and I appreciate that. And as crazy as it sounds, none of us would be at this table right now if you hadn't bullied Curtis. The boots, saving your life, the Speedsuit... Just that one thing set the stage for all of this. And the rest is history. Somehow all of this has worked out for all our good."

"You used to *bully* my son?" Miranda asks in her stern voice.

"*Uh, oh...*" Kelly says as Curtis and Treyshawn try to hide their faces.

"Did I just—Miranda, you didn't know?"

"No, Jim, I didn't."

"I'm sorry, I thought Curtis had finally told you."

"Curtis, I thought you two met and became friends the first day of school?"

"Technically Mom," Curtis counters, "Treyshawn responded to your question with 'we met the first day of school.' Neither of us actually said that we'd been friends. You made the *association* that we were."

Mrs. Powers looks at her son, then at Treyshawn, then back at Curtis before cracking a slight smile.

"Fair enough."

"Whew..." Treyshawn and Curtis let out a sigh of relief.

"Since everything turned out alright. I take it I'm the only one who didn't know?"

"Yeah," one of them says.

"Even *you*, Kelly?" Miranda asks.

"Yes..." she responds with a slight giggle.

"I can't believe it. I thought us girls were supposed to stick together!" They all laugh before Miranda stops. "Wait! Omar knew too?"

"We didn't want you to worry, so we decided not to tell you," Curtis said.

"Well…" She takes a deep breath. "What's done is done. I'm just glad everything has worked out. Speaking of which, Treyshawn? How are things going with you and your mother?"

"We really got into it back at the beginning of the school year. I told her I wouldn't be her excuse anymore. Since then, things have been better. They're not perfect, but we're both trying. She went and got a job, so I'm excited about that!"

"That's great news, Treyshawn!" Miranda says, "You should be so proud of yourself."

"I am. But you should thank, Curtis. Even though I treated him like dirt, he still treated me like I mattered. He believed in me… and now I believe in me, too."

Treyshawn and Curtis shake hands across the table as he replies.

"When my dad died, I wanted to die with him. I didn't think I could make it. But my mom told me that God had taken the time to make me for a reason. He believes in me, even more than my dad did, and no matter how bad things looked, I should believe in myself, too."

Curtis turns to his mother, "So *I* should be saying thanks to you, Mom. Where would we all be without you?"

"I think I'm gonna cry," Kelly says sniffling.

"Good job at buttering me up, Son." Miranda says while trying to hold back her *own* tears and forcing a chuckle. "I'll take as many compliments as I can get. But seriously, we've all been through a lot. But, the key word is 'through.' We didn't remain stuck. And I'm glad to know that you have two good friends, a watchful brother, and an encouraging mentor. I thank God for you all and ask him to bless you, every night, in my prayers."

"And Kelly," Curtis says. "From the first day we met, you've been a real friend."

"Thanks Curtis, you make it easy to be your friend."

"And…" Mr. Grabowski adds, "You make it easy to be your teacher."

After some moments of small talk and finishing the meal, Miranda announces, "Who wants dessert? I've got chocolate cake and vanilla ice cream."

Later that night, Curtis writes in his journal...

Thursday August 26, 2010. Entry 1,562.

"I'm not even old enough to drive, vote or fight in a war, but now I know that young people can change the world. I never dreamed of being in newspapers or on television shows... I never thought about being on the radio or on the cover of magazines. I just dreamed of running and who would have thought running would have taken me this far?

"Never in my wildest dreams would I have thought I'd be racing bicycles, dogs, horses, motorcycles and cars. I never guessed that I would be standing before crowds of thousands—running before them and sharing my story—at schools and colleges, churches and corporate retreats; hopefully inspiring young and old to live out their full potential and realize that their mind and heart are their greatest assets... that we're here for a reason and can make a difference. Even with all of this, I know I have so much further to go. I feel like everything is just beginning!"

SHAWN ALLEYNE

Epilogue
Motion Blur

"ELEVENTH GRADE FLEW RIGHT BY AND twelfth grade is practically over! I guess that's what happens when you wear a suit that allows you to run close to 100 miles per hour. Our exposure has increased around the world, now, and with that exposure comes a lot of resources to aid in the development of new ideas.

"We went through another round of suit updates—moving from spring mechanisms to compressed air cylinders, to the first version of the electromagnetic repulsion boots. They really look promising! I even raced a cheetah and lost, just barely, but we're scheduling a rematch!

"We get tons of mail from kids *and* adults. They're so amazed that a person can run so fast!

Omar has one more year before he leaves the navy. We plan to work together, so watch out world! The Powers brothers are coming!

"Mom finished her business degree, got a better job, and moved us to a better part of town. Our new house isn't like the one in New Jersey, but it's nice to have a front and back yard again.

"Kelly's in demand as a dance teacher and performer! And we finally admitted our feelings for each other. It's funny to see girls at school who thought I was a nerd before, now want to hang around. But Kelly's been there from the beginning and that counts a whole lot!

"Graduation's almost here and Treyshawn, Kelly and I are looking forward to college. That's right; Treyshawn's graduating and going to college! He pulled his grades from F's to B's and even got an award for 'the most improved student.' Some of his friends from his block—those who are still alive—are trying to get their lives right... all because of Treyshawn's example.

"And Mr. Grabowski's class has exploded with more students than ever! He still has the reputation as one of the toughest teachers, but students figure if he can create something cool through physics, then maybe science isn't *all* that bad.

"Can you believe I'm about to graduate in two months? As big as that day is, the bigger day comes after that! Graduation is in June and then, in July, we all head to London for the Olympics! And the opening ceremony starts on my birthday! It's like one big dream that I never want to wake up from! I have no clue what will happen because of this trip, but I know I want all of us—me, mom, Treyshawn, Omar, Kelly, and Mr. G to enjoy our time together."

The 2012 Olympics: London. July 27th.

A single figure walks into the Olympic arena to non-stop, applause of more than fifty thousand people. The sun shines unusually bright as thousands of cameras preserve this moment in digital sharpness. Newscasters recount his story for the world—Curtis Powers the fastest man alive on two feet—setting new records at speeds over eighty miles an hour.

"Mom was right. God *does* have things for us that stretch beyond our imagination."

Curtis looks to the sky, through his gold tinted visor, and raises his arms, caught up in a moment that most in the stadium cannot perceive. A single tear streams down his face as the official announcer approaches him with microphone in hand.

"Curtis 'Speedsuit' Powers! You are the fastest man alive! You've carried the Olympic torch the last leg of the journey during the opening ceremonies and lit the flame. What's going through your mind right now as you stand here in the midst of such international accolades?"

There's a hush over the crowd as the audience waits eagerly to hear his response. The television cameras and photographers zoom in to capture Curtis' expression as he disengages the Speedsuit's hood, pulls it back and reveals his tears.

"My dad always said I'd make it here... I was wondering if he could see me from heaven. This run is dedicated to him." Curtis looks back up to the sky and declares, "I love you, Dad!!!"

A man rises in the stands and begins to clap—his eyes filled with tears. The clapping spreads like a massive wave across the entire stadium, as television reporters speak. "We've just heard Curtis Powers share his thoughts about this momentous occasion—citing his father, who died almost 7 years ago when he was in 6th grade, as his inspiration."

Curtis walks over to the starting blocks. The Olympic runners who will compete against him in this special exhibition event greet him. As final preparations are made, he can't help but think back to the beginning where this adventure began. Here he is, at the starting blocks, able to see his family and friends in the front row of the stadium seating nearby, as he stands next to some of the world's greatest athletes.

"Ladies and gentlemen, boys and girls from around the world... the 2012 Olympics presents to you... Jetstream!!!"

In this moment as the runners take their mark and the gun is about to fire, the sound of the crowd fades away into Curtis' thoughts, *I'm about to run into my destiny...* And with that, the shot is fired as the Olympic runners take off down the track!

Curtis stands motionless—watching the men travel down the track—waiting for the second shot, which will signal his time to launch. The runners approach the quarter mark, as Curtis takes his stance. The crowd roars as the second shot is fired and Jetstream lunges into motion—taking off down the track!

For the first quarter of the run, he can only use his K.R.B. boots. Even so, by the end of the first leg he has made up some ground.

As he crosses the threshold into the second leg of the run, Curtis notices the Olympic runners are passing the halfway mark. He is now free to use the Vortex Thrust Pack and wastes no time engaging it! Immediately, his body accelerates and seconds later his speed is twice that of the fastest runner!

The crowds cheer as the gap between the runners and Jetstream quickly diminishes! By the time the first runner passes the last threshold of the race, Jestream is fast approaching! He passes runner after runner as if they're standing still and then zooms past the lead runner, leaving a column of highly pressurized air in his wake!

Within seconds, Curtis crosses the finish line as the entire stadium and those watching by television and listening by radio jump to their feet and cheer at the top of their lungs! Moments later, the nearest runner—who is more than five seconds behind him—finally crosses the finish line.

Curtis engages the braking system, slows to a stop and then goes back to congratulate the Olympic runners. After receiving a large American flag, he poses with them as photographers take numerous pictures. Curtis pulls back his hood as they take a victory lap around the track—waving to the crowd. He then breaks away to embrace his mother, Kelly, Omar, Treyshawn, and Mr. Grabowski.

"You did it, little bro!" Omar yells as he hugs Curtis tightly. "Your dream came true!"

"We did it, Omar! All of us!"

"We did it with God's help!" adds their mother.

"Yeah!" Curtis exclaims. "With God's help!"

In the midst of the cheers and accolades, his thoughts drift back to that day when he, his dad, and Omar watched the 2004 Olympics.

"Dad said I'd make it here… and here I am."

Five months have passed since Curtis settled into college life in Atlanta, at Georgia Tech. Since his arrival on campus, he's been a celebrity of sorts; surrounded by many opportunities and temptations. But he remains strong and focuses on his future.

The first semester just ended and his mind aches, even though his last exam was two days ago. Between his class work and Speedsuit exhibitions, he already feels the need for a vacation, and looks forward to the Christmas break. But, there's been a nagging thought in the back of his mind, *there's got to be more to this experience than just my studies.*

The more he improves his Speedsuit, the more ideas he has for other inventions. Starting a technology firm seems like the logical choice; but what's crazy is *when* he wants to start it.

"Treyshawn, I know you're out in California at Design school, but I'm seriously thinking about starting a tech firm."

"After you graduate?"

"No, like next year. What do you think?"

"The tech firm sounds good—but what about your classes? You think you can handle it?"

"I think so—if I strictly work on the creative side and leave the business aspects to someone else. I just need some way to work out these ideas in my head and have a platform available for innovations needing patents, promotion, and distribution."

"It seems like a natural next step," Treyshawn says after giving the idea a moment's pause. "Maybe it can boost what we're already doing to help get kids into science."

"Bro, you read my mind—been thinking about that! I know you got class work and art events, but you think you'd be interested? Omar said he's in."

"You don't even have to ask. You *know* I'm interested. You told Kelly yet?"

"Not yet, I figured we can work out the details during Christmas break."

"You got a name for the company?"

"Yeah, Powersuit Technologies: Run. Leap. Soar."

The following is Select Concept Art and Storyboard Sequences that I did for the story and the film.

—*Allen Paul Weaver III*

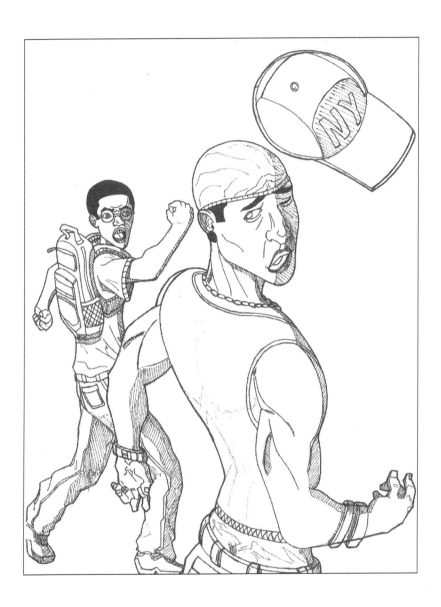

221

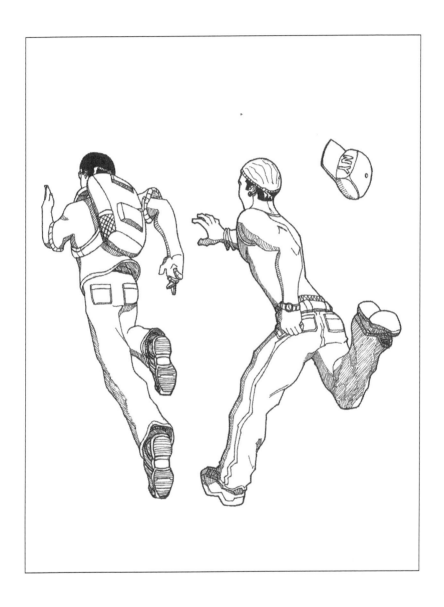

223

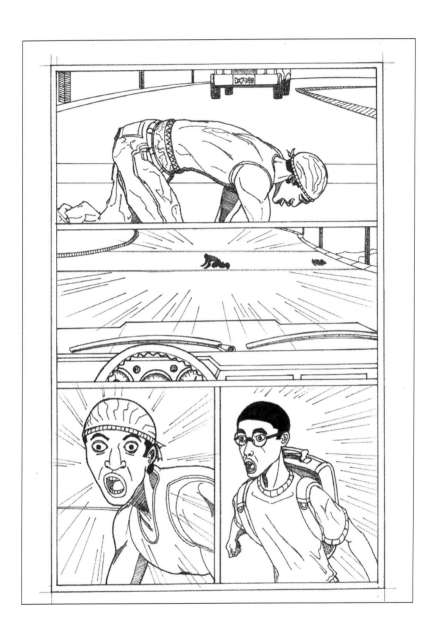

227

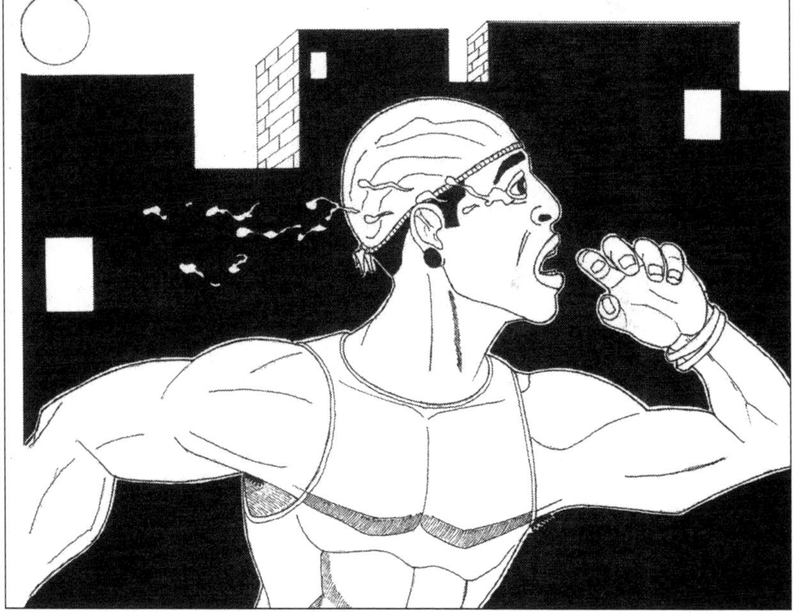

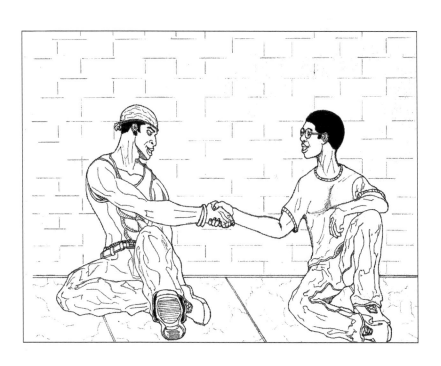

Hand Controls

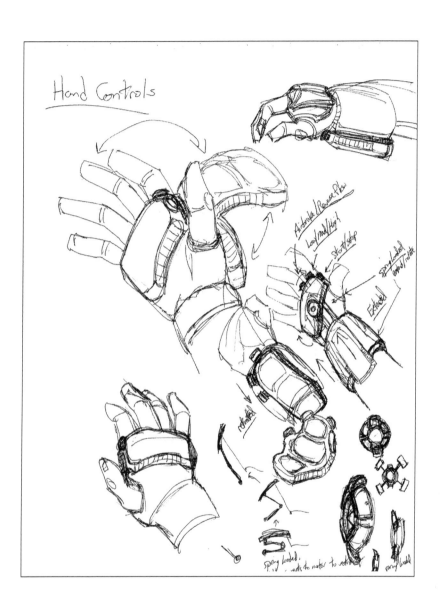

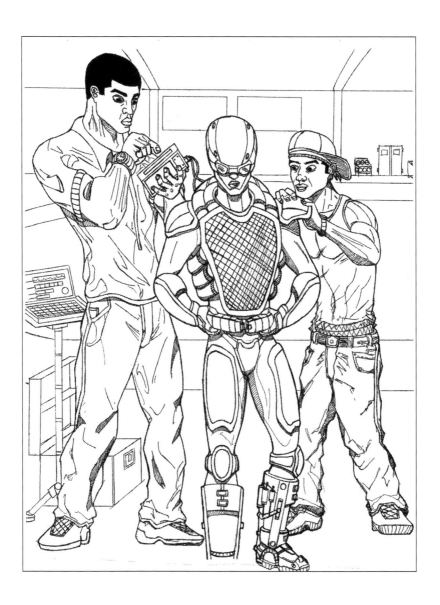

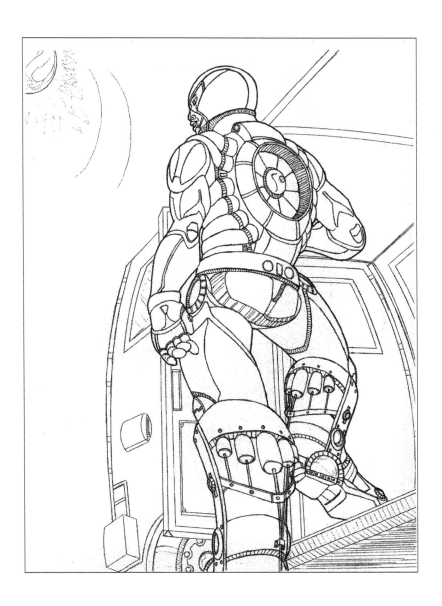

235

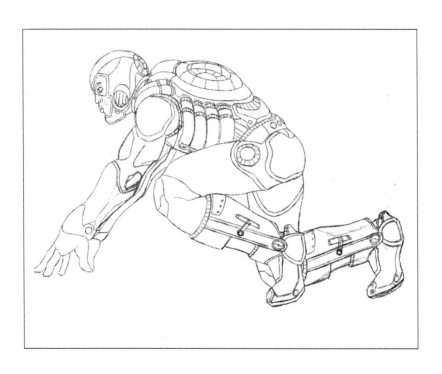

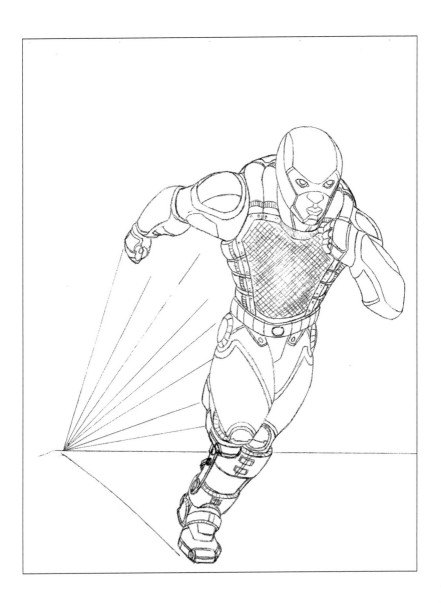

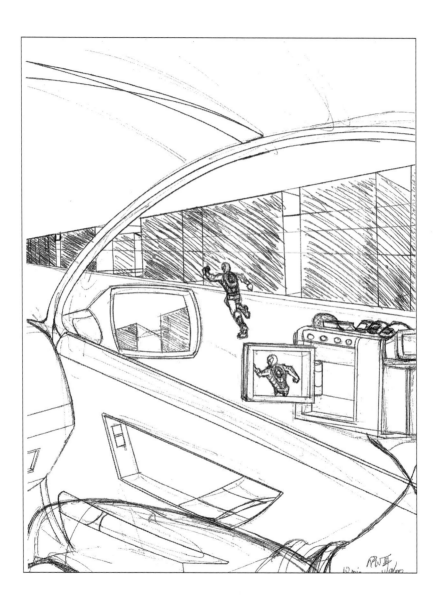

Reader's Guide
Selected Themes

Many themes emerge from the pages of this book. Consider them in terms of the characters' lives and your own. Here are three to get you started...

Theme 1:
The Power of Influence
Each character's life is influenced by someone else. Discuss how people have the power to positively and/or negatively impact someone's life. How can you help to influence someone else for the better?

Theme 2:
Purpose & Identity
Each character's life-journey leads to discovering part of their purpose and aspects of their identity. How can good and/or bad circumstances affect your purpose and identity? How can your gifts and talents help guide you towards your purpose?

Theme 3:
The Ability to Choose
Each character must choose the direction for their lives. Discuss when it is easy and/or difficult for people to make decisions about which way they should go in life. What steps can you take to make wise decisions for your life?

What other themes did you discover in the story?

Visit: **www.APW3.com** to enter the Powersuit world and find out more about the themes, story, characters and more!

Acknowledgments

I want to thank my wife, Ijnanya, who believed in me enough to say, "Write this story yourself, you don't need to hire a ghost writer." And thank you for listening to countless scenes and revisions and for offering your critical feedback.

I also want to thank my friend, Demetrius T. Veasy II, creator of the Lions 12 comic book line. You challenged me, back in April '08, to move beyond my fears and write this story down—which has lived in me for almost a decade.

I want to say thank you to Dorette Saunders, Miranda Smalls, Sheree Williams and Davina McDonald for editing earlier drafts of this story, upon which this book now stands. "Where would I be without you ladies?" And I want to thank Dr. Tisha Y. Lewis for all of your encouragement and phone conversations.

Also, thanks to my friend, Andrew Seltz, who provided various creative direction and ideas. You are truly the 'gotoguy!'

And finally to Tiffany, Shekara, Asa, Shaquan, Shellae, Tseohnni, Cyrus and Sadasia—thank you for taking the time to read this story from a teenager's perspective.

About the Author:

Allen Paul Weaver III is a Dreamer who grew up on comic books, science fiction and the Bible. He holds a BA degree in speech/mass communications and a Master of Divinity degree in theology.

Allen speaks to youth and young adults about developing creativity, linking experiences to opportunities and walking in their God-given purpose.

He is presently working on books two and three of the Powersuit Series (as well as several other manuscripts). Allen is also the author of *Transition: Breaking Through the Barriers* and *MOVE! Your Destiny Is Waiting On You.*

He enjoys drawing, writing, creating and producing short films, brainstorming innovative ideas with his brother, spending time with his wife, visiting new cities and countries, and flying in vertical wind tunnels.

Allen believes when your imagination is combined with action and resources, internal thoughts can become external realities! To have him speak at your event, visit: **www.APW3.com.**

READ THE SECOND BOOK IN THE SPEEDSUIT POWERS TRILOGY! SPEEDSUIT POWERS: THE OPPOSITION

Behind the Story:

An interview with Author, Allen Paul Weaver III

Q: Tell us a little about yourself.

APW3: Well, I'm from Florida, but grew up in New York. I graduated from New Rochelle High School and went back to Florida for college at Bethune-Cookman Universtiy, in Daytona Beach. I love to write, draw and travel... among other things. And my wife and I have one son.

Q: What exactly is Speedsuit Powers about?

A: There are many themes in the book, but if I had to sum it up I'd say, Speedsuit Powers is about how unplanned circumstances and obstacles can open the door to unexpected discoveries and opportunities for growth. Or—what can happen when experience and opportunity meet.

Q: What are some of the issues that characters face in Speedsuit Powers?

A: Identity and Choice are huge in this story. Each character wrestles with, "Who am I? What am I good at? What am I supposed to be doing with my life?"

Bullying and Running are other key issues. We all are running from someone or something and we're running somewhere—even if we don't know 'where' that is. In bullying situations the focus is often on trying to get help for the person being bullied, but the bully needs help too. This book takes a look into the motivations behind the bullying as well as solutions for the victim.

The power of Influence is another theme. We're all influenced by others and influence others. This happens based on the choices we make. For example, both Treyshawn and Curtis have to cope with not having a father (although for very different reasons). As they share their experiences, they discover commonalities. There are other issues, but I don't want to give them all away.

Q: When and how did you first conceive of the concept for Speedsuit Powers?

A: In high school, I had friends who ran track and because of my speed the track coach asked if I was interested—but I didn't have the discipline. Also, I didn't want to give up my afternoons to practice. But I enjoyed watching track and field. There's something about running that makes me feel free— and stories that deal with running often attract me.

I grew up on comics, so I've always wanted to run faster than humanly possible. In college, I began researching ways to run faster and discovered that others around the country were spending 'big money' researching the same thing. Shortly after that, I came up with my idea for a pair of running boots.

Around the year 2000, I began developing that idea and came up with a way to incorporate it into a story. I love stories where teens overcome great odds and go on to do amazing things in the world. Having worked with teens since 1997, I knew my story would involve a young African American male in middle school, transitioning to high school. That just seemed like the appropriate age to start—right at that middle ground—not a child, but not an adult—trying to find your way… It's amazing to think that I've kept this story locked away for so long.

Q: Curtis is basically a genius when it comes to school. How were your grades?

A: [Laughing] I always got A's in gym, music and art. I had B's, C's and an occasional 'D in the rest. But, one of my uncles always told me that he saw me 'shining' in college.

In 11th grade, I was failing pre-calculus and my mother (a school nurse who knew all of my teachers) forced me to go to extra help. At first I hated it because I didn't understand anything; but as my teacher worked with me, things started to make sense. I passed the final, which brought my grade up from an F' to a C'. The way my teacher and I celebrated, other students thought I got an A. I would have failed without the extra help. That was the best C of my life!

I also took Physics in 11th grade and got my first F ever. My parents were ready to ground me and I told them they didn't need to because I was so upset. All my playing around had caught up with me. I took the class again the next semester, studied hard and got an 81.

I'm a huge procrastinator and had to wrestle with this a lot in college, but I really started to 'shine' as I studied more. It was tough, but I ended up on the honor roll every semester and even made the deans list for one semester. I graduated Magna Cum Laude—with honors.

So I didn't start out as the best student… but with help from others, hard work, prayer and determination, I became a better learner.

Q: When did you start writing?

A: I started keeping journals somewhere around 6th or 7th grade. Writing helped me sort through my feelings. Of course I had to write essays in English class, but I also wrote a couple articles for my high school newspaper. When I got to 12th grade, I took my first Creative Writing class and fell in love with writing stories. Some of my early works are pretty cheesy, but everyone has to start somewhere. I also started writing poetry in college and wrote for the school paper for a semester. Then my first book, **Transition: Breaking Through the Barriers**, was published in 2006. It's an anthology that covers ten years of my life.

Q: Your book addresses issues of faith. How important is that to you?

A: As a person of faith, this is very important to me. I believe that God has me here for a purpose and I wanted to bring that out in the story. Everyone may not believe as I do—and that's fine—but I didn't want to compartmentalize my life and leave something that is very much a part of who I am, outside of a story that is very close to my heart.

Q: Who does all the drawings?

A: Typically, I do all of the initial concept drawings and then turn them over to a freelance artist to draw a more detailed version. Honestly, part of the reason I do this is because I'm just beginning to grow comfortable with my drawing ability. What's funny is that people compliment me on my drawings all the time and ask if I'm an illustrator or an artist. I laugh and say 'no'— mainly because I know so many artists who draw way better than I do. It's easy to see someone who can do something better than you and to not do anything because you feel you'll never be as good as the other person. But I've learned that there will always be someone who can do something better than you—but that doesn't mean you stop working to improve your gifts and talents. So I do all of the initial drawings.

Q: Will there be a Speedsuit Powers 2?

A: Definitely! Book 2 is about done and will release this June (2015). I can't tell you any specifics, but the story is bigger and dives deeper into each character, while introducing new characters into the mix. The book will examine bullying more deeply as well (physical, emotional, cyber and institutional). Oh, and there are new suits, too! Like the first book, it really has something for everyone. People won't be disappointed.

Q: Why did you want to write a teen novel with an African American main character?

A: There's no 'one' Black experience. Every Black person isn't poor, or rich, or from the ghetto, or educated, etc… Although we're similar, we're also unique; and I wanted to showcase this in the story. When people think urban Black teens, they think poor, at-risk, uneducated, etc… This is the case for some, but there are those teens that love school, study hard and work relentlessly to develop their gifts and talents—all while living in an urban environment. I wanted to address both of these realities and show how everyone can grow… if they make the choice to do so.

I also think it's important to have characters that look like you and believe in noble values. As an African American male, I often have to 'translate' characters that don't look like me—into my own experience. I have no problems doing this and never really cared until I began to read Milestone Comics back in the '90's. Here were characters that I enjoyed reading about—who looked like me, had their issues and were trying to make their way in the world. I devoured almost everything Milestone put out: Icon, Static and Hardware were my favorites.

Fast forward to 2009 and it's important for me to write a teen fiction novel with an African American main character who was male, because there aren't that many stories, targeting teens with positive male characters of color. I wanted to do a story about a character that had issues, but was really trying to live right and do the right thing by others. I think it's needed today.

Q: It's funny to hear that you are a reluctant reader, and yet you've written a novel and several other books?

A: That does sound funny doesn't it? I can't fully explain it—I'm a reluctant reader who loves to write! I'm very visual and never really liked to read while growing up. It wasn't that I couldn't read, I just didn't *like* to read, unless it was something I was interested in—like comics or science fiction. That's the key when dealing with reluctant readers—finding subject matter that appeals to their interests.

During the summers, I would visit my aunt and uncle in Atlanta and they would give me math and reading assignments. I hated it! But they would also let me buy comic books—if my work was done. I read a book and wrote a report every week and did better on books that were related to something I liked or I could relate to my own experience. Then I slowly began learning how to think critically about books and life—which expanded into new genres.

I'm still somewhat of a reluctant reader, but I have a larger range of interest now. Speedsuit Powers is 229 pages long and I believe that other reluctant readers will enjoy it. The current record for finishing the book is 4 hours! A mentor once told me: "Always finish the books you start." Doing so provides a sense of accomplishment.

Q: What do you think is unique about your book?

248

A: That's always an interesting question—what makes you unique? People are pretty much the same and yet different. What makes *this* story unique is the vantage point from which it's told. It's an urban story, but it doesn't glamorize street life, nor does it have explicit language and sexuality in it. A lot of people know what it's like to experience the negative aspects of urban life, so I felt the story didn't need to 'go there'. Since the book was written for teens, I wanted to create a story that all teens could read—one where adults didn't have to worry about language and sexuality. There's enough of that in the environment already. What makes this urban story intense isn't necessarily the words of the character, but connecting with the emotions of the character. This book is unique because every character is on a journey; everyone has to choose which road they will follow.

Q: Were you afraid to write this story?

A: If it weren't for the challenge put to me by my friend, Demetrius Veasy and his manager, this story would still be locked up inside me. I'd still be walking around with drawings and an outline—too afraid to do anything with them. Even through the writing process, I take things one-step at a time and focus on the end result… a story that could help change the lives of youth for the better. I think many of us are afraid to do things with our gifts and talents. We need to press beyond the fear and bless others with what we can do. This journey has been amazing so far, and I would have missed out on it all—if I had given in to fear.

Q: What's your ultimate vision for the world of Speedsuit Powers?

A: My ultimate vision is that the world of Speedsuit Powers will help inspire youth towards their greatness. Of course to do this, I have to finish the 2nd and 3rd books of the trilogy! Book 2 should be out by Summer 2014 and Book 3 by Summer 2015.

The world of Speedsuit Powers is definitely larger than the three main books. There are other books in development that will follow other characters, like Treyshawn and Kelly. Also, new characters and storylines will be introduced that fall outside of the three books--yet relate to them in some way. We produced an independent film entitled, Speedsuit, back in 2012. It was screened in 14 venues to a few thousand people. I would love to have the Speedsuit Powers Trilogy picked up by a major studio and produced as either a television series, made-for-televion movie, or a major motion picture.

The Speedsuit Powers message is powerful. I believe it could seriously impact the world, if provided the right opportunities.

Q: Why is this story so important to you?

A: This story is important to me because I almost didn't live to write it. I attempted suicide in 1992, just after graduating from high school because my self-esteem issues seemed so large. I just wanted the pain to stop. Had I been successful, there would be no story. After that experience, God began to reveal my purpose and my gifts and talents—one of them being writing. I know how hard life can be for young people. I remember meeting a 16 year old male on his birthday and asking him what he wanted to be when he grew up. He looked me straight in my eyes and said, "I don't think I'll be anything." This blew me away. I don't ever want to hear a teen say that again. Hopefully, Speedsuit Powers will help inspire youth towards their God-given purpose.

Inside the mind of artist, Shawn Alleyne

Q: What were your thoughts when you first heard about the Speedsuit Powers story and concept?

SA: I was very intrigued with the Speedsuit world from my first encounter, both as a freelance artist interested in new clients and as a fan of the whole sci-fi/superhero genre. From the start the idea seemed like a fresh concept that would bring back some of the classic comic book elements of the Golden Age.

Q: How did you approach creating illustrations based off of Allen's concept drawings?

SA: I approached the illustrations pretty much the same way I do all my other projects: try to be faithful to the creator's vision, but incorporate my own design sense into the equation. Above all, my main ingredient is to have fun with the characters. When that didn't work I copied Allen's designs and took the credit. (SMILE)

Q: What was your favorite part of the drawing process for the Speedsuit Characters?

SA: As a broke artist getting paid was high up on the list, but I would have to say my favorite part was capturing a "real world" feel to the characters. In the sense of, how might the Speedsuit look in reality? How might the characters stand? That sort of thing.

Q: How long did it take you to do the drawings?

SA: The time periods depend on many variables—backgrounds, feedback from Allen, complexity, etc...

Q: How did you get started with your drawing?

SA: I woke up, sharpened my pencil, sat down... uhm what?... too long... oh... sorry... I had already drawn the Speedsuit at the New York Comicon where I met Allen, so I felt a little comfortable with the character already. It was just a matter of finding out what the creator wanted.

Q: What tips can you give young readers who aspire to be artists themselves?

SA: Three simple things that will turn anyone into a great artist:

1 – Draw everyday.

2 – Draw everything.

3 – Repeat steps 1 and 2.

Q: Is there anything else you want young readers to know?

SA: Just some advice someone once gave me: "never stop being a kid and having fun." Never lose that sense of wonder that will have you seeing the magic in everything around you even when you're old and grey. And don't forget to floss.

As a published author and filmmaker of a story that seriously tackles the issue of school bullying, I seek to provide answers for how our communities can counteract this disturbing trend and help our young people discover and pursue their purpose. Below is an article I wrote to help provide solutions-based-thinking for the school bullying epidemic in our country.

MOVING BEYOND BULLYING:

Laying Groundwork for Discovering School Bullying Solutions that Work for Everyone

By: Allen Paul Weaver III (copyright 2012)

WE HAVE A PROBLEM...

Media reports - including Anderson Cooper 360, Oprah, Dr. Phil - and perhaps our own experiences have made us aware of tragic school bullying stories where deaths are often the result. According to the US Department of Justice bullying report, the situation is so dire, that 160, 000 youth create excuses to skip school every day for fear of torment from bullies. Sadly, many young people are too disillusioned to expect solutions from adult leaders and adults are often too shocked to see beyond the problem.

Is there any way for our communities to move beyond bullying? By saying "beyond" I do not mean we ignore the problem and try to get on with our lives. Rather, we must begin to imagine a reality where the value of each individual is affirmed – thereby nullifying bullying. Then we must implement solutions to move us to that reality.

Let me say, there is no simple solution to this issue. Bullying is a very complex, growing epidemic in our culture; and due to Internet social media, it's mutating – much like a flu virus. No matter how fearful we may feel, we cannot allow the problem to 'frame' the solutions, but rather the solutions must systematically challenge and dismantle this epidemic at every known level. However, if youth and adults unite in meaningful discourse, we can create solutions.

DEFINING THE TERM

Every generation has a tendency to redefine terms used by previous generations. The problem reveals itself when different groups use the same term, but in reality consider the term to mean different things. For genuine discussion and discourse to occur, all parties involved must first agree to the meaning of key terms. The word 'bullying' is one such term.

To some groups of people bullying is seen as teasing and occasional harassment between peers. ("Occasional" because in the past, the harassment usually stopped once the victim came home from school). It is an unfortunate "part of growing up" and a "rite of passage" into adulthood – something you endure and go through. However, to this current technology-driven generation (with access to information and the ability to communicate with one another instantly and constantly), bullying goes beyond teasing and occasional harassment. Bullying, through cell phone and Internet technology, has been elevated to include new forms of mental and emotional torture that happens at school, at home and in almost all locations in between. The result is that many of our youth consider, attempt and succeed at taking their own lives in order to relieve the pain they experience on a daily basis.

Few would deny that the world is an increasingly complex place. Part of that complexity is seen in the following ways: 1) Internet and cell phone technology have enabled youth to make vicious statements with detached anonymity. 2) Youth have an increased lack of anger management, problem solving and coping skills, which leads to an escalation of violence. 3) There is an increasing disregard for the value and sanctity of life among young people and adults. 4) Adults seem unable to stop the bullying - especially in situations where the parents of the bully encourage or support the negative behavior.

CREATING NEW ENVIRONMENTS

We need new environments where bullying is not the norm, but seen by all as a correctable abnormality. One way we create such an environment and move beyond bullying is by striving for authentic relationships. A genuine relationship is one of mutual dealings between two (or more) people; anything else is manipulation. We must learn to establish relationships with identified bullied individuals as well as the bullies themselves. In reality, both the bully and the bullied are victims - just of a different sort. While the bullied is tormented by external factors (the bully); the bully is often tormented by internal issues which may also be a result of their own external factors (home life, self-image, etc...) Both need people they can trust, relationships that promote character development, and visions of a better-alternate reality to the one they are currently experiencing.

Once authentic relationships are established, they can be strengthened through mentor programs focused on the development of the talents of the youth involved - in relation to one another. Within the framework of honest relationships, character building and interpersonal talent development, a new community environment can be fostered where conflict is mediated, differences are celebrated, and common ground is discovered. By implementing positive relationship building through peer-to-peer and adult-to-teen mentoring, this new environment can be created.

Our main obstruction to this new reality is not our youth, but rather the repeated examples of adults (in almost every sphere of life) who no longer value civility as a key ingredient for relating to one another. Our current culture continues to lose sight of what genuine positive relationships look like and how to develop them. As people mistreat one another and don't care to solve conflicts, the result becomes selfishness that causes disparate communities. Society focuses on self-advancement and gratification at the expense of others.

3 KEY CONSIDERATIONS

First, bullying is a symptom of a deeper issue. Every bully has a context for their bullying: family trauma, internal turmoil, inferiority or superiority complex, desire to climb the social ladder of their peers, etc... Context plays a major factor in triggering bullying outbursts. To miss this is to make a grave error.

Beneath context, lies a root issue common to all persons who bully: a lack of value for life. If we are at war with ourselves – we will be at war with others. But if we have a healthy view of ourselves, we will have no reason to cause chaos in the lives of others. We must find a way to help bullies deal with this foundational reality – while taking responsibility for the pain and damage they cause. To understand why they lash out is to open up an entirely new realm of possibilities for positively changing their behavior!

Second, we cannot merely react to bullying. Reacting will always put us behind the problem, because a person cannot react until acted upon by an internal or external force. We need to act – meaning: make decisions based on the facts of the situation; foresee possible outcomes; take preventive measures to structure a bully-free environment; and have appropriate measures in place for when bullying takes place. In short, a proactive approach is necessary.

Rash "knee-jerk" actions often cause more harm than good because they are uninformed actions. The more time we take to examine bullying and walk through practical steps for a variety of scenarios, the more likely we will take appropriate actions when the time comes. The less time we spend seriously considering the reality and outcomes of this bullying epidemic, the more we put ourselves and the lives of our youth at risk. Everyone has his or her own opinion (whether informed or not) about what constitutes "appropriate" action. What standards of determination should we use? The question I propose - regardless of the bully prevention program being used or ignored - is this: "Is this action a "win-win" situation for both the bullied and the bully?" If not, then we must seek additional alternatives.

Third, we must help the bullied AND the bully. If we try to help the bullied, while only removing the bully from the equation, we ultimately participate in a win-lose situation. The bully will be left to his or her own devices, often carrying that negative behavior into adulthood, which puts others at risk, including themselves.

This approach is different from an anti-bullying/zero-tolerance perspective. While anti-bullying/zero-tolerance can be helpful and necessary in many circumstances: removing a bully from the immediate situation – its inherent failure is in its "one size fits all" stance. Zero tolerance says "no bullying will be tolerated under ANY circumstances." The result is a punishment that often doesn't fit the crime. So a first-time bully is given the same punishment as a person who constantly bullies others. And the person who has been a victim of bullying who lashes out because they have no other recourse, is punished just as if they were the bully themselves (often resulting in the actual bully being perceived as the victim!)

In almost every sphere of life, we regard the circumstances of others in an effort to discover context and motivations for actions and best practices for navigating through society. Take parenting as an example: a child's motivation behind an action will greatly influence the type of reaction presented by the parent. If a parent discovers that their car -which they lent to their child the night before - now has major damage, knowing the circumstances behind the damage is crucial! Was their child intoxicated? Or did someone else run a red light and crash into them?

Yet, Zero tolerance disregards circumstances and leaves the bully and/ or bullied without a resolution for their present and future. Zero tolerance, as a win-lose approach, may work on some level; but it does not work on all levels. To work on all levels, we need a win-win approach incorporated into this "bullying equation." We need an environment that inspires winning for all instead of winning only for a few.

WHERE IS THE BYSTANDER'S POWER?

Bullying has a negative affect on the bystander community that witnesses such adverse behavior. It creates an atmosphere of fear where well-meaning youth and adults are paralyzed by a sense of powerlessness. A sort of "tunnel vision" takes place, which causes bystanders to feel isolated. Fear often triggers their self-preservation instincts (Fight or Flight) as thoughts play out in their mind, "What if the bully targets me?" The result is that many bystanders will either quietly retreat from conflict or - in an effort to keep themselves from being targeted - will join the negative behavior. What is lost is the fact that bystanders may often outnumber the bullies - providing them a greater advantage for positively changing the situation. "There is strength in numbers."

So, does the bystander have power? Yes. The power comes from the strength of their moral character and their ability to empathize with the person who is being bullied. Bystanders can use their power to influence the outcome of a bullying situation by directly getting involved, indirectly calling for help or providing some type of distraction that helps the bullied child to escape.

The bullied, bully and bystander each have their own power to influence, however, the greatest share of that power is realized by bystanders who unite. If one person musters the courage to intervene, then others will most likely do the same.

When I was a freshman in college, a fellow student had an extremely bad asthma attack in the lobby of my dormitory. When I arrived on the scene, the entire room full of students seemed paralyzed and helpless. To make the situation worse, the student's inhaler was nowhere to be found! We all just watched as the student wallowed on the floor, until one student had the courage to try and help him. As this upperclassman tried to calm our asthmatic classmate down until the ambulance arrived, she yelled out, "Don't just stand there! Somebody help me!" Immediately, I felt compelled to act and jumped to her side. As we tried to calm our fellow classmate, some other students ran outside to try and look for the ambulance.

While this was not a case of "bullying," it does illuminate a point about the nature of group dynamics. Almost all of us were bullied that day - internally coerced by fear and externally restrained by everyone else's lack of action. We felt powerless, but this was a false sense of powerlessness, which was exposed the moment the first student took action and called us to do the same. Bystanders must no longer see themselves as non-participants, as if their inaction has no bearing on the outcome of events.

Sometimes circumstance requires involvement. Instead of "By-standing," those youth and adults who witness bullying must begin to see themselves as being on "Stand-by" - ready to give their assistance when needed. Often bystanders do nothing because they are unsure of the actions they can take. We can help change this reality by clearly presenting ways that they can help.

CAN EVERYBODY WIN?

Our society thrives off of winners and losers. Sports empires and the fans who support them illustrate this fact. Big Business and the consumers who are cheated by them also illustrate this fact. Criminal enterprises are motivated by this fact as well. Somehow, deep down in the back of our psyches it has been ingrained that someone has to lose in order for someone else to be successful. The perception is that there are not enough resources for everyone to be successful. It is "survival of the fittest" and those who are strong enough simply take what they want regardless of the effect it has on others.

But what if we began to ask ourselves, "How can everybody win?" What possibilities would we discover as we looked at the situation from a completely new perspective? What if we were solutions-oriented instead of problem-focused?

Can everybody win? Is there a way for everyone to get what they truly need and not just what they have been coerced into believing was their lot in life? Our young people are dying and if we fail to answer this question correctly and envision a new future that they can see for themselves, then we will all be lost. The task seems insurmountable, but if enough people - youth and adults - can work together– then the dream of a new day will no longer be some future fairytale possibility, but will become a bright new present reality.

Can everybody win? Yes. Everyone CAN win if we are all willing to work together to make the impossible possible.

Made in the USA
Charleston, SC
04 December 2016